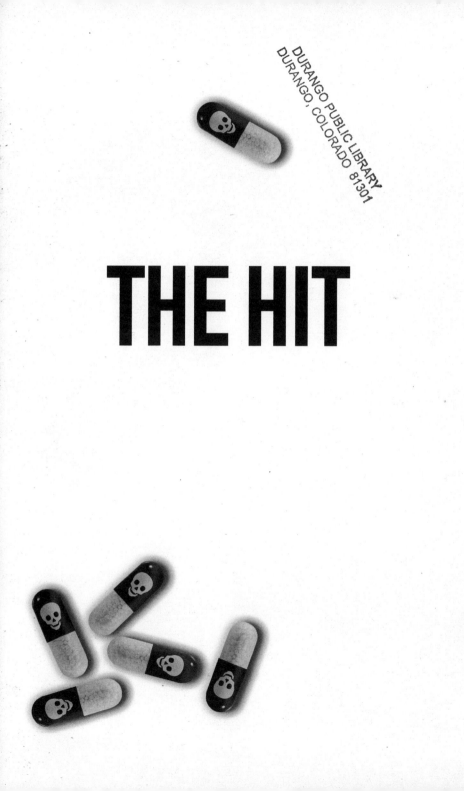

THE HIT

THE HIT

MELVIN BURGESS

Chicken House

SCHOLASTIC INC.

NEW YORK

PART 1

DEATH

CHAPTER 1

THE VERY PUBLIC DEATH OF JIMMY EARLE

WITH JIMMY, IT WAS ALL ABOUT THE FANS. PEOPLE OFTEN say a performer gave everything, but no one ever promised more for a show than he had tonight.

Adam didn't believe it, but he still felt part of something special. Jimmy Earle had been the big thing for years, his shows were legendary, but nothing before had ever been like this. People had flown from California and Beijing to be here. This was going to be the concert to end all concerts, the one experience no one could ever repeat.

"Like human sacrifice," said Adam. "They should tear his heart out, like the Aztecs. Now that would be cool."

"You won't be making jokes if he really does it," Lizzie said.

Adam shook his head. It would never happen. Jimmy had everything — wealth, youth, good looks, talent. You could understand the losers and lowlifes in the projects taking the drug called Death. They had nothing and never would. Why not go for that one crazy week in the blazing light? But Jimmy Earle? No way.

"He wants to join the 27 Club," said Lizzie excitedly. "Brian Jones, Jimi Hendrix, Janis Joplin, Jim Morrison, Kurt Cobain, Amy Winehouse — and Jimmy Earle. All twenty-seven years old. That's what they're all so scared about it. Look at 'em!"

It was true, Adam thought as they filed into the arena. There were security guards everywhere, big men standing in the aisles. They all looked on edge.

"He'll be remembered forever if he dies tonight," Lizzie said.

Adam grinned. "Yeah. And we'll remember this concert forever."

"Gosh, buying tickets — something else you're good at!" she teased. Lizzie never let him get away with a thing, but he couldn't help boasting. The glory that was Jimmy Earle was Adam's glory, too, tonight.

"Where were you the night Jimmy Earle died?" he said, acting it out. "I was there. I *saw* it." He grabbed her hand. She smiled back and squeezed. Adam felt his head go. He fancied her that bad.

Lizzie was out of his league, really. They used to know each other years ago at primary school. They'd been good friends — hung out, gone to the same parties. Then his dad had to leave his job, Adam had to change schools, and they'd lost touch until they bumped into each other again in town just a couple of months ago. It was like magic — they'd got on in a flash, as if they'd never been apart all those years.

He'd been delighted and amazed when she let him kiss her a week later. In a world where there were so many people and so few jobs, it was serious stuff for someone rich to go out with someone poor. Families hoarded their wealth like dragons. So look at him now! He felt like the King of the World with her at his side. He'd bet not one of her rich friends could have got her a ticket for Jimmy Earle like he had tonight.

Actually, it was his brother Jess who had got the tickets for him. God knows how — Jess never went anywhere or did anything. No need for Lizzie to know that, though . . .

They made their way toward their seats. The noise was already deafening. People were shouting at the stage, even though there was no one there to hear them.

"Jimmy, I love you!"

"Don't do it, Jimmy!"

"No, do it! Off yourself. Save me the price of your next crap album," yelled a bloke near them. He snickered at his mates, who laughed uncomfortably. A tearful girl yelled at him to shut up. A couple of rows down, a man offered to punch his lights out if he spoke up again.

The whole place was too hot, too edgy. Lizzie slipped her hand out of Adam's as they pushed through to their seats. She sat down and stared around her, trying to take it all in.

"Do you think anyone here's taken it?" she asked.

"Bound to," said Adam.

Lizzie laughed nervously. *She's scared*, he thought, and realized that he was scared, too. Deathers were dangerous. They had nothing to lose. That was the whole point.

Death had started out as a euthanasia drug, to give the terminally ill one week of great quality of life and a clean way out. No one ever imagined that the young would take it, too; but then, no one imagined what it would give the young — super youth. On Death you were better — mentally, physically, sexually, anyway you cared to look at it. It was the biggest high there was.

So they said. And, of course, at a price. Death cost thousands per pill.

And there was no going back. No one had found an antidote and most scientists didn't expect one to emerge. Jimmy Earle was a big star — the biggest — but in this respect he was the same as everyone else. If he'd taken Death, he was as good as dead. He'd gone on about it for ages, in the press, on his website. The concert had been canceled twice since he had announced that he'd finally gone and done it. The authorities were terrified. Death had already caused the biggest wave of suicides ever recorded among the under-twenty-fives. Only when he'd withdrawn his statement and sworn it was all just a publicity stunt had they allowed the concert to go ahead.

The question was, who was Jimmy fooling? The authorities, or the fans? Was he or wasn't he on Death? And if he was — *why*?

"The bucket list," said Adam. "Oh yeah!"

"Not the point!" exclaimed Lizzie. "It's not what you do, it's how you experience it. Everything is for the last time. Every little thing matters. That's the point. When you enter the Death phase, life becomes so intense. Most people wait till they're old and tired. Jimmy decided to do it while he's still young . . ."

Adam snorted. "That's such a girl thing to say. Did you *read* his list? I mean — come on!"

Jimmy Earle's bucket list was a thing of legend. It had cost over twenty million pounds. He had slept with a hundred girls in one week; at least twenty of them had come out of it pregnant. He had traveled round the world, eaten two kilos of caviar in one sitting, drunk thirty gallons of champagne, snorted a pound of cocaine, been into space, killed a man, hunted snow leopards, climbed Everest . . . the list went on.

Of course, it was a fantasy. No one person could have done all those things in a single week. Or could they? Death didn't just kill you — it loved you up better than ecstasy and boosted you at the same time. With strength, fitness, and belief on your side, you could do anything.

Maybe, just maybe, it was all true.

Nah, thought Adam. *Publicity, that's all it is.* But how great would it be if someone, somewhere, really had done all that stuff in just one week? And how much greater if that person was him . . .

Lizzie fixed him with a look. "Would you do it, Adam? If you could have his bucket list? Really?"

Adam tensed up. He hated being put on the spot. If it was true, Jimmy Earle had done more in a single week than he would in his entire life. More girls. More fun. More everything. That was an amazing thought. But what Lizzie really wanted to know was if he'd jump up and start shagging all the girls he could find. It was her he wanted . . . But if you only had one week to live — well. You would, wouldn't you?

"Dunno. What's *your* bucket list?" he asked her.

Lizzie smiled. "I'd have sex with as many attractive people as I could find," she said. And Adam, to his surprise, felt hurt.

She snorted with amusement. Winding him up. She got him every time.

It was all right for her. Her dad had a good job; she had it made. All Adam could see ahead was hard work, never earning enough to do what he wanted. It would have been different if he'd done better at the football trials he'd had a few weeks ago. He was a brilliant player, but now he was having to come to terms with the fact that there were too many others more brilliant than him.

But he wasn't beaten yet. Practice, practice, practice — that's what he had to do. He could still make it if he tried hard enough.

The arena filled. Everyone was so wound up. A few fights broke out, but they were quickly put down, often by other people in the crowd. Even now, with every seat sold, the concert could be called off at any second.

When Earle came on the stage, the noise welled up like a climax before a single note had been played. He held out his hands and waited for the uproar to subside.

"We're going to play you a few songs," he said. "And it's going to be the performance of a lifetime."

He turned around, lashed out with his arm, and the band burst into the first number. The crowd roared.

"He's great! He's so great!" screamed Lizzie.

"He's fantastic!" yelled Adam.

The people, the adrenaline, the noise. He'd never seen anything like it. He wondered if anyone ever had. Around them the crowd surged to its feet, and they jumped up with it, everyone laughing, weeping, yelling, dancing. And this was only the first song.

The concert was brilliant. Jimmy seemed to be singing his whole life up there in the space of a couple of hours. The noise got louder and louder as they neared the magic time — ten thirty — when he was supposed to die. Death was accurate; you could work out when you were going to go pretty much to the minute. Was he mad enough — committed enough — to have really taken Death?

With Jimmy, you could never tell.

As the last few minutes ticked by, the band launched into their current single, "Something to Live For." Jimmy howled and strutted his way through the song. Ten thirty came and he sang on. It was all a publicity stunt — of course!

But just when everyone was certain, the song died in his throat. He staggered. There was a gasp from the crowd. Jimmy almost fell, but then drew himself erect, and clamped the mike to his chest. The band petered out. Out of the speakers came a rapid beat.

Babangbangbangbangbabangbangbababababang bang.

Jimmy's heart. It sounded as if it was trying to hammer its way out of his chest.

BANGBABANGBANGBABANGBANGBANGBANGBANG.

The band started a countdown. "Ten . . . nine . . . eight . . . seven . . ." The crowd went crazy.

"Don't do it, Jimmy! Don't leave us!" someone yelled.

". . . four . . . three . . . two . . . one."

Nothing.

Jimmy Earle looked up at the crowd and grinned. He spread his arms as if to say, *Fooled ya!* Then he tipped forward and fell flat on his face.

There was a moment of stunned silence. People stood at their seats, waiting for him to get up. Was it another trick? It had to be another trick. A beefy paramedic rushed onto the stage, flipped Earle over onto his back, and started chest compressions. They could see it all up there on the big screens, a hundred times larger than life. The guy was pounding on Earle's chest like he meant to break his ribs.

The crowd started up again, a different noise this time — a deep, nervous buzz, punctured with shouts and screams, building quickly. Onstage, one of the guitarists crossed himself, unplugged his guitar, and walked off. The drummer climbed down from his seat, came to the front, and said something into the mike. They couldn't quite make it out, but it sounded like, "Congratulations." The crowd was getting louder by the second. Someone nearby yelled, "I love you, Jimmy, I love you!" A girl just in front of them screamed, "Take me with you, Jimmy! I want to go, too!"

Some Red Cross people came running up the aisles but they didn't make it to the stage. Chaos broke out. The crowd surged forward and up toward the stage, trying to get to Jimmy. People were begging him to get up, begging him to live, demanding their money back. Security reacted furiously, lashing out, throwing people down.

In the middle of it all, flat on the floor, eyes wide open, beyond any excitement or fun or sadness or pleasure or pain, Jimmy Earle lay, his chest violently pounded by the big paramedic. The air was going in and out of his lungs, the blood pumping in all directions in and out of his shattered heart. Not one drop of it was ever going to do him any good again.

CHAPTER 2

MANCHESTER BURNING

THE BIG SCREENS BLANKED OUT SO THAT NO ONE COULD see what was going on, but it didn't stop the chaos. Things were being thrown. Shoes, cans, even bottles were flying through the air and down into the crowd. There were screams; people were getting hurt. Fights broke out; security was getting overwhelmed. It was turning into a full-blown riot. There were warnings over the PA that the whole place was under CCTV surveillance and vandals would be prosecuted, but the violence didn't stop. It was doubtful anyone even heard.

Then there was another announcement — Jimmy was alive! It was just a stunt after all. *Everyone, just calm down, please.* It seemed to work for a minute or two. People milled around in confusion. After a short wait — there he was! Jimmy Earle, walking onto the stage, waving, and smiling. But it was pathetic — it was obvious it was just a look-alike dressed up in his gear. If anyone had any doubts that Jimmy Earle really had died, those doubts were put to rest there and then.

Things got suddenly worse. Seats were being torn up and thrown about. People were trying to storm the stage to loot the equipment — it would be worth a fortune after this. But then the doors banged open and police came in, squads of them, storming up the aisles in full riot gear. They fought their way to the stage, turned to face the crowd — shields up, batons drawn — and began to edge their way forward. They were going to literally push the audience out onto the street.

There was another announcement; there would be a refund available online to anyone not prosecuted. The management apologized and asked everyone to leave quietly. At last, things began to calm down.

Herded by the police, the crowd began to shuffle toward the exits.

Adam and Lizzie had good seats, close to the front, so they were among the last to leave. They heard the sirens going off while they were still inside, and by the time they got outside, things were already kicking off. Thousands of overexcited, upset fans, suddenly thrown out into Manchester on a Friday night, with nothing to do — there was bound to be trouble. The venue was safe, but now there was the whole of Manchester to run riot in.

Out on the streets, the atmosphere was electric. People were running to and fro in groups, groups merging into gangs, gangs into crowds. As Adam and Lizzie walked toward Piccadilly Gardens, some kids chased past, barging them out of the way.

"Hey!" shouted Adam. But the gang had already gone. They walked on to the middle of the block, and saw what it was — a shop window, smashed, and the police gathering to stop the looting. Someone stumbled past them with a huge cardboard box held in front of him, leaning right over backward in an effort to keep his balance, like a man in a cartoon. Farther ahead another gang appeared out of nowhere and started throwing bricks and stones at the police.

It was like a Jimmy Earle song turned real. His music had always been about love and sex, loss and hope, about rioting and looting and fighting back against poverty and failure — and here it all was, sizzling hot in the drizzle of a Manchester night. Tonight the streets belonged to his fans, and they were going to make the most of it.

Adam and Lizzie ran on. The city was in flames. The shops had given up the ghost, the windows smashed open, people running freely in and out. On the corner of Princess Street, someone was pounding the back doors of a van with a piece of broken paving stone. There were shouts and sirens, clouds of smoke, the stink of burning rubber and gasoline. It was a war zone. But for what?

Adam felt dizzy with excitement.

"Looting! Hey, what about it?" he hissed in Lizzie's ear.

"Wow. Look at it. Look at it!" yelled Lizzie, staring about her with bright, big eyes.

"You scared?"

"No! I love it!"

Lizzie had lived all her life safe and sound, protected by her parents' money. Sometimes she felt as if life was going to grind to a halt. Now look! The city going up in smoke and here she was, right in the middle of it.

They made their way up Princess Street to Albert Square. It was heaving. There was some sort of struggle going on in front of the town hall, a mass of people fighting their way forward showing no mercy. The police were there, trying to hold them back from storming the building. They were acting more like soldiers than law keepers, lashing out at people with their batons. But they were outnumbered, and the crowd against them was swelling rapidly. Suddenly they'd had enough and made a run for it, pushing their way out of the crowd, which parted to make way for them. A roar of victory went up, and the vanguard at the front began smashing the windows of the town hall and pounding at its heavy oak doors, trying to get inside.

The police re-formed a line and tried to push their way back to the town hall, but it was no good. The doors were giving way and people were already crawling in through smashed windows. The banks and the headquarters of the big companies around the square were under attack as well. Bottles and bricks were in the air. There were no peacemakers. Anyone who wanted out had already left; it was just the hard core now. In the shopping streets and malls around them, the looters were still busy at work, but here in the square, people weren't interested in wide-screen TVs and crates of beer. They wanted more. They were trying to tear the whole city apart with their bare hands and start again.

And they were organized. From where Lizzie and Adam stood, they could see people wearing rat masks. Adam hissed in excitement. Zealots! Half madcap protest group, half armed rebels — right here in Manchester, fighting to take over the seat of the city government.

"It's not just looting," yelled Lizzie. "It's a revolution, Adam!"

Across the front of the town hall, there was a ripple of movement. They looked up as a huge banner, a hundred feet wide, unraveled like a wave of water down the height of the building. It showed a gigantic rat clutching a can of red paint, staring angrily into the crowd, with the Zealot slogan painted red behind it: OUR TIME WILL COME!

The crowd in the square roared their approval. Above the noise, an amplified voice boomed out: "The town hall is ours. Free cheese for everyone!"

Around them, people screamed in delight. High up on the roof, they could see Zealots in rat masks looking down at the crowd. One of them shook a machine gun in the air. Was it real? Adam wondered. The Zealots were everywhere — pushing back the police and hauling them off as if they were under arrest. One group had taken a jackhammer to Barclays Bank on the corner; someone else was squirting glue into the locks of the NatWest. Loud music started blaring out a Jimmy Earle number, "The Rats Are Taking Over." The crowd around them jostled and surged. A man banged into them and thrust a handful of pills into their faces.

"What is it?" Adam asked, reaching out. Free drugs! Ecstasy, maybe?

"Sweeties," said the man, grinning at them. "Courtesy of Jimmy Earle. Last point on his bucket list."

Adam handed one to Lizzie and they looked closely at them. On each pill, neatly printed in black, was a tiny skull.

"It's Death!"

"It can't be . . ."

But it was. Everyone knew what the pills looked like. Adam could see the man moving on, passing out handful after handful of the deadly little pills. It must have cost a fortune.

And people were taking them. He could see them tipping back their heads and flinging the pill down their necks. "Live fast, die young!" yelled the man. He laughed and threw a handful of the pills into the air. Around him, people scrabbled to pick them up.

"We could have taken it without realizing," exclaimed Lizzie.

Adam stared at the black-and-white pill in the palm of his hand. What would it be like to know — to *feel* like Jimmy Earle for one brief, sweet week . . . ?

He flung his hand to his mouth, then grinned madly at Lizzie. He swallowed. She started back, shocked — but then he showed her the pill in his hand.

"You bastard," she yelled, and laughed. She stared at the small capsule of craziness in her palm. All those people, just swallowing it! "Do you think it's the real thing?" she said.

"Could be, if Jimmy Earle paid for it. He has the money."

They looked at each other, shocked by how tempting it was. They'd been there with Jimmy. They'd seen it, they were part of it! If they took Death tonight, they'd be living it, too.

"It's not worth it," said Lizzie. She flung her pill into the crowd. Adam did the same. Death, on a night like this? He wanted to live.

15

Only, some people said, that was exactly what Death made you do . . .

From some way off, they could hear sirens. Reinforcements were on the way. The city was a dangerous place tonight. There was the sudden rat-tat-tat-tat of machine-gun fire. Instinctively, Adam and Lizzie ducked. Up on the roof of the town hall, rat-masked Zealots waved weapons in the air. On another part of the roof, there was a small blaze of fire moving about. It stumbled a few yards, then fell; it looked like slow motion from that height and distance. The crowd gasped as the fire rolled down the steep ledge of the roof, over the edge, and down to the ground.

It was a person. Self-immolation. There were the jokes about cheese and the rat masks, but the Zealots were prepared to die for their beliefs. Every few weeks someone died, killing themselves with fire, or going up as a suicide bomb. It was crazy — but you couldn't help respecting them for their commitment to their cause: freedom and food for all!

Above their heads, the loudspeakers began to spit out slogans: "Equality! Freedom! Power to the people! Down with corporate profits and greed! The government is in the pockets of the corporations — fight for the right to govern yourselves."

Firearms spat out again from somewhere. People were running to get away. Adam and Lizzie dropped to the ground and followed the crowd out of the square and into Crown Street. Behind them, gunfire started up in earnest. There would be deaths tonight. This was no place for tourists.

*   *   *

Outside of Albert Square, there were hardly any police at all and the looting went on unopposed. The Arndale shopping center was in pieces; you could walk in and just help yourself. People had brought in cars and vans to carry stuff away wholesale. Adam and Lizzie wandered about the blazing streets, diving in and out of the broken shops, following the crowds. They picked up some scarves from a looted department store, and the anonymity it gave them made them feel untouchable, as if they could spend the rest of their lives living off stolen food like beasts running feral in the transformed city.

Later on, the police came back to try to chase the crowds off and make arrests; maybe the war in Albert Square was over. Adam and Lizzie got caught in a camera shop and had to run for it with the uniforms on their tails. But the police got sidetracked by some kids smashing a car. There were so many crimes being committed tonight, the authorities didn't know where to turn.

The night came to an end abruptly. They were tagging along with a crowd running down one of the narrow streets, pursued by a couple of riot police, when another policeman dashed out on them from the side. Adam slipped sideways and got away, but the man grabbed Lizzie by the arm and held on to her.

Adam stopped. He wanted to help, but he didn't dare go near.

"We were just watching," he yelled.

The policeman pulled the scarf from Lizzie's face. To Adam, it looked like a film — the burly policeman, covered in body armor and riot gear; and slight Lizzie, hanging off his arm like a rabbit.

The policeman stared at her for a moment. "For fuck's sake," he snarled. "You want to end up in the nick, you silly bitch?"

He flung her down into the road and stalked off back to the main road. Adam ran to help her up and dust her down.

"Time to go," said Lizzie shakily. Adam nodded. Beyond the fires, the sky was growing pale. It was getting light. They were both really shocked by their narrow escape. The last time there had been riots, people had been locked up for months just for being there. Lizzie suddenly dived into her pocket for her phone. It had been on silent ever since the gig. She looked up. "Mum and Dad are going crazy," she said. "It's three A.M. They haven't got a clue what's been going on . . ."

Adam got out his phone, too. Same thing.

"We're in the shit now," he said.

They both grinned sheepishly at each other.

"But that was great, wasn't it?" he asked.

"It was the best night of my life," said Lizzie fervently.

They kissed. Adam felt a thrill when their lips touched. Wouldn't it be great if they could go somewhere and make love now, while the fires still burned! But there was no chance . . .

"It's all changing," Lizzie said. "Not just here. The whole world. People have had enough."

Only a few hours ago the future had seemed so fixed. All the money was owned by the banks and the big corporations, the economy was falling apart, there were no jobs, social services were a joke.

For decades everyone had complained but nothing had changed. Now, suddenly, it was all up for grabs. The Zealots had shown the nation how to seize the future by setting fire to the present. Who knew what tomorrow would bring?

"When will I see you?" asked Adam. All he wanted was to stay with Lizzie. It was unbearable to think that everything was going to go back to normal as soon as they went home.

They wandered a hundred yards up the road, but they knew it was over — for tonight, anyway.

"I better ring Dad, get a lift back," said Lizzie at last. She paused with her phone in her hand. "Shall I ask him to give you a lift, too?"

"No way!" Her parents hated Adam. "They'll kill me."

She nodded and rang her dad, arranging to meet him on Oxford Road, by the university, away from the trouble. Adam walked her there and waited with her. Her dad glared furiously at him when he turned up in his Jag. Lizzie kissed Adam passionately on the mouth, then ran to the car and drove off. Adam began the long walk home.

He felt jubilant. He was falling in love, and the future was his.

CHAPTER 3

THE MORNING AFTER

ADAM COULD FEEL HIS PHONE BUZZING AWAY IN HIS POCKET as he walked. It was his dad.

"Where are you? What happened?"

"The police locked the town up. I've just got out now."

"Have you seen Jess?"

"No." Adam was taken aback. His brother was as straight as a stick of rock, working as a research chemist for Pak-Hilliard, one of the giant corporations that owned half the world. He was always there, always working, always earning. Their dad was an invalid, their mum worked nights at telesales. If it wasn't for Jess, they wouldn't be able to pay the bills.

"He's not come back from work. I can't get in touch," complained his dad.

"Must be doing overtime."

"Not at this time of night."

"Something to do with the riots, then."

Adam was surprised, but not worried. Dull old Jess. What was he doing out so late, while the shops were burning, and rioters and policemen were dying on the street? Hiding in a basement, probably, working on some formula to make plastic gaskets last longer.

His dad was still up when he got home, standing by the kettle with a blanket over his shoulders, drinking tea. It was cold. He always turned the heating off when Jess was out. The Great God Jess. As soon as he walked out the door, the shivering started.

There was still no news.

"You haven't rung Mum, have you?" Adam asked.

"Of course I have. She wants to know what's happened to her son."

Adam groaned. His dad was always ringing her up at work with his stupid worries.

"You have to stop worrying about everything," Adam said.

His dad shuffled from the counter to the table, with a cup of tea in his good left hand, supporting himself with the other on the back of a chair. "You should be doing the worrying for me. I have nothing to do but worry," he said, and smiled grimly.

It was a typically bitter little joke. Adam sighed. The old man was going to be up all night now, but there was nothing he could do about it. Jess was bound to be safe. He'd run a mile at the slightest sign of trouble.

Adam went to bed thanking his lucky stars that he wasn't Jess.

His life was going to be different. He'd glimpsed the future and the future belonged to him.

Adam was brought round the next morning by his phone alarm at ten A.M. Saturday morning: football. There was a text from Lizzie waiting for him.

What a night! You and me, Ads! xxxx ps don't txt dad's taking my phone.

Adam hugged himself and turned sideways in his bed to look at himself in the mirror on the side of his wardrobe. His blond hair was curling over his eyes. His skin glowed in the light coming in between the curtains. He smiled at himself. How could she resist? After he'd failed his trials for Man U and City, it had seemed that his life wasn't going to be the golden dream he'd always hoped for. But the tide had turned. The death of a rock star had made him shine.

But it wasn't just about Jimmy Earle. It was about Lizzie. It felt so right, being with her. But it was not just a romantic dream. The fact was, if they fell in love it could change his life. "Money opens doors," his dad always said. Adam closed his eyes and wished. He wanted so much to be in love with her and for her to love him, but he knew it was stupid. They were only seventeen. Anything could happen.

He sighed. Life went on anyway. He slipped out of bed, took a shower, and went downstairs.

*   *   *

Jess was there, of course. So was his mum, sitting with his dad at the table eating toast. Jess looked pale. His mum was exhausted, as usual, with dark eyes. Adam came across to kiss her good morning — except it was good night for her. She always waited to see him in the mornings, even when she was desperate for sleep.

"What happened to you?" Adam asked Jess, helping himself to cereal and sitting down.

"I went into town for a drink and got stuck," Jess said.

Adam laughed. "You picked your night," he said. Jess hardly ever went out — and then when he did, Manchester exploded!

"You need to be careful," his father scolded. "Anything could have happened to you."

Adam was exasperated. "What's he supposed to do, never go out in case there's a riot? Give us a break, Dad."

"Adam's right," his mum said. "Jess needs to get out more."

"Did you see it? The whole place was up in flames. Where were you?" Adam asked.

"We holed up in a bar," said Jess.

"Didn't you even go out to have a look?"

"It was dangerous!" said Jess. It was typical. The world was changing — and he was holed up in a bar, keeping safe.

"The Zealots were there. It was amazing! They occupied the town hall."

"Looting and destroying property," insisted his father. "According to the TV, the Zealots were handing out Death. Irresponsible thugs."

"It was paid for by Jimmy Earle. I didn't see any Zealots handing it out," Adam said.

"I wouldn't put it past them," said his mum.

"They aren't just looters," said Jess. Despite the fact that he was scared of life, he was passionate about politics. It was just that he never did anything about it. "Everything the Zealots do is about trying to make people think — trying to wake them up."

"Yes — by looting and encouraging young people to kill themselves," sneered his dad. "Very political."

Adam shook his head impatiently. "They were on top of the town hall. The police came in after them. There was gunfire." He shook his head at the memory. What a night!

"Nothing about that on the news," said his dad.

Jess scoffed. Everyone knew the news was owned by the government. You had to look on the Internet and on social media if you wanted to get to the truth.

"Well, I want both of you to stay well away from it," his mother announced. "Over twenty deaths in Manchester last night. And they think thousands of those pills were handed out." She shook her head, appalled. "I wonder how those young people are going to feel about that this morning?" She stood up. "I'm going to bed," she said. "Keep the noise down, you two."

That was to Jess and Dad, who would have argued furiously about politics for hours if they could. She went around the table, bestowing kisses.

Adam got up to go, too. "Footie," he explained. He cadged some money off his mum for bus fares, under his father's disapproving eyes.

"Waste of time," said his father as soon as she was out of the room. "Big fish in a small pond." He looked up at the little TV rattling away on the shelf, and slurped his tea. Adam stood there, dumbfounded.

"I love you, too," said Adam. He turned and left.

Jess ran out and caught him by the gate.

"What is it?" Adam asked.

"Nothing. Just — look after the old pair, won't you? Dad loves you really."

"He's got a funny way of showing it."

"Yeah." Jess laughed self-consciously. He looked awkward. "Take care, mate," he said. He nodded.

Adam shook his head and shot off.

He seethed all the way to the playing fields. It had nearly broken his heart when he failed to get in to Man U or City. He was still hoping to get in elsewhere — Burnley, maybe. Blackburn even. But his dad treated him like a failure already.

The crooked old bus jolted and crashed its way across the potholes on the edge of the road. As Adam looked out, the posh bus went past, long and high in the fast lane, the one that carted the rich kids to rich school, with rich lunches in their bags and a rich education at the other end. Six years ago, Adam used to catch that bus. Then his dad had had an accident at work and everything had changed.

"We can't afford to pay for two of you to go to uni, and Jess is the better bet educationally," his dad had said.

Adam hadn't minded at the time. He'd thought sport was going to be his way out. He wanted to fly, not toil. But now . . .

Big fish in a small pond.

At least there was Lizzie. But how long would that last?

At the playing fields, everyone was talking about Jimmy Earle and the riots. That was more like it. Man — he'd been there! The boys clustered around him while he gave the details of the concert and the events that followed.

One thing was for sure — Earle had hit a nerve.

"Have you read his blog?" someone asked. "He was high the whole time. Off his face."

"No! He didn't need drugs. Everything was hyper-real. Like, he spent an hour just looking at stuff."

"My idea of fun," said Adam.

"You don't get it. You don't need big experiences if you're like that inside. Everything is a high. He may have only had one week, but none of us will ever experience anything like he did, no matter what we do."

"But the bucket list. *That's* what it's all about," said Adam.

His mate Jack licked his lips. "Do you really think all those women slept with him? There were a lot of A-list celebs there. I bet he doesn't even know half of them."

"If you've only got a week to live? What sort of bitch would say no to you then?" said someone else.

They laughed.

The talk turned to what they would do if it were them. *What would* your *bucket list be?* Most of the lists started off with sex. Names were mentioned. After that, drugs, money, travel.

"I wanna stand on the moon."

"Get someone pregnant."

"Get rich."

"What for? You're going to die."

"So I can spend the money, you idiot!"

"Leave something so people will remember me."

"Kill someone."

"Who?"

"Someone bad. That way, at least you do something good."

Shag a princess. Write a book. Fall in love. Blow up the government. Die with a smile on my face.

"Leave my family with enough money so none of them have to work ever again."

Everyone nodded. Of course you'd want to do that.

"What about the riots?" said Adam. "The Zealots were there."

One of the boys shook his head. "Bunch of losers, cashing in."

"Ah, come on. They were attacking the banks. They took over the town hall," said Adam. "'Free cheese for everyone!'"

The boys laughed uneasily. The Zealots were a laugh, but they were so deadly serious as well. No one knew what to make of them.

"They didn't hold on to the town hall," someone said.

"No, but they had to send the army in. The police were fighting among themselves," said someone else.

Jack nodded his head. "This is big," he said. "When the police won't do as they're told, the government's in real trouble."

An argument broke out between those who supported the status quo and those who believed the whole state needed to be overhauled and changed. Adam listened. All he wanted — all any of them wanted — was a life. The question was: Where could people like them get one? Not in a world like this, where other people held all the cards, that was for sure.

Then the coach turned up, and he forgot about the Zealots and got going with the game.

The amazing thing, Lizzie thought, was how quickly life went from total adrenaline rush to utterly boring. Last night with Adam she had felt the future in the palm of her hand. Every window smashed, every door kicked in had seemed to be tearing down the prejudices and conventions that hemmed her in on all sides. She'd left Adam feeling as high as a kite, climbed into her dad's car — and had to endure half an hour of misery straightaway.

"Out with the lowlife . . . destroying property . . . vandalizing the town," he'd ranted. "What are you going to do — give it all away and turn out like your precious boyfriend, with no future and no hope?"

"You don't know what you're talking about," she told him. "We were all out there trying to make something happen. It's about hope. Changing the future. Not hanging on to as much as you can for yourself."

"You have a future," he told her. "I just wish you'd grow up and realize it."

At home she'd had her phone taken off her and was sent to bed like a child. She was too tired to argue. The next morning, the consequences were announced. There were never any punishments in her house, just consequences. She was not to see Adam again. She was grounded for two weeks. No pocket money. No Internet connection. No phone for a day. No this, no that.

Grounded — at seventeen? What were they on? The sooner she left home the better.

Later in the afternoon, she'd sneaked out to a neighbor's house. They had a daughter named Sarina about her age. Lizzie wanted to use her computer to make a call to Adam.

Sarina was not exactly sympathetic.

"Why do you care?" said Lizzie, settling herself at the screen.

"Of course I care. Your parents are friends of my parents. What if my mum and dad find out you've been using our equipment, when you're supposed to be forbidden to go on the Internet?"

"Oh, leave it, Sarina! No one will know, will they?"

"I know."

Lizzie flicked through, trying to find the site she wanted.

"Your parents have rights, too," wittered Sarina. "You can't blame them. Those riots caused millions of pounds worth of damage. You could go to jail . . ."

"I told you, I never nicked anything and I never smashed anything. It's not illegal just being there."

There it was. Fone4free.com. Lizzie clicked through and signed on.

"Anyone with any sense would have left at once. Mum and I were going shopping in Manchester this week. Now it looks as though we'll have to go to Leeds instead." Sarina peered over her shoulder. "Lizzie, what's that website? That's illegal!"

"Sarina! This is important. It's my boyfriend. Are you seriously trying to get in the way of true love?" she asked, swinging round to face her.

"They can trace that sort of thing. Now we're going to get into trouble because of you!"

Lizzie put her hands over the keyboard to stop Sarina getting to it. The little phone icon did a dance in the middle of the screen. *Come on, Adam, pick up!* she thought. She had to talk to him. Suddenly she was terrified that somehow, for no reason, he'd gone off her in the night.

"Hello?"

"It's me."

"Lizzie! You OK?"

"Yeah. You?"

"Yeah."

There was a pause while they both grinned at their end of the phone.

"Hey, guess what, Ads? I can't see you ever again. I'm banned."

"Really?"

"You want to see me?"

"What do you think? I'm just missing you. It's like . . ."

Behind her, Sarina was fidgeting. Lizzie tried her utmost to pretend she wasn't there.

"It's like we had that night and now it's all wrong, being apart," Adam said.

That was it. That was it exactly.

"What are you doing tomorrow?" she said. "My cousin Julie's having a party. She's loaded — it'll be amazing! Mum wants me to go; she thinks I'll meet a better class of boyfriend there. I can even have my phone back." She laughed. "She'll tell Julie you can't come but Julie won't care. She's got this nicey-pie image but underneath it she's so, so bad . . ."

They agreed to meet up outside the cinema in Stockport. Lizzie would pick him up in her little Fiat. And . . .

"And Ads?" she said. "That'll be the night . . ." Then she put down the phone before he could say anything.

Sarina, who had been sitting there soaking it all up, stared at her.

"What did that mean, that'll be the night?" she asked.

"Mind your own business," said Lizzie. But she couldn't help smiling.

Sarina smiled back. "Are you in love with him?" she asked.

Lizzie ducked her head. She wanted it — but it was too soon.

"You won't be really, because you're too young," said Sarina. "You just think you are, I expect. But it's still very sweet. Have you got your contraception sorted out?"

"You know all about that, do you, Sarina?"

"I already had sex. Two months ago. It was with a boy I met at a party. We did it in one of the spare bedrooms."

"Were you going out with him?"

"No. I was just curious."

Lizzie laughed. She was an odd one, Sarina. But Lizzie was curious. "Did you like it?" she wanted to know.

Sarina made a face. "I expect it gets better as you get older."

*   *   *

Lizzie made her way back home. Tomorrow night. Her parents had already agreed to let her go to the party. Julie was rich, and rich was good, as far as they were concerned. They were hoping she'd meet up with some dull boy with loads of money. No chance. It was her and Adam, all the way. *All* the way.

The thought sent a little thrill of excitement down through her stomach. When they'd first met up again, he'd seemed a bit of a pain — thought far too much of himself. But now she knew there was so much more to him than that. And then last night. The gig, the death of Jimmy Earle, the riots afterward, had blown her away. It had brought them together in a way she couldn't even describe — it was so thrilling.

Was it love?

She wanted it to be. Last night she had been sure it was, but what would it be like next time they met, in the cold light of day?

She climbed in through the bathroom window. *Let it be love,* she thought. She slipped past the sitting room, where her parents were watching rubbish on the TV. *Let it be love. Let it be something. Let it be anything rather than this.*

CHAPTER 4

COME THE FALL

ADAM GOT BACK HOME HAPPIER THAN HE COULD EVER remember. *That'll be the night,* Lizzie had said. She could only have meant one thing. He felt like a kid on Christmas Eve.

It was Saturday night and he could have gone out with his mates, but he gave it a miss. He wanted to be fresh for tomorrow, and anyway he didn't have the money for two nights out in one week. His mum was still in bed when he got home, but his dad was up, fretting in front of the TV. Jess wasn't answering his calls again.

"So where is he now that's so secret?" he wanted to know.

"At work," said Adam. "He never picks up at work, you know that."

It was infuriating. Adam was always allowed to do what he wanted, but Jess was guarded like the crown jewels. Adam never knew whether to be offended or delighted, but he was determined not to let his father's mood puncture his own.

"Hey, maybe he's got a girl. He doesn't have to report everything to you, you know."

His dad grunted — the nearest he ever got to admitting he might be wrong. He flicked through the Internet channels and found the news.

There were more riots going on.

"Again." He shook his head. "Manchester will be in ashes by the time they finish with it."

But it wasn't just Manchester. The Zealots and some of the other rebel groups had put out a call for people not to loot, but to protest. And people had heard them. Crowds were gathering in Leeds, London, Birmingham, Bristol, Newcastle — all the major cities. There was a crowd of over twenty thousand already in Albert Square — far more than the night before. All sorts of people had come to show support — students, workers, professionals. It was the biggest protest for decades.

Jimmy Earle's death had started something. Discontent had been growing for years; now it had found a spark. Unrest was flaring up all over the country.

Once again, the Zealots had occupied the town hall and made it up to the roof; once again the police had turned up to try to get them out — but this time there were many more people getting in the way. There was no violence, no throwing bottles and bricks. The crowd just stood there, facing them down, standing between them and the Zealots. Someone had a huge banner up, spread halfway across the square: YOU SHALL NOT PASS.

The police had made a commitment to the crowds, apparently:

Don't attack us and we won't attack you. So far, both sides seemed to be honoring it.

Adam was fascinated. Even his dad had to admit this was something new.

"Maybe now the government will act to do something for the ordinary man," he said.

Adam got to bed late, after two. He went to sleep with a smile on his face. Tomorrow was the day. Big party. Rich people.

Him and Lizzie.

He had everything to live for.

He was planning on lying in late, but his dad came in at ten with a cup of tea and put it on the bedside cabinet by his head. He stood looking down at him until Adam couldn't bear it anymore.

"What?" he moaned.

"Jess hasn't come back."

"No, Dad!" Not this again. He curled back over. The whole house had to sit up every time Jess had a night out? It was crazy!

"Didn't you hear? Jess is missing. No call, no message, nothing. Get up, get up."

"What for?"

"To help." His dad turned and left the room. So annoying! Jess had found a girl, at last, and turned off his phone so he didn't have to listen to their dad going on in his ear while he was on the job. So what? God's sake!

"You're bonkers!" he yelled.

"Come down. Your mother is up, too," shouted his dad from the stairs. "Does that make you start to worry now? Up, up! This is an emergency."

Adam wanted to go to sleep again, but he was too cross. The old fool had woken his mum up as well. But it was a little odd, he had to admit. Jess always rang home — always always always. Adam dragged himself up and went downstairs to see what was going on. His mother was leaning against the kitchen counter, watching him as he came in scowling, still feeling grumpy from being disturbed.

"I think this time we have something to worry about," she said.

His father, of course, had been up all night waiting and worrying. At about six in the morning he'd started to make calls. Eventually, about an hour ago, he had hunted down Jess's workplace, which was the one thing Jess had kept from him. It turned out that Jess had left four months before.

"He's been lying to us all this time," said the old man.

"Not lying, necessarily," said Adam's mum.

"What else do you call it? He said he was working there."

"Maybe a white lie. Not wanting us to worry . . ."

"He's probably just changed jobs," said Adam. "You know what you're like, Dad, always worrying. Maybe he got demoted or something. Less money, you know? He wouldn't want you to worry about it, would he?"

"He's not succeeded very well," said his dad.

Adam looked hopefully at his mum. But this time, she was scared, too.

His dad tried to report Jess missing to the police, but they didn't want to know. He'd have to be away for over a week before they'd do anything. His mum cooked breakfast for everyone to fill in a bit of time, then went to bed, hardly able to keep her eyes open anymore. It was a mystery, but Adam still found it hard to worry about it. Nothing ever happened to steady Jess, his boring older brother.

He was wrong. The answer fell through the mail slot at midday.

Adam found it on the mat — a plush white envelope with a black band around it. He knew what it was at once. He'd seen them on TV before. The Zealots sent them out to the relatives of fallen fighters.

Jess? A fighter? It was beyond belief.

The envelope was addressed to his mum and dad, but there was no stamp. It must have been delivered by hand. Adam opened the door and ran out into the street, but there was no one to be seen. Whoever had put it through the slot was already gone.

He took it through to his dad in the sitting room.

"What is it?" his father asked, looking up at him, small and frail in his chair.

"The Zealots."

His father looked terrified. He tore the envelope open and scanned it. His face crumpled.

"This is impossible. Not Jess."

He glanced up at Adam, then down at the implacable print that would never change its story. "No, no, no," he murmured. "No, no, no, no."

Adam read over his shoulder. At the top was the Zealots' logo —
an angry rat with a pot of paint — but the slogan had changed. Before
it had been: "Our time will come." Now it read: "Our time is now."
Underneath, it announced that Jess Whitely had given his life in the
fight for human rights and self-determination, at the Battle of Albert
Square on Saturday night.

"One of their pranks," murmured Adam. How could this be true?
He knew his own brother, didn't he? But his heart was telling him he
knew nothing at all.

His father struggled suddenly to his feet and ran up the stairs.
"Sharon, Sharon! They're saying our boy is dead. Sharon!"

Upstairs, Adam heard his mother exclaim sleepily. He sat down
on his own at the kitchen table and waited to see what would happen next.

The rest of the day was spent in a state of shock. His mother kept
leaking tears, which, more than anything, began to convince Adam
that something terrible had really happened. They went over and
over everything they knew, but none of them could believe that
Jess really was a Zealot. He'd got caught up in the riots, he'd been
kidnapped, he'd been arrested by mistake. Any minute now he'd
ring them up and explain everything. But the day went on and no call
came. Adam's dad made more phone calls — the hospitals, the
police, Jess's work again. The police came around as soon as they
heard about the letter and emptied Jess's room, searching for evidence.

They took all his stuff away, even the letter. They told them that they'd check dental records, DNA, anything else they could to try and match the remains they had collected in Manchester the day before.

"Remains?" said his father. "My son will still have a face, won't he?" The policeman shrugged and said it was just procedure, but Adam knew what he meant. Officially, it was never admitted, but he had seen it for himself: a Zealot self-igniting on the roof of the town hall. There had been more last night apparently, setting fire to themselves on the roofs of the houses in two or three cities around the country. Could one of them have been Jess, staggering across the roof and pitching down in flames to the crowds below?

The day dragged on; the news sank in and became real to them. At about three in the afternoon his mother couldn't bear it any longer and went back to bed. Adam kept his dad company in the front room, trying to watch TV. They sat there staring at the screen, going through the motions, trying to distract themselves from the exhaustion of grief. His dad made cup of tea after cup of tea, and finally broke down sobbing, sitting in front of the latest news bulletin. Clumsily, Adam sat on the arm of his chair, put his arm around him, and tried to comfort him.

"But where had he been going for so long?" his dad said through his tears. "He's been giving me money all the time. Where did he get it from? Tell me that."

"Maybe the Zealots have been providing it for him," suggested Adam.

His father shook his head. He could not believe it. For Adam, too, it was impossible to take in. All his life Jess had seemed so ordinary — colorless, even. Now it looked as though they knew nothing about him at all.

"What does it mean?" he asked his dad.

"For you?" asked his father. "That's what you're thinking, isn't it?"

Every now and then his father came out with these mean little remarks. Adam should have been used to it by now but they took his breath away every time.

"It means work. No more school for you. We have to find you a job. Unless you can find one for me, of course." His father held up his ruined hand and shook it in the air.

Quietly, Adam got up and went to his room to lie down. Some time later, he heard his father go in to see his mother and she began to weep again. He could hear his father's voice softly murmuring, trying to console her. He felt his own grief at the back of his throat like a hard lump, but there were no tears, not yet. He lay there for a long time and tried to imagine what had happened, and what it meant, and found that he wasn't able to do it. After a time, he began to cry, too. Then he fell asleep.

At about six o'clock, he woke up from an otherworldly dream and realized that he was late. Tonight was the night. He had a party to go to.

As quietly as he could, Adam got up and began to dress in his best clothes. He knew he shouldn't go, but he also knew that he wasn't going to stop himself. Already, through the grief and shock of what had happened, he could feel the world closing in around him. No school, no education — no life. He was going to end up like his mum, working the phone at the call center for fourteen hours a day. This party might be his last chance. As for Lizzie — anyone could see she was too good for him. He wasn't going to tell her what had happened, or what it meant. It was too humiliating.

Before he went out, Adam rooted around under his bed and pulled out the condoms he kept hidden in a little cardboard box. He put them in his pocket, all except one, which he took to an old electrical socket in the wall that had been disconnected ages ago. He unraveled the tiny copper threads sticking out of the wall and used one of them to pierce a hole in the condom. It was tiny; you'd never know. Sitting on his bed, he texted her.

Getting ready to go, he wrote. And then he typed in the magic words: **I love you.**

Such a little phrase, *I love you.* What did it mean? It meant: *I want to spend my life with you. I want you to give me your life. Please love me back.*

He got up and crept downstairs like a thief in the night. He caught the bus out to Stockport to meet her. On the way, a text came back.

I love you too Adam.

Adam put the phone in his pocket. The bus pushed forward through the end of the day. He leaned his head against the window and felt tears leak out of his eyes. He wiped them away with the back of his hand. In his pockets, the condoms were coming along for the ride — the good ones in the left, the bad one in the right.

Of course he wasn't going to do it. Of course not. How could he do that to Lizzie? Even though, with Jess gone, she was his only way out.

CHAPTER 5
THE CONTAINER TERMINAL

A YOUNG WOMAN WAS BEING BEATEN UP IN A SHIPPING container.

The container was one of several thousand in a vast open-air facility close to the railway line in east Manchester. The boxes were stored two, three, or more high in long lines, row after row of them stretching off into the distance toward the vanishing point, as if some gigantic autistic child had arranged them this way. It had. The child's name was industry. A few decades ago, the place had been buzzing with activity, tractor trailers driving to and fro up the aisles, forklift trucks lifting the boxes on and off the flatbeds, stacking them, storing them, emptying them. Now, with the recession in its twentieth year, all was still — on the outside, at least. Hidden away inside many of the boxes it was a hive of activity.

The young woman doubled up from a violent blow to the stomach, but didn't fall down, as she was held up from behind. Someone delivered her a blow to the kidneys; another at the front punched her in the face. Then they let her fall. She hit the carpet with a thud.

"Ready?" said the stocky man with graying hair who was directing the beating.

The young woman shook her head, dribbling blood and spit onto the carpet. With a grimace, the older man stamped on her thigh and she curled up in pain.

From the inside, you wouldn't know they were in a container at all. It was carpeted, decorated with striped wallpaper, furnished with a desk and executive chair, coffee machine, and other office equipment. Around and about, other containers had been converted into dormitories, living spaces, more offices, a gym, cafeterias, and several laboratories. This was a factory. They made Death.

Florence Ballantine sat back on his desk and gestured with his finger for the lads to carry on. Either the girl was tougher than she looked, or else she genuinely did know nothing about it, but Ballantine was certain of one thing: The Death that had been handed out in Albert Square on Friday night had come from his facility. There were going to be a whole lot of kids dying suddenly next week. That was fine by him — except that instead of buying it in the post-Jimmy euphoria, they'd got it for free, at his expense. That was another matter altogether.

The stuff had to be his. Apart from the fact that he was the only man on the planet making cheap Death, he kept tabs on every single pill that left the production line, and he was several thousand short.

"Smack her in the kidneys or the tits. I don't want any damage to her beautiful mind," said Ballantine to the heavy working on the girl. The last thing he wanted was for her to be unable to work. He needed her, at least for now. This girl and her friend, who had already been through this procedure, were Zealots, contracted in to oversee the manufacture of black market Death at Ballantine's facility. Why the rebel group would want to help him make Death was beyond him, but he certainly wasn't going to say no — at least until he'd worked out how to make it himself. But that was proving harder than he'd thought.

The heavy delivered a good one to the kidneys. The girl collapsed onto the ground, groaning, and was sick on the carpet. Fuck! Guys just didn't know how to deal out violence these days. The office would stink of disinfectant for the rest of the day.

Ballantine bent over her with his hands on his knees. "Your boyfriend told us, anyway," he said. "We just need to corroborate his story. Might as well," he said temptingly. "This is just violence. You wouldn't want me to tell these boys to step it up a notch, would you?"

"But I don't know!" insisted the girl, and she started to cry.

Ballantine nodded. One of the lads kicked her in the breast. She curled up around it, panting with pain and writhing around. But she still wasn't talking. It looked like she really didn't know.

In that case, it had to be one of his own guys who had stolen the pills. Ballantine could feel his blood pressure going up at the mere thought.

"My turn," said a voice behind him. "I got something I want to try . . ."

That was Christian, his son. Ballantine looked distastefully at him. He looked like a freak — forty-five years old and he dressed like a kid in baggy jeans, a baseball cap, and a T-shirt with a picture of a girl in a bikini snowboarding. What sort of gangster dressed like that? Fuck's sake.

"You leave her alone," he said. No way was he going to let Christian have a go at her — he'd ruin her for good, knowing him. It was just his bad luck to have a psycho for a son. He peered into his eyes suspiciously.

"Are you taking your fucking meds?"

"Jesus, Dad, do we have to talk about this in public?" Christian whined.

"Is he taking his fucking meds?" demanded Ballantine, addressing a big man standing by Christian's side — Vince, his bodyguard.

Vince nodded. "Absolutely, Mr. Ballantine. Every day. I take them out of the packaging myself."

Ballantine glanced again at his son, who was seething at being reminded in front of the boys that he was a psycho on meds. Then he looked down at the girl, who had got herself up onto her hands and knees, bleeding from her nose and mouth.

"I'm telling you, kid," he said, "if you're lying to me, it won't just be you. It'll be your family, it'll be your friends, it'll be the people you met on the bus coming to work this week. OK. Until we find out who's been stealing from me, you stay at the terminal. You don't go anywhere. You don't go for a shit without telling me about it. Now get her out of my sight."

The girl was dragged out. Ballantine didn't like people outside in daylight, but it wouldn't do any harm for the rest of the staff to see someone limping about. Good for discipline.

One of the guys shook his head. "Tough kids," he said.

"Tough kids?" sneered Ballantine. "They're chemists, right? That's both of them we've done good and not a word. They only got out of university a year or so ago; they don't have it in them. Which means, gentlemen, that one of you, or one of your staff — which amounts to the same thing — is stealing drugs off me. I am not a happy man."

The guys shuffled their feet and looked anxious.

"We have a leak." Ballantine thought about how angry it made him and he started yelling. "Have you any idea what this operation cost me? This is a fucking big risk and I am being let down badly here. People are taking this stuff for free. You hear me. Fucking free. Jesus!"

"Mr. Ballantine, those kids are lying. They have to be lying. Everyone else is watertight; they're the only ones we never worked with before."

"Where did kids like them learn to take a beating like that? University? They teach getting beat up as a chemistry unit at university? No. So you better find out who it is before I do it myself, OK? Because when I do find out, I am going to sack whoever was involved, and I am going to sack whoever was in charge of them. It should never have got this far."

The guys shuffled their feet awkwardly some more. Getting sacked from this firm meant losing a good deal more than your job.

"Back to work. Christian, Alan. Distribution. I want that drug on the street before it starts to occur to people that it's not a good idea to take it. And this time, I want them paying for it."

Sulkily, the guys edged out and hurried off to work on their own staff. Someone was going to have to take the rap for this. All they cared about was that it wasn't going to be them.

CHAPTER 6

THE PARTY

WHEN LIZZIE RECEIVED ADAM'S "I LOVE YOU" TEXT, IT TOOK her by surprise. It didn't make her feel happy though — it made her anxious. How come? Wasn't it exactly what she'd wanted?

She did want it. But . . .

The thing was, it was so quick. She hadn't even thought about love until the night before last, when Jimmy Earle died onstage in front of them and they'd spent the night out on the streets, caught up in the riots. It had been the most amazing night. If he'd had said it then, she'd have believed it. But now, in the cold light of day, she was less sure. If this was love, she was still falling. Why did he need to rush in and make out that it had already happened?

It made her feel cross, with herself as much as him. There were a hundred voices in her heart, and ninety-nine of them were overjoyed.

But one was going, "Yeah? Ya think?" And Lizzie being Lizzie, ninety-nine out of a hundred just wasn't good enough.

She picked him up at the cinema, and he looked dreadful.

"You OK?" she asked.

"Yeah, great, I feel great. Hey, I'm so looking forward to this," he told her, and he shot her a smile so sickly, so unfamiliar, she was shocked.

By the time she got the car on the highway she'd worked out exactly what was going on. He'd told her he loved her and now he was regretting it. Just like a boy. Just like Adam! One minute you were the center of his world, the next he treated you like you'd pissed on his chips.

One thing was for sure — he'd still be wanting the shag she'd promised him. *See about that, then,* she thought. She pulled out into the fast lane and put her foot down, ninety miles an hour. Maybe the atmosphere would improve at the party. The sooner they got there, the better.

Julie's house was set back from the road, so they passed it twice. There were electric gates, painted black and gold, and a drive winding up through young rhododendrons. Then they turned the corner and saw the house.

"Ta-da!" said Lizzie.

It was ridiculous. It was half mock Tudor, half Swiss chalet, but with turrets. Adam and Lizzie sat and goggled at it. Was it fabulous or was it hideous? Adam had no idea.

"It must have been built by a footballer," said Lizzie.

There was a bit of field set aside for the parking lot, full of expensive cars — a couple of Ferraris, an old Roller, any number of Porsches and Jags. Lizzie parked and looked over at Adam. He gave her another ghastly smile.

"I love you, Lizzie," he said.

"Ads . . ." she said.

"What?"

"Nothing."

She got out of the car and led the way toward the house.

Lizzie's cousin spotted them as they came in and rushed over to meet them.

"Lizzie! You made it."

"Julie! This is Adam . . ."

"Guys! Excuse me, I just want to borrow her for a moment — hey, Adam, get a drink, they're over there." She waved a hand over to the left and moved off to the right, pulling Lizzie with her. "We won't be long," she said.

Lizzie just had time to turn a surprised smile on him before she was hauled away into the crowd and hurried up the stairs.

"You are not going to believe some of the people I've got at this party," said Julie. "They practically own the world!"

"Is this your parents' place? What happened to that nice house in Knutsford?"

"Daddy got seriously rich."

"I thought he already was seriously rich."

"He got seriously richer."

"That was such a great house! This place looks like it was designed by a footballer."

"It was!"

They collapsed laughing up on the stairs.

"Do they know?" asked Lizzie. "Your parents? Won't they go mad when they find out you've had a huge party here?"

"They're away in . . . on holiday somewhere. They'll never know. The cleaners will come in. Professionals."

"But stuff gets broken. Stuff always gets broken. They'll know."

Julie stopped and put her finger on the side of her nose.

"No one would DARE. I have people at this party who will absolutely deal with anyone who gets out of order. If anyone so much as sneezes on the pizza, they will literally get turned inside out."

Lizzie laughed, a little uncertainly. "What sort of people?"

"People you would not believe. I won't even introduce you to them. *That* sort of people."

Julie was drunk, and her bright eyes indicated alcohol wasn't all she'd had. She pulled Lizzie into a little room, and fetched a mirror out of a drawer with several lines of white powder on it and a fifty-pound note rolled into a tight tube.

"Be careful. It's not cut."

"What is it?"

"XL5."

"What's that?"

"Rocket fuel. Try it."

Lizzie paused, then bent down to sniff up the end of one of the little lines. "Wow," she said.

"Isn't it? Get this — I'm not paying for any of it. The booze — anything!"

"Who is?"

"Older men."

"Julie!"

"Not *that* sort of older men. Not like they want favors. Like, I want a party and they want a party, and I have the house so they provide the drinks and the . . . 'nasal comestibles,' you know?"

"Oh my God."

"What?"

"My brain. My whole body!"

"Yeah, innit? Come on! I'll introduce you to some of them."

"But not the older ones."

"No! Not the older ones. Not the ones I won't introduce you to. The guys you're going to meet will all be top-notch, high-quality boyfriend material."

"I have a boyfriend. You just pulled me away from him. Can I take some of this down for him?"

"That's not a boyfriend. In entertainment terms, he's a night in with a bag of chips and Netflix." Julie slipped her a blister pack from the back of the drawer. "I mean something with a bit more of a kick. I'm talking about nightclub boyfriends. I'm talking about boys who know parts of your body you didn't even know existed. That one is *so* generic."

"You're an idiot."

"Come on! I'll introduce you."

Adam had rarely felt so out of place. All around him, the beautiful people draped themselves on items of expensive but badly chosen furniture, or gathered in groups across the expanse of cream carpet. A girl in a pair of jeans that cost more than Adam's dad's monthly pension sucked on a joint and watched Adam's best leather jacket — it had cost over a hundred pounds secondhand — turn into a laughable rag on his back.

The beautiful people averted their beautiful eyes.

He made his way to the bar, a long table carpeted with bottles of every form of alcohol known to man. A barman in a white suit on the other side raised an eyebrow at him.

"Er. What do you recommend?" Adam asked.

A couple of minutes later he was standing with a pint mug in his hand, with a drink called a Zombie in it. A cube of sugar burned weakly on top of a mound of ice. He stuck a can of beer in one pocket and a small bottle of vodka in the other — he had a feeling he was going to need friends tonight — then headed off to find Lizzie. He found her soon enough, killing herself laughing with Julie in the middle of a crowd. Everyone was tall, slim, tan, and expensively dressed. By the look of it they were pretty amusing, too. Lizzie was having the time of her life.

He walked past a couple of times in the hope that he'd catch her attention, but she didn't notice him at all. In the end he just shouldered his way in among them, and went, "Ta-da!" as if he'd just pulled off a trick.

At least it got him some attention. The beautiful people stared at him, then burst out laughing. He had no idea if they were laughing with him or at him. Then they started jabbering away again, glancing sideways at Adam as if he was made out of mud. But Lizzie found time to squeeze his arm before Julie dragged her off again.

"See you in a bit," she hissed. She shoved a little paper packet into his hand, winked, and vanished. Adam tried to make conversation.

"What do you do?" one of the girls asked.

"Still at school," he said.

"What does your father do?" she said.

Adam thought about it, and decided he couldn't be arsed trying to impress. "He used to be a stonemason, until he had an accident at work," he told her, and watched the girl's face fall.

"You're joking."

"Nope."

"So you . . ."

"Don't have any money. Yet. *Yet*," he said.

"So what are you doing here?" she wanted to know.

"I'm a tourist," he told her.

She smiled. "So we're . . ."

"Yeah. You're the zoo."

The girl's face fell, for the second time. Adam waltzed off. It didn't feel great, but making a fool out of someone else was better than feeling like a fool himself.

He needed to pee, so he got himself to a toilet and snorted up the entire packet of powder Lizzie had handed him.

Wow, he thought. Suddenly, he was in the mood to party. He ran straight out of the toilet and into the first group of people he could find. Everything was great! All his earlier anxieties about fitting in were gone. He was witty, attractive, full of ideas and jokes. In fact, he'd rarely felt so good in his entire life. His problems — Jess, his parents, his whole life — all disappeared into a sparkling fountain of happiness and well-being.

It lasted about fifteen minutes, going up all the time. Then — panic attack. It took him almost without warning. One minute he was chatting away happily to a girl in the hallway, then his heart began beating too fast, and before he knew it his head was about to explode and he could hardly breathe. He put out a hand to steady himself on the wall next to him. The girl he was talking to looked at him curiously.

"You OK?" she asked.

He looked back at her, his mouth opening and closing like a gold-fish, with nothing coming out.

The girl laughed shrilly.

"Look at this guy," she shrieked. "It looks as if his brains are going to come out of his ears."

Adam turned and fled, stumbling out into the garden, his heart going like a jackhammer, his brains boiling in hot fat. What was going on? That powder he'd hoovered up? And he'd been drinking cocktails. How many? At least three. He checked his phone for the time. They'd been at the party less than an hour and he was already so off his face he was hardly able to speak. How had it happened?

There was no way Lizzie could see him like this. He had to hide.

He headed off across the lawns into the night. There were lights around the edges of the flower beds, and a big, waxy yellow moon overhead, so at least he could see where he was going. Eventually he came to some water, with a dark, overgrown tree hanging over it. He crawled right under the dense canopy, where the thick leaves hid him completely. He lay on the ground in the dark shadows and waited for his heart to stop leaping around his chest like a rat in a trap.

Gradually, his breathing stilled, his heart began to beat rhythmically. But then, one by one, as if they were things he hadn't thought of up till now, the events of the day came crowding in on him. His parents weeping at home while he'd run away to have a good time. The pin-holed condom in his pocket — and Jess! Jess! Somehow he'd managed to forget about him altogether for the past couple of hours, but now the dreadful reality drove into his mind like an iron bolt. His lovely brother, gone, whom he'd thought he looked down on but in fact admired above anyone else. He'd thought Jess was someone he could rely on, even more than his mum and dad, but now he was dead and Adam had never even known him. Nothing was as it had seemed. All the hope and optimism of the past couple of days turned to despair. His life was ruined. He would never see his brother again.

Rolling over onto the dead leaves beneath him, Adam drew his knees up to his chest and held his breath. He hung on to the air as long as he could, but he had to breathe in the end, and when he did the tears came — great wracking sobs that tore at his chest, and which he was utterly unable to control. He lay in the dirt, bawling like a lost soul, astonished at both the intensity of his grief and the fact that he had somehow been so unaware of how bad he really felt.

Julie was right when she said there were some interesting people at the party. In the space of an hour, Lizzie had been introduced to rock stars, drug dealers, lawyers, a high court judge, politicians, and any number of hopelessly cool people involved in various kinds of money management. It was fun, but she was getting worried about abandoning Adam. She and Julie were on the stairs babbling with an offshore accountant when she spotted him pushing his way across the room on his own. He looked lost.

Full up with XL5 and fizz, Lizzie's heart melted. He was a boy. He wouldn't know what a feeling was if it got down on its knees and bit his bottom. He was confused! Poor baby.

It was up to her to reassure him.

"Fun, huh?" said Julie. "See anyone here you like . . . just meow!"

"I told you, I already have a boyfriend."

"Aw, you really like him, don't you? Are you . . . ?" Julie rolled her eyes and rocked her hips.

Lizzie laughed. "Not yet."

"Are you going to?"

"I guess I am."

"Of course," Julie added, "boys like that are just practice, you know? But it's a good idea to get a lot of practice in, if you see what I mean. So it's your first time with him? Has he been around much?"

"No. It's going to be his first time."

"Oh my God!" Julie stopped dead and stared at her. "And you . . . ?"

"My first time, too," Lizzie admitted.

"That's so sweet! Right. Come here."

She dragged her off to a quiet spot on the landing, rummaged around in her bag, and dug out a key.

"I was keeping this for something special. It's the key to the summer house. It's in among the trees; there's a fridge, some champagne on ice. Nice little sound system. You know? It's very private, there's a huge duvet . . . the moon is out, it's by the lake. Hey! What d'you think?"

"Is there really a moon?" Lizzie peered out the window — and yes, there it was, big and yellow, hanging among the trees.

"It's full, too, almost," said Julie. "Kinda cheesy, huh?"

"It's perfect!" Lizzie beamed and took the key.

Julie beamed back. "Go for it, babe," she said. "Be gentle with him," she called as Lizzie ran off. She sighed happily. Lizzie was so naive, she'd been worried about inviting her. There were some very dodgy sorts here tonight. But it was all right. She only wanted her sweet little virgin boy.

Lizzie spent the next twenty minutes running around the party with the key to the summer house in her pocket, trying to make Adam's dreams come true, and failing. Irritating! Where was he?

She was aware she was being a little unfair — she'd been off on her own for ages, after all — but it did remind her that she was annoyed with him anyway. *I love you.* Really? Just like that?

Her mother had warned her that he was a gold digger.

"I thought gold diggers were girls," she'd said.

"No, Lizzie. Gold diggers are *poor*," her mother replied.

Ridiculous. So how come she suddenly got the feeling he was playing her? He was probably just desperate to get into her pants. Fine. So where was he?

She ended up on the mezzanine floor, where she hoped she'd spy Adam below, but instead she got pounced on by a pair of really odd guys — some of those older men that Julie had been boasting about, perhaps. One of them was a huge, powerful-looking man, built like a house. He was wearing a suit so sharp you could have tied his lapels to your shoes and skated on them. He looked hopelessly out of place at a party like this.

The other was somewhere in his forties, quite handsome at first glance, but you could tell as soon as you looked closely that he'd had loads of surgery to make it happen. The oddest thing about him was the way he was dressed, like an American teenager out of an eighties movie: baggy jeans hanging down his bum, T-shirt with a gory picture of Metallica on the front, high-tops, and, most ridiculous of all, a baseball cap with the bill halfway around his head. At first she thought it was a costume, but from the way he was preening himself, he obviously thought he looked cool. His eyes, which had trouble meeting hers, kept dropping down to her breasts. All in all, he was one of the creepiest guys she'd seen in a long time.

It turned out that Vince, the sharp suit, was actually employed by the elderly teenager, whose name was Christian.

"As what?" Lizzie wanted to know.

Christian smiled. "Whatever I want him to be," he said. "Right, Vince?"

"You bet, Mr. Christian."

"You mean he's some sort of servant?" she asked. "Like Jeeves and Wooster? He's your *butler*?" She snorted.

"Kinda," said Christian. "And my bodyguard."

"Wow," said Lizzie. She looked at the sharp suit. "What do you need a bodyguard for?" she asked.

Christian shrugged. "I'm a rich man," he said, gazing vaguely at her groin. "Rich people get kidnapped, attacked, robbed. All sorts of bad things." He shook his head. "There are always people around who aren't happy about stuff."

Lizzie thought about it. "Would he take a bullet for you?" she demanded.

Christian seemed struck by this thought. "Would you?" he asked, turning to Vince.

"That's what I'm paid for, sir," said Vince.

Christian smiled. "I pay him a fuck of a lot of money. He's carrying. Show her," he ordered.

Obediently, Vince turned slightly away from the crowd and opened his immaculate jacket, revealing a holster with a gun tucked inside. Lizzie was so shocked she almost choked on her wine.

"Me, too. But not a gun." Christian lifted up his T-shirt to reveal a stout-looking knife with an odd, short blade.

"Why's the blade so short?" she wanted to know.

"Specialist item," said Christian. But he didn't offer to tell her what for.

Lizzie was both scared and mesmerized. "Wow. But what do you *do*?" she asked. "How come all these people want to kill you?"

Vince coughed discreetly. "A lot of people would think that was a silly sort of question to ask," he said.

"Lizzie's not a lot of people," said Christian. He smiled at her, revealing a set of teeth that looked at least twenty years younger than the rest of him.

Vince made a soft but exasperated noise, like an irritated parent.

Christian ignored him. "All sorts of stuff. Drugs. Weapons."

"You're a gangster?!"

He shook his head. "Businessman!" he said.

"You don't look like a gangster," Lizzie said to him. "He does," she added, nodding at Vince.

"I might be in disguise," said Christian.

A joke! It wasn't all that funny, but Lizzie laughed anyway, out of kindness as much as anything. Christian was delighted; he beamed at her.

"I like you," he told her, reaching out and touching her lightly on the arm.

It was a pass, definitely. "That's very nice, thank you," said Lizzie. Time to escape. She began to edge away but he plucked at her clothes.

"Do you want another drink?" he demanded. "What do you want? Vince'll get it for you, won't you, Vince?"

"But he'd have to leave you on your own, wouldn't he?" Lizzie said. "What if an assassin comes? Hey — what if *I'm* an assassin?"

"Are you?"

"No," she admitted.

"I didn't think you were. So, what'll you have?"

Lizzie shook her head. "Sorry," she said. "I've got to go and find my boyfriend. Another time, eh?"

"Hang on . . ." Christian fished a card out of his pocket and handed it to her. "Give me a call sometime," he said.

"Thanks. Great," said Lizzie brightly. She turned and made her way downstairs.

Behind her, Christian nudged his bodyguard. "I like her," he said. "She'd make a good girlfriend. Follow her."

Vince looked suspiciously at his employer. "Sir, excuse me for asking, but did you drink your milk this morning?"

Christian was furious. "Fuck you, Vince," he said. "This is a party. We do not talk about milk at a party. For your information, yes, I did drink my fucking milk, as you well know since you stood over me watching me swallow it. How much do I pay you, Vince?"

"A fuck of a lot of money, sir."

"Right. So go and do as I tell you."

"Yes, Mr. Christian," said Vince, and he edged his way into the crush after Lizzie.

CHAPTER 7

LOSING IT

SHE FINALLY CAUGHT UP WITH ADAM IN THE ENTRANCE HALL.

"Where've you been?" she demanded.

Adam gave her a wobbly smile. "Couldn't find you. Went for a walk," he said.

He looked really odd. He had leaves and mud on his clothes. "What's been going on?" she asked.

He laughed awkwardly. Suddenly she was struck by a dreadful suspicion. Leaves on his clothes . . . ?

"Looks more like you went for a roll," she said primly.

"No! No, no. I had to lie down. I got in a mess. That stuff you gave me . . ."

"XL5," she said. She looked at him more closely. His eyes were red. "Have you been crying?" she asked.

"No!" insisted Adam. He hurt so much, he couldn't admit it to anyone — least of all Lizzie. "I just took too much of that stuff, that's all."

"How much did you have?"

"All of it," he admitted.

"All of it? Adam!"

"I had to go for a walk, it blew my head off."

Lizzie hovered for a moment between anger and pity — anger because he'd hogged the lot, pity because . . .

"You're only supposed to have a tiny little line. It's uncut."

"No one told me," he said, and his voice sounded tearful. Pity won.

"Oh . . . Come here." She linked arms with him and planted a little kiss on his cheek. "Poor soldier. Beaten up by drugs." He grinned at her — another wobbly, uncertain grin. Sweet! "Feeling better?"

"Bit better."

He looked so upset, she laughed. "Come with me."

She led the way out of the house and down the steps. A bottle of champagne, some relaxing music, a snuggle up under the duvet. If that didn't make him feel better, nothing would.

The moon, the balmy air, the music drifting across from the house. Adam was pretty much out of his head, coming down now, in grief for his brother, his life, God knows what else, and still feeling panicky; but even so, he knew that this had to be his time with Lizzie. He squeezed her arm. It was going right again. He felt really weird, but it was going right. With his other hand he touched the doctored condom in his back pocket. He was going to lose his virginity and try to make his fortune in one go. It was so pathetic he snorted in amusement at himself.

"What is it?" demanded Lizzie.

"I'm having such a good time," he said, but it sounded like sarcasm. He hurried on. "Hey, look. Why don't we sneak upstairs and find a room?"

But Lizzie shook her head. "You just come with me," she said.

"What for?"

"I want to go for a walk." She guided him across the lawn toward the lake, but Adam held back. It was the wrong direction. He wanted the house, a room. He wanted sex.

"I've already been this way," he said.

She shot him a curious look. "Just for me," she wheedled.

But he stopped walking. "No, let's go in and find a room. You haven't changed your mind again . . ." Despite himself, his voice was sounding sulky.

"Adam . . . don't do this to me, not now . . ." But he was already certain she was putting him off.

"You're always making promises," he complained. "And then you back off. It's always the same."

"Adam, stop it!"

"Are we going to do it or not?" he demanded.

She let go of his hand and shook her head. "You know what, Adam? No, we're not. Just . . ." She turned abruptly without finishing and stomped off back across the lawn.

"You never had any intention of it, did you?" he shouted after her.

She spun on her heel. "This," she said, taking it out and shaking it at him, "is the key to the summer house. There was going to be champagne on ice, nice music, and the moon over the lake. I wanted it to be like that, and all you wanted was a fuck. So find someone else to fuck. OK? Because it isn't going to be me!"

She stormed off.

"Liar!" yelled Adam. He stood still and watched her go, then put his head in his hands. Was it true? Of course it was true! He'd talked himself out of it. Everything was turning to shit. Everything he touched — everything he even thought about, he now realized — all turned to shit.

He had to make it all right. He had no idea how. Just beg her to forgive him. Tell her what a dick he was. Tell her how much he loved her, before she found out the truth and gave him the boot anyway.

Turning, he ran back to the house and through the crowds, searching, searching, searching for her. But she was nowhere to be seen.

It just went to show. You could have a perfect night in a perfect setting with the perfect moon by the perfect lake listening to the perfect music, but if you tried to do it with an idiot, it wasn't going to work.

Lizzie wasn't inside more than a few minutes when she bumped into Vince, who told her that the boss would like to have a drink with her.

"No, thanks," she said. She went to sit in the loo for a bit to have a cry, and when she came out, Christian was waiting for her, with

Vince by his side bearing a couple of very elegant-looking cocktails on a tray. She was so taken aback that she accepted one and ended up tucked away in a bay window in one of the reception rooms, while Vince kind of floated in the background, which she supposed was what servants did. She was aware that they were really rather hidden. What if Adam came looking for her? Well, let him look. He could find her if he tried.

Adam had not yet totally imploded into his own misery, but he wasn't far off it. He should have been at home, grieving with his parents. Instead he'd tried to trick his girlfriend into giving him a future for free. Grief, betrayal, self-disgust, and an avalanching sense of failure were overwhelming him. He quickly gave up trying to find Lizzie, and was leaning against a wall, sinking fast, swigging beer from a can, when Julie passed by and spotted him.

"What are you doing here?" she demanded. "I thought you were off with Liz. Where is she?"

"I don't know," he said.

Julie cast an expert eye over the hopeless mess before her. "You've had a row," she said.

Adam hung his head.

"Shit. Where is she?" Julie grabbed him by the arm and trailed him off to hunt her down. They found her eventually, trapped in a bay window talking to a weird-looking guy dressed up in fancy skate-board gear. Adam cringed back and glanced anxiously at Julie, who was staring openmouthed at them. She began to hiss in his ear.

"Shit, shit, shit. This is bad, this is bad. See that guy talking to her? That's Christian Ballantine. He is completely predatory. I mean, the guy is a pervert, first class — and he's rich. No one can lay a finger on him. We have to get her away from him."

Adam shook his head. Julie ignored him.

"You go in this way, I'll go round the other side. Pincer movement. You are such a dick," she added in despair. "See the big guy in the suit? He's a gorilla, trying to stop anyone getting near them. You have to sneak past him. You got me?"

Adam peered around the big man. "Does she want me to?"

"Of course she wants you to. She's gone on you. She said. Go get her, tiger. Say sorry and get her away as fast as you can, before . . ."

"What?"

"Before he goes off with her and . . . interferes with her. She's *yours*, isn't she?"

Adam licked his lips. The pitiful remains of hope stirred sluggishly within him. He still had a chance!

"And don't let the suit see you," hissed Julie. She shoved Adam in the back and he went tottering off toward them, while Julie scuttled off to get around to Lizzie from the other side.

Jesus, she thought, *talk about the cavalry*. Christian was very rich, very weird, and very powerful. He thought he could do exactly as he wanted. There was a good reason for that: He could.

Lizzie was trying to work out how to escape again without being hopelessly obvious about it when Adam suddenly appeared at her side.

"Talk?" he said.

Christian twisted around and glared angrily at him. "Where the fuck's Vince?" he demanded.

Adam tugged at her sleeve; Christian grabbed hold of her arm. "You're not going anywhere," he said.

Lizzie had had enough. The pair of them were manhandling her like she was some kind of sandwich filling. She yanked furiously away. Adam let go at once, but Christian tightened his hold. It hurt. That was it. Lizzie took a deep breath and did what she had been told years ago to do on these occasions: She stared Christian straight in the eye and screamed as loudly as she could.

There was a shocked and sudden silence. All around them in the crowded room, people turned to look, saw who was involved, and turned quietly away again. In the silence, Lizzie let out a brittle laugh. Then things moved very quickly.

Adam stuck a drunken fist out at Christian and, by sheer bad luck, caught him on the ear. Christian let out a howl and Adam disappeared backward. At the same time, Julie materialized, beamed at Christian, and pushed Lizzie roughly away into the crowds.

"What? What's going on?"

"No. No, no, no, no, no," said Julie. "You are so out of here."

Adam, meanwhile, was on a short journey to the front steps, the back of his leather jacket clenched firmly in the huge fist of Vince. He carried Adam out of sight around the side of the house, dropped him onto the gravel, and gave him a short but expert beating; one blow to the head to knock him down, a couple as he collapsed, and three or four kicks while he lay on the gravel. Finally, he stamped on his head. Then he went back into the house. Shortly after, Julie came running out, pulling Lizzie by the hand. Lizzie was in tears.

"Just give me back my keys," she begged.

"No, you're not driving in that state," said Julie. "Here's Harold anyway, he's going to give you a lift home," she added as a car came up the drive.

"I wish I'd never come," Lizzie groaned. The whole thing was so utterly humiliating. Messed about by Adam, mauled by Christian, pushed around the place by Julie . . . and now, to top it all, she was being sent home early.

"It's your own fault, Liz. That boy is a wanker, a real wanker. And then you end up getting chatted up by Christian Ballantine of all people . . ."

"He wasn't chatting me up . . ."

"Yes, he was! Your mum is right; you're like a baby. Those people are gangsters! They're dangerous. You don't have any sense at all, no radar. You're like a rabbit in the headlights. He spotted you limping into his territory a mile away."

Lizzie blubbered helplessly. The car pulled up next to them, and Julie guided her into the backseat.

"I'll get the car back to you tomorrow, OK? Don't go anywhere. Straight home," she ordered the driver.

"What about Adam?" Lizzie cried.

"I'll sort Adam out," said Julie grimly. "And, Liz — don't see him again. He's a tosser. You're better than that."

She shut the door, and the car pulled away. As it did, a figure staggered out of the shrubbery and ran forward.

"Lizzie!" screamed Adam, holding out his hands for them to stop. The car drove quietly around him and off down the drive. "Lizzie!" he groaned.

Julie came marching up and shoved him in the chest.

"You wanker!" she yelled. "You complete, total wanker. If I catch you anywhere near my cousin again I'll have you beaten up properly, you hear me?"

"I'm sorry," wept Adam.

"You are so pathetic. Just . . . fuck off." She stormed back to the house.

"I don't have any money to get back," Adam called after her.

"God." Julie rolled her eyes. She dug in her pocket and fished out forty pounds for him. "Don't let me ever see you round here again," she said, and disappeared inside.

Adam put the money in his pocket and went back to weep in the shrubbery for a while. Then he phoned for a cab home.

CHAPTER 8

GARRY

IN THE TAXI, ADAM CONTINUED TO CRY. THE FUTURE HAD
been smiling at him only yesterday. Now it was leering at him like a
rotting skull, stinking, filthy, and full of fear.

You thought I was yours? it leered. *Well, I'm not.*

What had he done to deserve this? It wasn't even his fault! If it
was anyone's fault, it was Jess's. Jess, who had pretended to love his
family. Jess, who had lived and died a whole other life without any of
them knowing about it. Jess the liar, Jess the fraud. His parents had
kept telling him just how important his brother was, but he had never
really taken it on board. Now he'd gone, and he'd taken Adam's entire
life with him. Adam had trusted him, and he'd been let down. Suddenly
he hated Jess with all his heart. He wanted to stamp him to a pulp, to
kick him, hurt him, dig him up out of the ground and strangle him.

Even more than that, though, he wanted to ask him — why? Why had he fooled them all for so long? Why had he lied? What had he been doing all that time?

Who on earth *was* he?

He would never know. Jess had pulled off the ultimate escape from all questions, all blame, all guilt, all pain. Perhaps the thing that made Adam angrier than anything was the fact that Jess had put himself so totally beyond reach, and there was nothing he could do about it.

His kidney ached. His ankle was swelling up and growing stiff, his face red raw from the gravel. He'd cracked a rib, too; it hurt every time he breathed. Lizzie was gone; he'd blown every chance he ever had. He found the little bottle of vodka that he had stolen off the table and swigged at it, ducking out of sight of the cabbie, who was already eyeing him suspiciously.

What next? Go home? What for? To begin his new life? What a laugh! He didn't need work, he needed answers. Someone out there must know what Jess had been doing all this time — known him the way his family never had. But who? In all those years Jess had only ever had one girlfriend, a girl named Maryse who had disappeared to London when she was eighteen and never been seen again. There had been one or two school and university friends . . . Garry, for instance. He remembered Garry. Bearded bloke in a wheelchair. He'd even been around to the house a few times.

Now that he thought about it, Adam was sure he'd heard Jess and Garry going on about the Zealots a few times, years ago. Conversations and arguments with his dad, about how cool the Zealots were, how at least they were doing something. That sort of stuff.

He was a nice guy, Garry. Stuck in a wheelchair, but he never let it get him down. Played basketball.

And . . . Adam knew where he lived. Sort of. On the way back from a trip into town with Jess, they'd stopped by to see him. A dingy little place in Fallowfield. Him and Jess had been good mates for a while. Garry was in on it as well — betcha! If anyone knew what Jess had been up to, it was him.

Adam wasn't sure exactly where Garry lived, only the street. Once he'd paid the cabbie and got out, he wasn't even so sure about that anymore. The last time he'd been there was years ago.

But he was in luck. As he finished off the remains of the vodka and limped up the road a bit — there it was. He recognized the color of the drainpipe, which was painted purple.

There was a light on upstairs.

He tapped on the door. No reply. He banged. Nothing. He stood swaying outside for a moment.

Fuck this, he thought, *I'm dying here.*

"Garry!" he bawled suddenly. "Garry!" He began to weep again. No one appeared, but he thought he heard a noise at the window.

"Let me in!" he yelled. Above him, the curtains twitched. "Where's my brother? What happened to Jess? Garry! Answer me! You know. I know you know."

He kicked at the door and to his surprise it bent easily. It wasn't much more than plywood. He leaned back and flung his shoulder at it. The lock broke through the thin wood and Adam stumbled in, gasping at the pain in his ribs. Upstairs, someone shouted in surprise. He was standing in a cluttered sitting room. There was a stairway with a stair lift through an open door opposite him.

"What the fuck's going on? Jesus . . ."

He ran and looked up the stairs. Garry was on his way down on the stair lift. "Who the fuck are you?" he screamed. "What are you doing here? Get out of my house!"

Adam ran up to meet him. "I'm Jess's brother. What happened to him? He's supposed to have died with the Zealots. You know, don't you, you know . . ."

There was noise above him. Someone else was up there. He peered up. "Who's that?"

Garry was furious.

"You idiot, the police could be round. I don't know anything, Adam — go away!"

Garry didn't seem able to stop the stair lift, and continued past Adam and down. He grabbed out at Adam's sleeve with one hand, fiddling with the controls of the stair lift with the other. Adam pulled away.

"You used to talk about the Zealots. Where is he? Who's up there? Is that him?"

"No, of course it's not him. Adam, come here, come down here and talk to me. Jesus, this fucking thing won't work!" Garry leaned backward and snatched at him as the chair carried past on its way down. "Adam! How do I know what happened to him?"

"Who's up there? What's going on?" In Adam's addled brain, everything that happened was about him and his brother. He pulled himself free and went tearing up the stairs, while Garry, howling in rage and frustration, continued down at a snail's pace. Adam burst into the bedroom. Someone was on the bed, covered up by the duvet. Adam dragged it off. It was a half-dressed girl. She let out a wail, and ran out of the room and off down the stairs.

"Stella! Don't go. Come back. Stella!"

Downstairs, the door slammed.

"Adam!" roared Garry.

Adam stood next to the bed looking wildly around him. He was certain Garry knew something. He began ransacking the room, looking for some sort of a clue. On the bed, on the floor, on the chair, on the table . . . He pulled open a cupboard by the bed and something spilled out. A bag of pills. He snatched them up. There was another roar behind him. Garry, flushed with rage, was clinging on to the door, his hairy face distorted in a fearful grimace.

"You stupid little fuck!" he screamed. He staggered toward him, grasping for the bag. "Give me that . . . Give me it . . ."

Adam danced out of reach. Garry was dealing drugs, was he? "Tell me what happened to him! What do you know?"

"I don't know anything. What's wrong with you?"

"You know what's wrong with me!" Adam, to his shame, began to weep again.

"You little prick, Adam. Give me that! What are you doing?"

"This can pay for it — this can pay . . ." cried Adam. He pushed Garry out of the way, and the crippled man fell to the floor. Adam ran out of the room and down the stairs.

"Adam, no! You don't know what you're doing. Come back!"

But Adam was gone, out the door, on his way. Garry's yells stopped abruptly. Adam ran on. He ran and ran and ran, until the adrenaline stopped and the pain in his ribs kicked back in. He bent over, gasping for breath. When he'd recovered enough to move on, he put the bag of pills in his pocket and crept home.

It was over a mile back, and every step was agony. Halfway, under a street lamp, he took the bag of pills out and had a better look.

They were unmistakable. Little white caps with a crude black image printed on each one. A skull and crossbones.

It was a bag full of Death.

But it couldn't be. Death cost a fortune, everyone knew that. What was a poor man like Garry doing with this? There must have been fifty pills in there. They were worth . . . It was crazy! Thousands. Tens of thousands. Some sort of fraud? It had to be . . .

Adam put the bag back in his pocket and carried on home. When he got there, the house was still. He crept upstairs as quietly as he could and lay on the bed. He stayed still, trying not to think. He tried texting Lizzie.

I'm sorry. Please talk to me.

Nothing.

Please, Lizzie, please. I need you.

He stared at the screen, texted again. The same thing.

That was it. It was over. He was never going to see her again.

Adam took out the bag of pills and held one in the palm of his hand. He turned the TV on. It was an old film. A man and a woman kissed. She rested her head against his neck and sighed deeply.

Some kind of scam, those pills. Not real. But the news had said it was the Zealots handing the stuff out at Albert Square. If Garry was connected with the Zealots . . .

Could be. Maybe, maybe not. Who knew?

Adam popped the pill into his mouth, but didn't swallow, just held it there. It was an answer, wasn't it? One glorious week. What else had he got to look forward to now?

"We need a place of our own," said the man on the TV. The woman reached up and kissed him again. She sighed.

He could sell the rest of the pills and have the time of his life. Why not?

The pill was dissolving in his mouth. It tasted acrid. Adam reached over to the glass of water by his bed, took a mouthful, and swallowed.

He lay there. What had he done? *Not much*, he thought. What had he got to lose? *Not much.*

A shit life.

He knew he should get up and stick his finger down his throat, but he didn't. He lay there and lay there and waited to see if he would, but he didn't. It was a relief, really.

Then he closed his eyes and fell asleep.

PART 2

THE LIST

CHAPTER 9
DAY 1

WHEN ADAM WOKE UP THE NEXT MORNING, IT HAPPENED SO suddenly he was astonished. His eyes snapped open. He felt so clear-headed. His blood was fizzing. He was *happy*.

What's going on? he thought — and there it was, the past few days laid out before his eyes with total recall, every second in high definition. The concert, the riots, Jess, the party, Lizzie, how bad he'd cocked it up, Garry, the girl, the stair lift . . . and then right at the end of it, like a car crash, smack into a brick wall . . . Death.

He'd taken Death.

Adam leaped out of bed and stared at himself in the wardrobe mirror. His eyes sparkled. His skin was flawless — even the little spots on his forehead had vanished without trace. He was going to die? Impossible! He'd never felt so alive.

But how come? There'd been a fight. He'd been pulped! He felt where his rib had been cracked. There was a small, sharp pain there. Last night it had been agony.

The battering hadn't been a dream. This was Death working its magic, filling him up to the brim with life before it took it all away. He was transformed. He was quick, smart, and strong. He was capable of anything . . .

And then he was going to die.

Adam stared at his reflection. This was him. A week to live? He tried to imagine himself dead and gone, tried to feel the stab of fear that must be in there somewhere. But he was too full of life. *This* was what it must have been like for Jimmy Earle. Now he got it. He stared at his fingers, the whorls on the tips, the flesh and blood and bone of them. They were a miracle of engineering. *He* was a miracle. Life itself was a miracle. The pattern of the wallpaper, the colors on the carpet. Outside the window a bird sang. That was a miracle. The whole glorious pageant of life was beating, beating — waiting for him to start up and go. And he was a part of it.

One week, eh? Death was on his heels, was it? He'd out-run it, out-gun it, out-smart it, out-live it — and then welcome it like an old friend. He gasped as another rush sped through him, smooth, fast, flawless. And it was still getting better! One week was plenty of time to do all the things he needed to do. How much real living did the average person get through in eighty or ninety years? How long did they spend staring at the wall, ashamed, asleep, doped up, stupid, whatever? How many of them were truly alive, the way he was alive right now? How many of them understood the glory and beauty of it? Hardly any. Maybe none at all. One week was time enough to do everything in the world so long as you lived hard enough, fierce enough, young enough, true enough. The rest of it was just waiting to die.

The waiting was over. It was time to live — right now!

No regrets. Regrets were for the little people. Hope was for the angels. For one week, Adam was one of them.

He wanted to run out into the sun and start at once. Even sitting here, just breathing, just being alive was good — but the precious seconds were ticking past so fast.

The bucket list! His last deeds on earth. He grabbed a pencil and some paper and began to write.

Fall in love.

What was he talking about? He *was* in love! Start again.

Sex with Lizzie. Get her pregnant.

Yeah. He wanted to leave something behind. A son! He wanted a son. He'd always thought he'd have children one day. Not so soon — but now he didn't have time to waste. He had to *make* it happen.

Loads of sex with loads of girls. Several of them at once.

Too right! He had a lifetime of shagging to get done in one week. One girl wasn't going to be able to keep up with that.

. What else? Money. Yeah. He needed some money to spend. The life he was going to pack in didn't come cheap. And . . . his parents! People were going to miss him. He had to make it all right for them after he was gone.

Get rich. Leave my parents and Lizzie with enough money so they'll never have to work again.

Unable to stay still any longer, Adam jumped up and skittered around the room. He was wasting time! He had to get moving.

He got back to his desk and finished the list with a flourish.

Drink champagne till I can't stand.

Do cocaine.

Drive a supercar around Manchester.

Kill someone who deserves to die.

Do something so that humanity will remember me forever.

Die on the Himalayas, watching the sun go down.

Adam read it through. Yeah. It was a good list. It was a great list. It was a life's work, and it was doable. No problem. First off — Lizzie. Love. He wanted her at his side while he lived his last week on earth. He took out his phone and rang. No answer. OK. She was still cross. Yeah, well, so she'd had a bad time, so had he. Was he sulking about it? No, he was not. And shit, he was going to die!

He was going to die . . .

Don't think it, don't think it. Don't think anything. You don't dare. You have to live.

He texted: **Lizzie, I love you! Got grt news! Rng me!**

What next? Money. Hey! He already had some. He rummaged about in the covers for the pills he'd stolen from Garry. Death. Magic! These were worth a fortune. He was going to be living like a god for the next seven days.

Adam leaned into the mirror and grinned at himself. Despite the life that was fizzing inside him, his face looked back at him like a grinning grim reaper. He stared in horror for a moment, then flung himself back into action. He put on his clothes and hurried downstairs. He had to keep moving; he had to keep going. But as he vaulted down the last three steps, he felt a hard, hot little fizz burrowing its way around and around his stomach. What was that . . . ?

It was fear. Fear that he'd thrown away his one golden gateway into this stunning, unaccountable universe. Even now, when the drug was at its height inside him, filling his senses with love and joy, there was despair as well. It was part of the deal. Adam stood at the bottom of the stairs and panted with terror as he thought of how much he had thrown away.

There's no antidote, he thought. *Don't waste time even worrying about it. No regrets!* He swung round the banister and into the kitchen. *Don't think, just live.* That was what life was all about. That was what life had always been about, if only he'd had the courage. Well, now he had no choice.

Don't think. Don't care. Just do.

His dad was sitting at the table studying something on the laptop. He was always taking courses, trying to find a way back into work. It was languages now. What a joke. His dad was rubbish at languages. He'd never liked studying — his brain was in his hands, his mum always said. It was just fate that when he'd had an accident, it was his hands that caught it.

"Where's Mum?" asked Adam. She always waited to greet him, every morning.

"Gone to bed." He looked up coldly at Adam. For a second Adam was confused — what had he done wrong? Then he remembered. Jess. The party. Shit.

"I'm sorry," he began, but then he was angry, too. He had one week to live. What was he supposed to do, sit around holding hands with them because of bloody Jess?

"I don't understand you. Your brother is dead and you run away from us. This is a time we should be together," said his father.

"He lied to us about everything, that's not my fault," said Adam. He stood by the counter, thinking, *What am I doing here?* He was wasting time.

"Your mother is upset," said his dad. As he spoke, his eyes filled with tears and Adam's heart went out to him. He'd made his family his life's work. First his hands had been broken, then his eldest son had died. And now Adam, too, was going to leave him. What did the old man have left, out of the treasure chest of his life? A surge of love ran through Adam. He ran across and seized his father around the chest.

"It's going to be all right. I have a plan. Gonna hit the big time, Dad!" It was what his dad always used to say, back in the day.

His dad shook his head and pushed weakly against Adam's arms. He looked so broken. "No, no, I understand how you feel, Adam. You having to leave school to support me. It's wrong. I've let you all down . . ."

Adam laughed. His dad thought everything was lost. How wrong could you be? Brilliant! "No. Really! I have a plan. We're going to make the big time."

His dad's brow creased. "Work . . ." he began.

"No, not work. A proper plan. You'll see. I love you, Dad." He leaned forward and planted a great big kiss on his dad, right on the smacker. His dad almost jumped back. They weren't a kissing family.

"Oh my God!" he said. But then he smiled and hugged Adam back. "I love you, too, Adam. I never say, but I do. Always remember that."

For a moment Adam wanted to tell his dad everything, but he didn't dare. Instead, he turned and ran. "There'll be enough money for everything," he shouted over his shoulder.

Behind him his dad rose to his feet, alarmed. "What are you doing? Come back! No trouble, Adam! No trouble . . ." But Adam was out the door and away, off to fulfill his destiny, off to make his dreams come true and turn the world into a better place for everyone who loved him. He had one week to do it.

You don't dare think and you feel so much and you feel so good and you're so scared, and you so much want to live but you're not going to. And the life is fizzling out of your fingertips and if someone came up to you right now and said, "You can have your life back but you won't ever feel like this again" — what would you say? Because this is Death. Death is the cost of life, of all this beauty and joy and love. No more joy forever, not like this, not real joy . . .

No! No! No! Of course you'd say no. Yes to joy and love and beauty and Death, and no to year after year of being half-alive and never knowing what life is about. You have to look life in the face now. You have no choice. You made your choice when you swallowed that little pill. So no, you wouldn't swap this for all the world, you can't, not for your mum and dad whose hearts will be broken, not for Lizzie, not for yourself. Not for anything.

And you ride the bus so full of joy and tears and youth and life and death, you hardly know what to do with yourself, except that whatever it is, it has to start now, right now, because this is it, my friend, what you're doing now, right here, this moment, this one precious moment in time called now. It's all you have. Don't waste it. There's so little of it left.

The bus sped along. Adam tried not to think. *Regret it, forget it, regret it, forget it*, his brain sang and sang and sang, all the way out to Wilmslow.

Lizzie rose out of sleep like a turtle surfacing in a sewer. She felt disgusting — sick, headachy, and anxious, too, as if the events of last night were still happening. Someone was banging on the window.

It had to be her dad. *Have some respect for the dying.* She pulled the covers over her head and tried to ignore it. It would go away. The world would go away. Even this headache would go away, eventually.

No. Louder than ever! Unbelievable, what selfishness. It was right by her ear, right by her damn ear! In the darkness she ground her teeth. Monday mornings during break were not for consciousness. He knew that. He was being a bastard.

She lifted her sore head. "Go away!" she roared. But even as she bellowed she remembered that her room was way up high on the second floor. She peered over her shoulder. There was a gap in the curtains just big enough for her to see that the bastard was Adam. He was standing outside her window, grinning at her like a maniac.

Lizzie stared at him a moment, then laid her head back down. Clearly she was still asleep, dreaming.

The events of last night came avalanching back to her at the exact same moment as she realized that this was real. She clawed herself around and stared. Yep. Adam, balancing on her window ledge, twenty feet up — Jesus!

She started to leap out of bed to open the window and save his life, when she realized she had nothing on. Conscious of how pathetic it was to let someone die rather than let him see her naked in his last seconds, she wrapped the comforter around herself and shot over to the window. Adam looked completely comfortable. He grinned and let go of the window frame so that he fell slightly backward, making her stomach vault inside her as she fumbled at the catch.

"You idiot," she hissed.

She opened the flap at the top of the window, scared that if she opened the main one she'd knock him off. As she did so, the comforter fell half off her and she had to snatch at it. Adam smiled happily and let out a low whistle.

"What are you doing? How did you get up there?"

"I climbed."

"No, you didn't." Lizzie peered out. How had he done it? When she was little she used to look out her window when she'd been locked in her room, imagining the climb down. There were a few old screws that had once been used for wires to hold up a climbing plant. Apart from that, nothing.

"How did you do it?" she demanded.

"Let me in," pleaded Adam.

She had no choice. She opened the window. He stepped in and went to grab her, but she twisted away. "You must be off your head. Get out of here!"

"Lizzie — please!"

"I mean it, Adam. You were a total shit last night." She peered at him, aware that she looked a mess and, despite herself, feeling a bit of a tingle at his closeness to her, here in her bedroom, while she held on to the comforter to hide her nakedness.

"I know I was. But listen — Jess has died."

"What? Jess . . . ?"

"I was scared to tell you."

"Adam . . ." Lizzie made a face and fell onto the bed. She was hardly awake. This was bending her brain.

"I've got to leave school. Dad has no money. Jess earned everything."

Lizzie shook her head. "I need some painkillers. Hang on . . ." She went to her table, still clutching at the comforter, and swallowed some aspirin. She got back into bed, folded the comforter tightly around her, and glared at him. Adam slowly sat down beside her and gave her a lopsided grin. Lizzie shook her head, but inside she felt a lot less cool than she made out. He had scaled the wall of her house to reach her window. It was like *Romeo and Juliet*. He was in her bedroom.

No one knew he was there. He looked gorgeous. His blue eyes, a bit of a sweat on him. Actually, truth be told, he looked really gorgeous — more so than normal, and she had really fancied him right from the off.

And his brother was dead. Shit. It began to sink in. Something dreadful had happened. But how come he was looking so happy?

"Go on, then," she said. "This had better be good."

As Adam's story unfolded, Lizzie felt a column of panic rising inside her. Jess dead. No wonder Adam was so weird at the party. Having to leave school and get a crap job. It all got worse and worse and worse, but normal worse. And then — Death. He'd taken Death.

When he said it, she laughed. It wasn't pleasure; it was fear. She couldn't take on what it meant. This sort of thing happened to other people. It was not possible that something like this could enter her own life.

"I don't believe you," she said.

"I climbed your wall," said Adam. "Just the gaps between the bricks, with my fingers and my toes. I'm like — I'm alive for the first time. Really, really alive. Look."

He had the evidence in his face, in his looks, in the speed and fire of him. But he had concrete evidence as well. He rummaged around in the little backpack on his shoulder and pulled out the little bag of pills.

"Oh my God."

"See?"

It was true. "Adam! What have you done?" It sent a chill of excitement and fear right through her. He was doomed — and he looked so alive! "Why did you do it?"

Adam looked appalled. "Don't say that," he said. "I have my week, Lizzie. It's going to be the best week anyone ever had. And I want to spend it with you."

"Oh my God." She put her hand to her mouth and shook her head. She wasn't saying no, but Adam nodded at her anyway — willing her, willing her, willing her to say yes! Yes to everything. He was breaking her heart — right now, breaking it in pieces. She could feel it cracking inside her. She hadn't even known she was in love.

"Say yes. Say yes," Adam pushed on relentlessly. "I want to be with you for the rest of my life. I love you," he said. "Just love me back. For one week. Say yes. Please, Lizzie."

She heard the desperation in his voice and shook her head. "What do you want from me, Adam? I can't save your life."

"I don't want to be saved. I told you. I want to spend my last week with you. How can you say no?"

Lizzie clutched at her head. She was trying to think, but her mind shied away. "It's too much," she said. "You're asking . . . I don't know what you're asking!"

"I'm asking for one week of your time."

"It's not one week! It's your whole life! You're asking me to watch you die. It's like — getting married or something."

"Pretty short marriage," Adam said, and despite herself, she snorted with laughter.

"You're something else, Adam, you know that?"

"I am now," he said seriously.

She was about to tell him that he had always been something else, that he always had been worth it, but what was the point? It was too late for home truths. Lizzie couldn't help being flattered and deeply moved. He had one week to live and out of all the things in the world, all the people, all the places, he wanted her.

One week, she thought. *So little time to live your life.* Could she do this for him, and then just walk away and get on with her own life with only memories to keep her company? But what memories they would be!

An idea suddenly hit her. "You've got a list, haven't you?"

Adam's eyes swiveled briefly as he tried to remember what was on it. How many girls . . . ? "I'm . . . still working on it."

"Hand it over."

"It's private, Lizzie."

"Private? You want me to drop everything for you, and what we're going to do is private?"

"I only did it this morning," said Adam. "It's not final."

Lizzie put out her hand. "Give."

Adam dug in his pocket and pulled it out. He cast a glance over it. "Sex figures pretty highly here," he admitted.

Lizzie snatched it out of his hand and scanned through it.

"At least I'm number one," she said. Then her eyes bulged.

"Pregnant? You want to get me pregnant? And then you're going to leave me to bring up a kid on my own? Well, fuck you!" She screwed the list into a ball, threw it on the floor. "You're not even going to be there for the birth, you bastard," she said, and again, despite herself, she started to laugh. It was just so ridiculous!

Adam grinned at her and picked up the list. "It's just the first draft. Come on, Lizzie. I mean, wouldn't you want to leave something behind?"

"Yeah, but I'd like to be around to watch it grow up." She shook her head. "Pregnant," she said. "I can't believe you. Give me that list. Right." Lizzie took the piece of paper and fumbled on her bedside table for a pen. She scribbled out pregnancy. "OK?"

"Yeah, OK. Whatever you say, Lizzie."

"*Sleep with as many girls as possible. Two or three at the same time,*" she read. She glared at him. "Three girls at once. You think I'm going to do that for you, do you?"

Adam hesitated. "Haven't you ever wondered?"

Lizzie's pencil hovered in the air above number two.

"Look," said Adam. "This week. It's got to be a total experience. Two hundred percent going for it. It's not like normal; it's like, everything. All the stuff you would have done if you went to uni, or if you'd gone to war, or if you married and had kids, or just went crazy. You know? You might say you don't want a threesome now, but what about forever? Because that's what this is about — forever."

"Forever in a week," said Lizzie. She shook her head. "Suppose I say no?" she demanded. "What then?"

"Then — I'll keep trying to convince you." He grinned weakly. "I could become a pain."

"Become? Huh. And if I say yes? All this — we have to do all this. That's the deal, is it? I have to do everything you want?"

Adam looked at the list. "We can go through them one at a time," he suggested.

"Thanks." She scanned down it again. *"Kill someone?"* she exclaimed. "You want to leave me with a murder charge?"

"No!" Adam shook his head. "OK, I hadn't thought it through. I mean, only if it was someone who really, really deserved it. Hitler or someone."

"Hitler's dead, Adam. We're not going to meet Hitler."

"A serial killer, then. We'd be doing everyone a favor."

"Except me. It's not up to us to decide who lives and who dies." She shook her head. "I want to be able to say no."

"Yeah. Yeah. No problem. We only do it if you agree."

"We go through these things one at a time."

"Yeah! I mean, you're in on it, too, right?"

"Right."

Adam looked at her. "You're saying yes."

"No, I'm not," she snapped. But she was, and she knew it. She turned to look at him sitting next to her, smiling and . . . hopeful? No. Hopeful wasn't big enough. It was like his whole life, his whole world, his whole being depended on her answer. She held all that in her hand. That was it. He had put himself, all of himself, body and soul, into her keeping. It took her breath away.

"I love you, Lizzie," he said.

Love — what was that? It wasn't like tripping over a brick and falling on your face in the road. Of course it had to be the right person — but you had to go for it, too, didn't you? You had to be prepared to jump in and drown. Someone, that special person, they didn't just come to mean everything to you by accident. Somewhere along the line, you had to give yourself to them, completely give yourself, be prepared to sacrifice everything for them. That was what Adam was offering, and that was what he was asking in return. That's what love was, wasn't it? Like Romeo and Juliet. Like Bonnie and Clyde. Your true love had to be worth more to you than life itself.

He'd climbed the wall to her window. He had one week to live and he'd come to her. He was going to take her places she'd never even dreamed of going. She was going to fall in love. It was going to break her heart. It might even kill her.

"Say yes, Lizzie. Please say yes."

And he was gorgeous, wasn't he? Gorgeous and doomed and mad and so, so sexy. And yes, sometimes she felt she was going to go out of her head with boredom and . . . and . . .

"I can walk away whenever I want, right?"

"Anything."

"I can say no."

"Anything."

"We do it one thing at a time."

"One at a time. Anything!"

"And . . ." She paused. Adam was beaming at her, just beaming like a light had been turned on in his heart. She was that light.

"I love you, Lizzie," he said again.

And she could have said, *Oh, come on,* or *Grow up,* or *Please!* Or just *I don't believe you.* But instead, she jumped up and wrapped her arms around him and hugged him so hard, and he picked her up and spun her around in circles and crowed like Peter Pan.

"And I love you," she said fiercely. She pulled him to her and snogged him, stark naked there in her room with the comforter on the floor. And . . . *Yes!* she thought. She was going to help him have the time of his life.

CHAPTER 10

MR. B

AT ABOUT THE SAME TIME THAT ADAM WAS CLIMBING THE sheer wall to Lizzie's bedroom, Garry, from whom he had stolen Death the previous night, was on the receiving end of a very difficult phone call with a man he knew only as Mr. B. It was the first time he'd dealt directly with Mr. B — usually he only got to speak to his underlings, but today he had been handed on to the big man himself. For that reason, he knew he was in some very serious, and probably very painful, trouble down the line.

"I'm sorry," he begged. "I got robbed. It was random. This guy turned up and did the house over. What can I do? Call the police?" He laughed weakly at his own joke.

Mr. B waited a moment before he answered. "I'll pop round tomorrow and we'll discuss the situation."

"You?" said Garry in surprise.

"I like to deal with any problems that arise personally."

"No need for that, is there?" No answer. Garry let out a high-pitched giggle out of pure nervousness. "I'll have the money for you, Mr. B, just give me a couple more days. I mean, even if I still had the stuff it takes a while to sell it. You're a businessman. You know that."

"Tomorrow, eleven A.M.," said Mr. B.

"That's not fair!" cried Garry.

"Be there," said Mr. B, and he hung up.

Garry sat still, staring at the phone in his hand. This was bad. He had been warned that Mr. B was dangerous, but he had been a poor man all his life, and the prospect of using his old Zealot connections to get his hands on some Death to sell had been too much to resist.

"I'm out of my league here," he muttered, chewing the ends of his beard. He was in a wheelchair. What was he supposed to do? Run around trying to hunt for the little shit? It took him half an hour just to get on and off the bus.

He picked up the phone and made another call — a call he had been told to make only under very exceptional circumstances. He sat a long time listening to the phone ring, before it went dead. Then he rang again. And again and again. He'd been sitting there for half an hour before he got an answer.

"This needs to be pretty important, Garry," said a voice at the other end.

"Thank God you answered," burst out Garry in relief. "Something's gone wrong. You're not going to believe this."

Garry ran through his problem, aware that he was getting an unsympathetic silence, right up until he mentioned . . .

"Adam?" asked the voice incredulously.

"Yeah! The little shit. What am I going to do about that, then, eh?"

There was a pause. "I can't help you."

"Come on! I'm seeing that guy tomorrow. Mr. B. You know what they say about him."

"I can't jeopardize everything we've worked on just for this."

"Just for this? This is my life we're talking about. You're making the stuff, for God's sake. Just divert some my way."

"I'm a Zealot, Garry. I follow the rules. I'm not going to steal from my own organization."

"It was getting handed out for free the other day in Albert Square."

"That was an operation. Look, Garry, I'm abandoning my family for this. If I can do that to them, what makes you think I'm going to stick my neck out for you? I warned you what you were getting into when I put you in touch with Mr. B and you accepted the risk."

"I just wanted a life, you know . . ." said Garry.

"I've given mine up," said Jess grimly.

"You had a life. Me, it takes me ten minutes just to go to the toilet in this stupid house. The stair lift keeps breaking; it gets stuck going up, it gets stuck going down. You try it when you're dying for a shit. I just wanted a life. I just wanted things easy for a bit." Pathetically, Garry began to weep. "Just have a word with Adam. How will that hurt?"

"He thinks I'm dead. It'll stir up all sorts of nonsense if he knows I'm still alive. What was Adam doing round at yours, anyway?"

"He was looking for you, what do you think? He was in a pretty bad way — someone had really beat him up. He's desperate, Jess, your whole family is desperate. What did you expect? They think you're dead."

"I am dead."

"Please, Jess, please?"

Jess sighed. He hated this so much. A gentle person, he had to push himself to be hard. "Maybe you just have to die, Garry. Quite a few of us are going to."

"But not like this," begged Garry. "Anyway," he said, a thought occurring to him, "what do I say to Mr. B? I know where Adam lives. Your whole family. I mean, you know, under torture? What about that?"

There was a pause. "You're threatening me," said Jess.

"No!" insisted Garry, but he was. "Look, I'm not a bad man. I don't want to do this, but he might make me. You know?"

"Garry, you bastard, I did you a favor!"

"Look, just . . . don't make me do this, right? Now you know how it feels," added Garry.

"I need to think."

Jess put down the phone abruptly. Garry sat there awhile longer. He wouldn't tell Mr. B where Jess's family lived. He'd sunk low, but not that low. But if thinking he would got Jess out and trying to get those pills back, so be it.

He wheeled himself to the kitchen under the stairs to make himself a cup of tea.

In a gym in the basement of a large house buried in a clump of woodland south of Manchester, Vince was lying facedown on a mat with Christian on top of him, studying the back of his neck. Both men were dressed in judo gear. Christian rubbed his finger down the vertebrae and counted under his breath while Vince waited nervously for him to finish.

"Can I get up now, sir?" asked Vince.

Christian stood and let him up. They bowed to each other, then battle resumed. Christian threw Vince around a bit, kicked his arse a few times, got him upside down on the mat, and punched him repeatedly in the back of the neck before he'd had enough.

"That's enough for today."

Vince got to his feet, panting.

"You're out of breath, Vince. You need to do some more work on your stamina," suggested Christian. "You're getting too easy."

"Sorry, sir. I'll do a run this afternoon," snarled Vince.

"No." Christian wiped his face on a towel. "I have a job for you."

"Is it the cripple the chemist put us onto?" asked Vince. "We should never have done a deal with him. Do you want me to sort it out, sir?"

Christian shook his head. "I'll deal with that. I have something else for you. I want you to get out there and find out where Lizzie's gone." He shook his head. "Running off like that. She could be in any kind of trouble."

Vince paused, not sure who they were talking about. Then he remembered — the girl at the party the night before. "Why are you worried for her, sir? She's not exactly your girlfriend, is she?" he pointed out.

"With that crazy ex-boyfriend of hers hanging around? I'm worried for her. Just do it. You can start with her friend who threw the party last night. Julie, wasn't it? Her. Sooner rather than later, if you don't mind, Vince," he added when Vince paused, looking at him curiously.

Vince shrugged. "I'll get right on it, sir."

Vince left his boss and went to his own room. Inside, he closed the door, stripped off, and went to look at the mirror. Magnificent black bruises blossomed all the way up and down his body, but the most serious injuries didn't show up as much more than a puffy swelling on the back of his neck, where Christian had punched him at least once a day for the past nine months. Every time, the same thing. It was doing him damage.

Christian was a nut-job. He'd have been in the Broadmoor loony bin years ago if it wasn't for the fact that he was the son of Florence Ballantine. In effect, Vince was less a butler/bodyguard, as Lizzie had suggested, and more of a butler/prison guard. His job was to serve Christian hand and foot — including the procurement of "girlfriends," when required — right up to the point where Christian went mad. Then — he should be so lucky — he had permission to restrain him.

Man! He wanted to restrain him so bad.

The big man finished his shower and went in to give Christian his afternoon milk before he left. There was the usual fuss. It went in phases. Just now, Christian was in a sulky phase. Vince would have loved it if he simply started refusing to drink it, because it was at that point that restraining measures might come into effect. So far, Christian had denied him that pleasure.

Even so, and despite the fact that he stood and watched Christian swallow the meds in milk twice every day without fail, his boss's behavior lately was beginning to worry him. This girlfriend thing, for instance. It was a worrying sign.

Vince made his way out to his car, a classic model Porsche, and paused outside to make a quick phone call to his real boss.

"Mr. Ballantine."

"Vince. How's it hanging?"

Vince paused, unsure how to put it.

"It ain't easy," sympathized Ballantine.

"He just beat me up on the mat again."

"Wow. I've heard about beaten wives, but a beaten bodyguard? Is there a support group or something you could join, you know? Share experiences, that sort of thing?"

In the background, Vince could hear raucous laughter. He shook his head and winced. "Always the neck. It's dangerous. He's going to do me an injury."

"Aw, come on, Vince. You're a big boy. You can put up with a little pain."

Vince paused, unwilling to admit just how much he dreaded those daily sessions.

"Did you really drag me away to complain about your working conditions, Vince? Is he still taking his meds? That's the only thing that counts. Vince, please tell me he's taking his meds."

"He is, Mr. Ballantine. It's not that. It's . . . there's another girl."

"So what's new? There's always another girl."

"Yes, sir, but this one, he's calling her his girlfriend."

There was a pause. "And is she?"

"No, sir."

"How do you know?"

"She keeps trying to get away, sir."

Ballantine thought about it. "Isn't that the sort of thing girlfriends just do, though, Vince?"

Vince sighed. Like father, like son. "Not if they really like you, sir."

There was silence. Vince could almost hear the shrug.

"You know what," said Ballantine, "there aren't many things normal about Christian, but the fact that he likes girls is one of them. It keeps him happy. And if he's happy, I'm happy. And — he's taking his meds! So long as he's taking the meds, it never gets that bad. Believe me — I've seen the results of no meds. You don't want to know."

"It's not nice, sir. I had to help him with the last one."

"Heheheh, it's a tough job, eh? Vince, how much do I pay you?"

"A fuck of a lot of money, sir."

"And how much does Christian pay you?"

"A fuck of a lot of money, sir."

"That's right. Now two fuckloads of money add up to . . . what? A fucking enormous amount of money, if I'm not mistaken. I'm using a technical term, here, Vince."

"I know, sir."

"How long have you been with him now?"

"Nine months, sir," said Vince. "Pretty much to the day."

Ballantine nodded. Secretly, he was impressed. That was a record. "Tell you what, Vince. I'll make you an appointment with my personal physician. Get the neck checked out. If it's really that bad, maybe we'll do something."

"A holiday would be nice, sir."

"Vince."

"Yes, sir?"

"You're whining."

"Sorry, sir."

"I'm sorry, too, Vince, because I have a whole lot on at the moment without having to listen to my son's babysitter complaining to me about his very well-paid working conditions."

"Sorry, sir," said Vince, but the phone was already off.

Vince shrugged. You could only try. He cricked his neck and shook his hands. Pins and needles. Ah well. Meanwhile, he had a job to do.

He climbed into the car and headed out to the M56 highway.

*　　*　　*

Just a few miles away, Jess was leaning up against the side of a shipping container in the company of Anna, the girl who had been beaten up the day before. Both of them looked the worse for wear — swollen eyes, fat lips, and bruises all over their bodies. Ballantine's men were professionals. Of course, nothing had been done that would stop them working.

Jess was seething. Anna listened sympathetically as he told her about Garry.

"So what are you going to do?" she asked.

Jess glared at her. "What *can* I do?"

"Go and sort it out."

"I can't, you know I can't."

"Yes, you can."

"Even if I wanted to, we have our orders. Stay here until we get a new mission. That's what I'm doing."

He fumbled in his pocket for his cigarettes. His hands were shaking, he was that upset, but he wouldn't lift a finger to save his own brother. He was such a goddamn soldier, Anna thought. Always followed orders, never crossed the line unless he was told to. The Zealots were his whole life.

"It's your brother," she said. "Don't you care? And keep your voice down," she added. She nodded sideways at the guard leaning up against a nearby container, who was watching them with interest. They'd started off as employees, on loan from the Zealots. Now, they were more or less prisoners.

Jess took a breath and forced himself to speak matter-of-factly. "I'm not putting everything at risk just because my brother is an idiot," he said. "I've made the break. That life is over. I'm dead as far as they're concerned. What would be the point of showing myself to any of them? I'm going to be dead for real in another week or so."

"You'd get Christian off their backs. I'd say that was a pretty good start."

Jess ground his feet on the tarmac in his agitation. "I've made the break," he repeated. "They're on their own. It's up to Adam to look after them now."

"Doesn't sound as if he's doing a very good job of it," said Anna.

"He's a selfish little —"

"He's young," she said.

Jess puffed furiously on his cigarette in agitation. So passionate, so clever, so committed. But there had to be time for yourself and those who mattered to you as well, or what was the point?

She glanced at the guard, who had relaxed back against the container, smoking a cigarette of his own. "We can get out of here if we want to," she said. "They think we're a pair of geeky kids. I've been keeping an eye out. No problem. You could go out and —"

"No! We have our orders."

"Jess, who's going to know?"

"I'd know." He sank down on his haunches against the container, to make himself stay still. "They think I'm dead. That's how it's going to stay."

Anna sank down next to him. For a while they smoked in silence.

"I had a message from Command," she told him.

"Did we get a target?" he demanded eagerly.

"No. Just to stay here and make sure the production goes smoothly. They want as much drugs out on the streets as possible until Friday."

"See?" Jess nodded. Point proven. Orders.

"Big day, Friday," said Anna.

"Yeah. It's still growing?"

"Oh yeah. Big rallies in all the major cities. Not just thousands — they reckon hundreds of thousands of people are turning up. They've called for a general strike. It's incredible. And Manchester's at the heart of it." Anna shook her head. "Just a few miles away. And we're stuck here missing it . . ."

Jess looked at her excitedly. "It's started," he said. "What do you think?"

"Maybe."

"I think so. I really do," he said.

Anna grinned. She licked her lips and said it: "Revolution."

The magic word. What they'd been working for all their lives. What they believed in, what they hoped for, what they lived for. What, as Zealots, they were going to die for.

The Zealots were always asking for volunteers. Both Anna and Jess had made the offer, and the offer had been accepted. Self-immolation, maybe, although that was less likely now that things were moving. It was a great way to attract attention, but once you had the ear of the people, it was time to act. Most likely, they would be asked to be bombs. Organizations like the Zealots always had a need for people prepared to die, to take out difficult targets.

This mission ended Friday, on the one-week anniversary of Jimmy Earle's death. The next mission: to die.

"Think of it," she said. "It's all happening just over there — and we're stuck here. Don't you think that's just crazy?"

Jess scowled. "Orders," he said.

"Oh, for fuck's sake, Jess. Tell you what — I'm not staying here."

He looked at her, alarmed.

"Come on. A day or two. What difference is that going to make? We're a part of it, Jess. We helped make it happen. If I'm going to die for the revolution, I want to see it. Every night there's a protest, bigger than the night before. By Friday it could be millions. It's the future and it's happening right there." She nodded across toward the railway line, where Manchester lay, the heart of the revolution. "We deserve it. We have a right to be there."

Jess made a face.

"Aren't you even curious, Jess?"

Jess shook his head slightly. Of course he was! But . . . orders.

"Get out there, Jess," she urged. "You've earned it. Jimmy Earle set it all off, but it wouldn't have spread like it has if you hadn't worked out how to make the cheap stuff. It's finally, finally dawning on people how bad things really are, that so many kids are prepared to kill themselves just so they can have one crazy week. That's down to you. Don't you think we deserve just one night out there with them? I'm telling you, I'm going. You should, too — you must. See your brother.

Get the drugs back so Christian is off your family's case. Spend a night out on Albert Square and get a taste of what you helped make happen. Then come back and no harm done. Why not? Just — do it."

"No," he said as she tried to interrupt, "I told my family I'm dead because I am, as far as they're concerned. This is how I do things." He stubbed out his cigarette. "Things can go wrong," he said. "Those orders are there for a reason. What if we got caught or shot? It would interrupt the supply line maybe. Anything could happen. If you're going, that's all the more reason for me to stay here to make sure the mission is carried out."

"We could go together. Jess, it would be so good! Why not?"

He stood up. "If you go, that's up to you. I'm staying here."

He left, back to work. He made her want to scream sometimes. They were both going to be dead very soon. The world was full of things she wanted to do and never would. She was prepared to give them up — she would give them up. But meanwhile she was going to snatch her chances when she could.

Such a soldier, she thought. *Such a monk, too.* Pity. He was a good-looking guy. It was a pity all around.

"Time to go, miss." The guard had stopped Jess from leaving, and was making him wait for her. She stubbed out her cigarette and followed them back toward the lab.

CHAPTER 11

HALF A VIRGIN

"THE COST OF CHAMPAGNE IS SHOCKING THESE DAYS," joked Adam.

They were walking back from the shops. Lizzie looked sideways at him. Shocking was right. The really good stuff, Cristal or Dom Pérignon, cost over two hundred pounds a bottle. Two hundred pounds, for a bottle of wine! Even the usual posh stuff, Bollinger, cost over a hundred. But as Adam pointed out, what was the point if you weren't going to go for it? What was he supposed to do? Save up for it?

Except it wasn't actually his money. Adam didn't want to wait until they'd sold the Death — that could take days. Lizzie had suggested nicking it — great idea! It was exactly in the Death spirit. Storm in and take what you want. Go for it!

But everyone knew what happened to Deathers if the police got their hands on them. They locked them up, refused bail, and waited for them to die. His last week, rotting in a police cell? Come on! He wasn't going to risk his freedom every time they wanted to go shopping.

Save the robbery for the big time. There was another, safer solution. Lizzie just had to pop back to her house and pick up her savings book. Six bottles of Bolly — six hundred quid. She'd been saving that money for a holiday with her mates; now she was spending it on Adam. He was the one on Death — how come it was her acting like there was no tomorrow? It was typical Adam. She was doing her best to think what a privilege it was to be the One chosen by Him to spend His last week with. She just wished it wasn't proving so expensive.

They were on their way back to her place. Her mum and dad were both at work; they'd have the house to themselves all day. The perfect place to get so drunk on champagne they couldn't stand up. And, of course, to lose their virginity.

Nothing had been said, but Lizzie knew it was expected. In a way it was fair enough — they'd talked about it often enough. Even so, she was feeling resentful. Maybe she was being selfish. Adam had, let's face it, cornered all the rights to be the unreasonable one here. Even so, having agreed to go on the ride, she was now realizing that somewhere down the line she had actually *become* the ride and it was making her feel sulky. At the same time she was feeling increasingly panicky at what she had agreed to.

This was all going straight over Adam's head, of course. He was having a great time. Once they got to her house, he started showing her all the things he could suddenly do on Death — bouncing a ball off the wall with his head while he spun in circles, walking around the room on his hands. He was hilarious and gorgeous, all at the same time, with his blond hair hanging off his head and his face turning red as he waltzed around on his hands in her bedroom.

Lizzie giggled, feeling hysterical by now. She put five of the bottles in the freezer to chill quickly, fetched a couple of glasses from the kitchen, and led the way up to her room, where she sat on the edge of the bed easing the cork out of the sixth bottle, while Adam cavorted around her.

Bang! Off went the cork. Adam cheered. Lizzie poured the wine and laughed at the bubbles frothing up out of the bottle, but inside she was horrified. What on earth was she doing, drinking champagne with a dead man? Because that's what it amounted to. His brother had just died and here they were celebrating — it was mad! He hadn't even mentioned Jess since he'd first told her what had happened. Where was the grief? When was it going to come out? What on earth was he going to do next?

Adam took his glass off her with a flourish. Celebration time! He knocked it back, then another, then another, all in about five minutes.

"Hold on. What about me? You're drinking it all."

"No, we've five more to get through." Adam tipped his glass up and licked at the drips. He was in a hurry. Lizzie grabbed the bottle and poured herself another before it all disappeared.

She looked across to Adam, who was now doing a handstand in the middle of the floor and muttering, "I love you, Lizzie Hollier, I love you, Lizzie Hollier, I love you, Lizzie Hollier."

It didn't sound like love to her.

"How drunk are you?" she asked suspiciously.

He flipped over onto his feet and beamed at her. He had a think.

"Not at all," he admitted. He grabbed the bottle and looked at it. "How strong is this stuff?" he asked.

"Wine strength, I expect," said Lizzie sarcastically, but Adam didn't hear. He was rushing off downstairs to fetch another bottle. Lizzie sat on the bed and sighed. Death seemed to be working in waves. One minute he was relatively calm, the next he was like a Ping-Pong ball on speed. It was exhausting.

I must stop being irritable, she thought. It wasn't fair on him. One week to live! It took her breath away. If only she'd known what was going on when they were at the party, she could have stopped him.

It was a thought that chilled her.

Adam came running back up the stairs with the bottle, popped the cork, and drank straight from the bottle. The wine fizzed down his chin onto the floor.

"I don't feel anything yet," he said. "Can *you* feel it?"

"Yeah."

He looked curiously at the bottle.

"Hey — maybe it's Death," she said. "You know. It makes you super fit, right? Maybe it makes you immune to booze as well."

"No!" Adam was genuinely shocked. Lizzie snorted in amusement.

"Your face," she giggled.

It was hilarious. Death was supposed to help you have a good time. Instead, it made it harder. They both burst out laughing at the thought. Giggles. A sign of hysteria. That was even funnier and for several minutes they were both holding their sides, hurting with laughter. Gradually it subsided. Lizzie realized she was feeling very drunk already.

"Do you think that's what it is?" asked Adam.

"Nah," she said, although she did. "It's because you're so excited, that's all. Sit down. You'll get sick before anything happens."

"Before what happens?" He grinned at her.

"Before *anything* happens. Sit down here."

Adam sat next to her on the bed. He put his arm around her and went in for a kiss.

"I love you, Lizzie," he said. "I love you, I love you, I love you."

"Go on, let's do it," she said. Suddenly she wanted to get it over with. Adam was busy with her boobs, then moving on already to fiddle with her jeans. She stood up, took them off, pulled her top off, and got into bed with just her bra and underwear on.

Adam got in with her and pulled his own clothes off under the covers. She did the same. Naked, he pressed himself right up against her, so she could feel him all along her body.

"That's nice," she said.

"Gosh," said Adam. He shook his head and made his eyes go big and round. She laughed and kissed him.

He fumbled around for a bit, then, too soon, he climbed on top of her and began to push. It hurt.

"Ouch," she said.

Adam stopped. "You OK?" he asked.

"It's all right, go on."

He pressed a bit more gently and got inside her. He began to move and suddenly, without any warning at all, Lizzie remembered that he was as good as dead. It was horrible. It just froze her blood. She turned her face away and tried not to cry, but the feeling was overwhelming.

"Why don't you . . . just stop it," she said.

Adam froze in surprise, then rolled off. "What?"

"I'm sorry," she said. She didn't want him to see her cry. She turned her back to him. "Feeling sick," she said. "Too much to drink."

Adam paused, not sure what to do.

"Feeling really sick," she said.

"Do you want a bowl?" he asked.

"Just let me lie here for a bit. Go downstairs. I'll be all right. Urgh," she added.

"OK. OK." He got off the bed and put his jeans on. "It doesn't matter, Lizzie. It's all right, I don't mind."

"I just drank too much. I'll be better in a bit."

"Sure. It's OK." Quietly, he left the room.

Lizzie glanced over her shoulder to make sure he was gone. Then she let the tears come. One week. What on earth had she agreed to? It was going to be unbearable.

*   *   *

Down in the kitchen, Adam was seething. Did it count? He'd been there — but for less than a minute. What did that mean? Was he still a virgin or not? He was some sort of half virgin. It was so unfair.

"I don't have time for this," he muttered. He went to the freezer, popped the cork on another bottle, and took a hard swig. The wine fizzed up in his mouth and made him choke.

This wasn't fun. Nothing was working.

He raised the bottle again and, as carefully as he could, drank the wine down. It fizzed and writhed in his throat, but he kept at it until he'd finished off the whole bottle, all hundred pounds' worth. When he was done he stood there, feeling . . .

Still sober.

Lizzie was right. It was Death, making him stay sober. It was like some kind of trick. Would he have to spend four times the money to get drunk? Maybe six bottles weren't even enough? This wasn't right. He was supposed to be in the middle of having great sex and then passing out from alcohol poisoning, and instead, here he was, half-virgin and still sober, without enough champagne to drink, while a naked girl lay upstairs in bed feeling too sick to have sex with him. How did this happen?

There was a laptop on the kitchen table. He opened it up and got on the net, surfing around for some info on Death.

He wasn't alone, that was one thing. Hundreds, maybe even thousands of people had taken the drug in Albert Square the other night. On Friday, there were going to be an awful lot of people dropping dead at the same time. And it was still going on. Death normally cost thousands of pounds per pill, but it looked as if someone had worked out how to make it cheaply. Overnight, cheap Death was flooding onto the streets. It had begun in Manchester, but it was getting everywhere — London, Birmingham, Leeds, all over the country.

Everyone wanted to die.

This was all interesting, but it wasn't getting Adam a shag, was it? He found a Deather site he'd heard of before, regretit-forgetit.com. There was loads of stuff there — places to post your experiences, your thoughts, your requests, answers to your FAQs.

Requests. Yeah. He needed a backup plan.

"Deather teenager wants girls to sleep with. I'll give you the time of your life, you give me the time of mine."

It was kind of crap, but it was also kind of true. Adam pressed "post." It was the right thing to do. You couldn't do half measures. You had to be sure. It was all about him. *Me me me me me me.* Lizzie would understand . . . but maybe not a good idea to tell her anyway . . .

He went on to the FAQs. There it was.

"Can I get drunk or high on Death? How much will I need?"

"Yes, you can!" the answer said. *"But Death means you'll have to drink more, faster. With drugs, quadruple your usual dose. With booze, same thing. Best thing — drink it down quick. Four bottles of wine will get you really drunk. Have fun!"*

Four bottles to get drunk, eh? Adam wanted more than just drunk. He wanted paralytic. Four bottles = drunk. Six bottles might just = not able to walk.

Lizzie was out for the count upstairs. No point waking her up. Day 1 was already disappearing fast. He needed to get a move on.

Opening the freezer, Adam removed the remaining three bottles of champagne and lined them up on the work surface.

Number one. He popped the cork, lifted it to his lips, and drank carefully. The bubbles were a pain — they stopped you drinking the stuff! It was a pity he couldn't make it flat. Wait — maybe he could. Digging about under the stairs he found what he was looking for — a bucket. He opened all three bottles and poured them one after the other into it. Yeah! A bucket of Bolly! Now you're talking!

He stirred it to get rid of the bubbles, then, lifting the bucket to his lips, started to drink it down. Better. It was still fizzy, but much easier than straight out of the bottle. Now he just needed to get it down him as quick as he could to get the maximum benefit.

Fifteen minutes later, with much belching and glugging, the bucket was empty. Adam did an experimental stagger around the kitchen. Yeah! He was pissed. Pretty fucking pissed actually. But . . . he could still walk — just about. Goddamn Death! He'd have been dead by now otherwise. *Hehehehehe*, he thought. *Hehehehehe.*

Hang on. Seeing double. Feeling sick. Feeling very sick. Walk. Door. Get up.

He took two steps to the door and fell over. He tried to get up and failed.

"Too drun to fucki stanup," he announced to no one. Then he was lavishly sick on the floor. Success!

And he passed out.

Adam awoke lying on the floor in a pool of cold puke. Lizzie was sitting at the kitchen table glaring at him.

"What happened?" he asked.

"You drank it all. You greedy bastard."

"Sorry." He picked himself up and tried to grin at her, but it was difficult when you had cold puke all down your front. "You were asleep," he mumbled. "I didn't have time. At least that's one thing out the way."

"'Out the way'?" she demanded. "Six hundred pounds' worth of champagne 'out the way'? Thanks, Adam. Any more things you want to get 'out the way' for me? My money, what's left of it?"

"You were ill," he reminded her. "And this is about me, isn't it? One week," he reminded her. "I'll pay you back, don't worry." She was making a fuss — spoiling it for him. "I'm going upstairs to shower. Hey — I'm going to need some more clothes, these stink," he added, and ducked upstairs before she could answer.

In the bathroom, Adam sat on the edge of the tub for a moment. He felt sick and incredibly anxious. The hangover, it must be. He found some painkillers and whacked them down. Then he got undressed and climbed into the shower.

Don't think don't think don't think. Thinking about what he'd done with a hangover was dreadful; it made his stomach lurch. Don't go there. What next? Sex, sex was next. He should have done that by now. He had to get on — he had so much to do and so little time to do it . . .

The water flooded over him, taking the sweat and stink off him and washing it away down the plughole.

Don't think — but you can't help thinking because that's what your brain does, thinking all the time, it won't stop. Don't think of the future because the future is disappearing before your eyes. Don't think of the past because that's going, too . . .

All your memories, gone, all your hopes and regrets, gone. Wherever you look, death is everywhere; past, present, and future, all gone, like water down the drain . . .

From the floor came a rattle of music. His phone in his jeans pocket. Leaning out of the shower, Adam picked it up and opened it up. A number he didn't know. He pressed answer and held it to his ear.

"Hi, Adam," said a voice.

It came as such a shock, he reeled back and banged into the wall behind him.

"Who is it?" he whispered.

"Don't you know me?"

Adam didn't answer, not daring. It must be some kind of mistake.

"It's Jess," said the voice. "We need to meet up."

*   *   *

Lizzie was drinking coffee in the kitchen when Adam burst in with the news. Jess was alive!

She goggled at him. She couldn't keep up with this. First Jess was dead — now he was alive. Ten minutes ago Adam had been lying unconscious in a pool of vomit. Now he was rushing round the room babbling like a lunatic.

"Adam, stop it!" He was practically bouncing off the walls. "Slow down. Jess is alive? Is he OK?"

"Yes! I don't know. He sounded fine. He wants the drugs back."

"What, the Death? How does he know about that?"

"Garry must have told him." Adam paced up and down, trying to work it out. "They said on the news that it was the Zealots handing out the free Death on Friday night."

"Jess was a chemist, wasn't he?" Lizzie thought about it. "This is deep, Adam. Jess must be wrapped up in it somehow."

Adam shook his head. "Why would the Zealots sell Death? Jess wouldn't do that." Or would he? Adam was finding out how very little he knew his own brother.

"When are you meeting him?"

"In a couple of hours, in Platt Fields Park."

"Ask him about the antidote," said Lizzie suddenly.

Adam swung around to face her, shocked . . . horrified . . . hopeful. "There is no antidote! You know that."

"That's what we're told. But he'll know for sure . . ."

"There is no antidote," he hissed furiously. "That's the point, isn't it? I'm going to die. Just get used to it. It's a good thing," he added.

Yes, he wanted it! Yes, he welcomed it! But the words choked in his throat and to his shame, emotion hijacked him, and he burst into tears.

"Hey. Hey, hey — come on." Lizzie jumped up, and he let her fold him in her arms.

"I can't," he told her weakly. "I just can't . . ."

"Can't what?"

"I can't think like that. Hoping. What's the point when there isn't any hope?"

"But what if there is?"

"No!" He pushed her away. "You don't get it, do you? I'm going to die. I've got my week, that's all I've got. That has to be enough. It HAS to be enough. Don't you see?" He wept and raged at her.

"Look, Adam. No!" she cut in when he was about to launch at her. "Let's have this conversation now — just once. OK? Just once. Because, Adam, we do have to have it. I have to have it. I have to know. It's . . . it's part of the ride, OK?"

Part of the ride. Adam stared at her.

"If there was an antidote. What then? Would you take it?"

There was a pause. "I can't think like that. I can't do that, Lizzie . . ." He squeezed his eyes shut and tried to squash the tears right down inside himself, where they didn't matter.

The tears were answer enough. "So look. Ask Jess. OK? Just ask him. He's involved in this somehow or other. The Zealots, Death, everything that's going on. If he says no, fine. We get on with your week. But if there is, we — I — am going to try and get it. Not for your sake," she insisted before he interrupted her. "For me. Because I don't want just one week with you. I want more. OK, Adam? It's not just about you. It never was, it never will be. It's about me, too. And it's about Jess, and your mum and your dad. All of us. We've got to stand here and watch you go. I'll do it for you, if I have to. But if I don't, well then, we're going to try and save your life whether you want it or not. OK? Deal?"

Adam felt like she was breaking him in half. But — OK. For her. For Lizzie. Not for him.

He nodded.

"Good." Lizzie smiled, and looked pleased. But what she was really thinking was if Jess was alive, Adam had taken Death for no reason at all. And how was he going to react when he realized that?

CHAPTER 12

MEETING IN THE PARK

ADAM BEGGED HER TO COME WITH HIM TO MEET JESS, BUT Lizzie steeled herself to say no. This was between him and Jess, she told him. But it wasn't that, really.

The fact was, she didn't believe in an antidote, either. You never knew, you heard the odd story, you had to hope — but the evidence was all the other way. No. Adam was going to die. He was dying now, even while he walked next to her along the road, fizzing with life like no one she'd ever known. She'd promised to spend the last week with him and she intended to keep that promise, but it wasn't going to be easy. Nothing else she was ever going to go through — love, sex, childbirth, her own death — was going to come even close to this in sheer intensity. It was going to be heaven and hell rolled up into one big, angsty ball.

She wanted a few hours on her own just to get her head around it. They would probably be the last few hours she'd have to herself before he died.

Adam got on the bus, turned his tragic white face to look at her, and grinned as if to say, *Yeah, this is what it's all about.* She stood and waved good-bye, then went back home to tidy up and pack a bag. There was no way she could stay at home. Her mum and dad could not be allowed to even guess what was going on.

Where they were going to hide out, she had no idea. This was going to require some careful planning. Once she got the place tidy, Lizzie sat down and turned on her laptop. The Internet was awash with Death.

It was amazing. Kids all over Manchester were following Jimmy Earle into the night, and with them was coming the biggest crime wave in history. Robbery, rape, murder. Suddenly there were thousands of people roaming the streets with nothing to lose and nothing to win but one week of fun. The police were desperately trying to track down the source of the drug, but meanwhile, it was flooding the streets.

She found a comment about a Deather who had committed murder online. Wow. She found the video of it easily enough — it had three million hits already, and it had only been up for two hours.

It started off straight enough — a well-known female reporter talking to some kid on Death. She was asking him why he'd thrown his life away like that.

He grinned. "How do you like it?" he asked the reporter.

"What do you mean?" the woman asked. In answer, the kid lunged forward and stabbed her in the stomach, hard. Lizzie jumped to her feet in shock. Murder — right there in her face. The reporter made a strange noise, half groan, half gasp of surprise. The kid shook the blade right in the camera — in her face, it felt like — splashing the lens with blood. The crew tried to grab him, but he was off, sprinting away, pushing them all back, and escaping easily.

Why had he done it? But she knew the answer, sort of. This was a poor kid who'd had nothing all his life. Now at least he had as much as that reporter — more, in fact, because she was dead and he had a few more days to live.

And because he could.

Her thoughts were interrupted by a call on her cell phone. It was Julie.

"Darling," said Julie. "How are you?"

"I'm fine," said Lizzie absently, still shocked from the images on the screen.

"No, you're not fine. You're in the deepest shit you can think of."

"What?"

For a moment she thought Julie had somehow found out about Adam. But it wasn't that. That guy at the party that Adam had punched? Christian? He was interested in her.

"So what?" asked Lizzie.

So what? Julie was furious. Did she have any idea who Christian was? Only the son of the biggest gangster in the north of England, which without doubt meant the whole country, since Manchester gangs were the worst of the lot anyway. Not only that, he was a dirty, sick pervert as well. These were the people flooding the country with cheap Death. Julie had already had a visit from his bodyguard, the big guy in the suit, wanting to know where Lizzie lived. This was very bad news indeed. Very bad. How had she been so stupid as to get talking to him at the party?

"How was I supposed to know? You invite me to a party with a gangster and then it's my fault?"

"I didn't invite him, he just came."

"Why didn't you warn me?"

"Because any idiot can tell at a glance he's not all there!"

"Did you tell him where I was?" demanded Lizzie.

"No, of course not. Well, not everything. I gave him your e-mail."

"My e-mail? You cow, Julie. Why did you do that?"

"Jesus. Lizzie! Why do you think? So I wouldn't get beaten up, for fuck's sake. God, Lizzie, you are being so selfish about this!"

Lizzie groaned. "So now I'm going to get bombarded by pervy e-mails from that freak. Great. Did you give him my Facebook as well?"

"Lizzie, Christian is not interested in sending you pervy e-mails. He's not that sort of a pervert. He's more the hands-on kind. I doubt that you'll get any e-mails. What you will get is a personal visit as soon as he's worked out where you live."

"Can he do that?"

"Oh yes."

"Shit. But what does he want me for? What does he want to do?"

"What do you think he wants to do? He wants to perv all over you, and don't ask me what that means because I don't even know."

"Well . . . what do I do, then? Call the police?"

"You do not call the police on these people! These people practically ARE the police. No way. What you do is, you go into hiding. Give it a few weeks, he'll probably get over it and move on to someone else."

"Go into hiding?"

"Yes. That's what I'm going to do and I'm not even the one he wants. Don't argue, Lizzie," warned Julie. "You don't have any choice. And your parents will have to hide as well. I'm ringing them next."

"No!"

"Yes! You want them beaten up and set on fire, too?"

Lizzie thought about it. There didn't seem to be much choice — and anyway, it might play into her hands. "OK," she said, "but I'm not going into hiding with them. It'd drive me mad. I need a place of my own, for a while anyway."

They argued about it for a bit, but in the end, Lizzie got her own way.

"But where?" she asked.

Julie had just the place.

While Julie was explaining things to Lizzie, Adam was on the bus to the park, allowing himself to think about his mum and dad for the first time since he'd taken Death.

Speaking to Jess had sobered him right up.

Lizzie was right; it never was just all about him. In effect, Adam had committed suicide. He was in freefall to the rope's end. It was a long rope, but it was going to end all too soon and he wasn't going to be the only victim. As sure as a soldier firing a gun, he had executed the hopes and dreams of his mother and father as well. He'd ruined their lives by ending his own.

But! Maybe not. They still had Jess, back from the dead. As ever, Jess was the one who was going to go back and pick up the pieces. Once he knew what Adam had done, he'd have no choice. Everything would be back to normal. On Jess's shoulders would be heaped all his parents' dreams and hopes. Jess would provide them with grand-children, help and support them in their old age, and give them the joy of watching their offspring growing old and wise.

Except it wasn't all back to normal, of course. There was one person for whom nothing could ever be changed again: Adam. By coming back from the dead, Jess had removed any meaning at all from his own death. Jess, the faker, had made even Adam's despair meaningless.

Unless . . . could it be true, as Lizzie had suggested, that there might be an antidote? Everyone said it didn't exist, but there were some stories going around — that the manufacturers only said there was no way out because the antidote cost even more than Death itself, or that the government suppressed the truth because, face it, without the death at the end, this was just one really good drug. Everyone would want it.

Hope. That's what Adam was feeling as he rode the bus across town. Hope. And hope, he was discovering, was the most terrifying thing of all.

They'd arranged to meet by a boarded-up shed that had been a ticket office for the boating lake years ago. When Adam saw his brother, he went running toward him — he'd never felt so glad in all his life. But when he got close, he felt angry again. He'd forgotten for a few seconds how Jess had betrayed him — betrayed the whole family. You could almost say that Jess had killed him.

They stood there looking at each other, not touching. Jess looked flushed, his eyes bright. His brown hair had been cut short and he was wearing unfamiliar clothes. A new Jess.

"You're alive," said Adam. He didn't know whether to hug him or hit him.

Jess nodded. "Have you got them?" he asked.

Adam was offended. This was his greeting, then. He took the pills from where he'd hidden them down his pants and handed them over. Jess snatched the bag and looked into it.

"Are they all here?" he asked.

"One short."

Jess shot him a sharp look. "You didn't take it, did you?"

"Do I look stupid?" Adam said it before he could think. He knew at once that the lie wasn't going to be as easy to take back as it was to give.

"You sold it?"

"Yeah."

For the first time, Jess looked Adam full in the face. He raised his eyebrows slightly. "Someone's going to die, then."

"What are you doing with this stuff?" said Adam. He wasn't going to take any stick from Jess. "Did you help make them?"

Jess ignored the question. "That was a stupid thing to do. You could have got Garry killed, do you know that?" he asked, stuffing the bag into his pants.

Adam stared resentfully at him. "So it's all my fault, is it?" he asked. Jess didn't meet his eye. "What's going on?" he demanded. "Why did the Zealots say you were dead?" He paused a moment. "Have you told Mum and Dad you're all right?"

Jess looked away, then back. "I'm not going to tell them, Adam," he said. "And neither are you."

"Are you joking?" Now he was getting angry. "Of course they have to know. What are you playing at, Jess?"

Jess took a couple of steps back, out of sight of the path nearby. "Keep your voice down. I'm carrying, remember?" He waited for Adam to step into the shadows before he went on. "I wanted you all to think I was dead," he said. "It would have been easier that way."

"Easier than what?" demanded Adam. How could anything be harder?

Jess grimaced and shook his head. He looked furious himself. "It's not about you or me or Mum or Dad," he said. "It's about everyone. The human race."

"We *are* the human race, in case you hadn't noticed. Your bit of it," said Adam bitterly.

"Do you think I don't love them? Or you?" Adam looked away. Him and his brother had never talked about love before. Jess reached out and grabbed hold of his arm. "You think it didn't break my heart to do what I did?"

"I know you broke their hearts, all right. Mum's and Dad's."

Jess looked appalled. "I'm sorry, Adam," he said. "I really am, but you can't tell them. It'd only break their hearts again. I'm going to die. I said what I did to get it over with."

Adam was horrified. "What do you mean? You haven't taken Death, have you?" he demanded.

"No. Of course not. I volunteered."

"What, to die?"

"I'm a Zealot. It happens. Self-immolation. Suicide bomb if I'm lucky."

Adam was struck dumb for a moment. It was unbelievable.

"When?" he croaked.

Jess shrugged. "Maybe tomorrow, maybe next week. Soon."

"But it's stupid! It's pointless," raged Adam. "What good will it do? No one's going to change their mind because you set fire to yourself, or blow yourself up . . ."

But Jess was shaking his head. He'd heard these arguments a hundred times. Adam wasn't going to change anything by going over it again.

"The Zealots," Adam spat. "So you're helping them make Death, is that what it is? And it was you lot handing Death out in the square that night, was it? That's great, isn't it? All those innocent people dying. Did they volunteer as well?"

"It's a war, Adam!" insisted Jess. "There's always collateral damage. And it's working. Have you seen the crowds in Manchester? People are heading out in the hundreds of thousands. This Friday, one week after Jimmy Earle died, it'll be the biggest protest yet. Maybe more than just a protest this time. The police are coming over to our side, even some of the army. It could be a revolution."

"They've brainwashed you," said Adam.

Jess made a dismissive gesture. "That's what they want you to believe," he said. "But it's you who's been brainwashed. The government is running scared. They know their time is up. I'm prepared to die for what I believe in. That's not being brainwashed. Maybe one day you'll believe in something, too."

"And what about Mum and Dad?" said Adam. Although, in his heart, what he wanted to say was — *What about me?*

Jess gave him a thin smile. "You want to make it hard for me. You can't make it any harder. I'm doing what I *believe* in, Adam. The human race is going down the plughole. People have been abandoned so a handful of investors can make more billions while the rest of us sink into the mud. There's enough capacity in the world to feed, clothe, and educate everyone, but it's all spent on banks and weapons. This is war. People get lost in war. Families get broken up. It happens."

"It's not war," insisted Adam. "You're just saying that to make it sound OK. You didn't have to go. You wrecked my life, Jess, you bastard. I trusted you, and you wrecked my life . . ."

Tears of self-pity filled his eyes, but Jess was having none of it.

"Oh, don't start. How did I wreck your life? By making you get a job? You were always going to get a job. Stopping you getting a place on a football team? You were never going to get a place on a football team. Did you think I was going to spend my life working like a slave so you could dream about being a big star? Wake up, Adam. Sorry it was me who rang the bell. Smell the coffee. It stinks. What did you expect?"

Adam was aghast. Was that what his brother really thought?

"It's called real life," said Jess furiously. "Welcome to it. They're not my rules; they don't have to be yours, either. Mum and Dad choose to follow them. I've chosen to fight back, and you know what, Adam? There's nothing to stop you from fighting back, too. You have a choice, same as me. Same as everyone. We can all fight."

"And desert Mum and Dad like you did?"

"Then do your bit and work for them! There's no space for dreams anymore, not unless you're prepared to make them come true. Look around you!" Jess swung his arm up, no longer bothered if people heard him. "People are dying. People are wasting their lives working for loveless bastards who own nearly everything already and *still* want more. Society is dying, three-quarters of the world is starving — and you want to play football." He spat the words out in disgust.

Adam had no idea all this venom was in him. "You never said . . ."

"I said all the time. You didn't listen. None of you ever listened."

Suddenly Jess grabbed hold of Adam and held him in his arms. "I love you," he said. His breath was hot on Adam's face. "Don't ever forget that. And I know you're going to work this out and do what's right."

Jess hugged him hard until Adam pushed him away and stood there looking savagely at him.

"OK," Adam said. "OK." He was panting with emotion. He had one last card to play — the trump. He played it. "That missing pill. What if I told you I *had* taken it?" he asked. "What then? Then you'd have to come back."

Jess frowned and peered into his face. "And did you?." he said.

"I did. I took it. So what now?"

Jess stood there awhile, thinking. Then he shook his head.

"Then you're a fool and I can't help you," he said. He laughed tiredly. He looked suddenly drained. "Just . . . at least make sure you get your full week in, if that's all you have left." He pushed his way past to the path. He was going. Adam had played his final card, and Jess was still going.

"You don't care about me. You never cared about any of us!" he yelled after him.

Jess shook his head again. There was nothing more to say.

"Jess — wait!" Jess paused midstep. Adam steeled himself to ask the million-dollar question. "Is there an antidote?" he asked.

"It's a one-way street, just like they say." Jess looked at Adam one last time — a long, searching look. "I love you anyway," he said. He paused a moment longer. "I wish I could help you, but I can't."

He walked rapidly away. Adam stood and watched him go. *At any moment,* he thought, *he's going to turn around and come back and sort this out.* That's what Jess always did.

But not this time. He walked along the path and disappeared behind some shrubs. That was it. Good-bye forever.

Adam stood there awhile on his own. *That's it, then,* he thought. Then he left and made his way back to meet Lizzie.

After leaving Adam, Jess made his way to Fallowfield to see Garry and give him the pills. It had broken his heart seeing Adam, but he wasn't going to let that change anything. He had given himself to the Zealots a long time ago, and what hurt him or pleased him was no longer his own concern. Anna had convinced him that he should have at least a few hours for himself and not the cause. He wasn't sure that she was right, but he had been unable to resist the temptation of seeing the drama unfolding in Albert Square — perhaps a foretaste of revolution itself, if things worked out. He had given his life for this. Wasn't it right that he should have just a brief taste of it while he had the chance?

It had been a mistake seeing Adam, though. It hurt too much.

After Garry, he would go into town, meet up with Anna, and have his one night of glory in the square, watching the end of despair and the beginning of hope. Then it was back to the container terminal, where Ballantine would doubtless have the shit beaten out of him and Anna — if she came back, that was. He suspected that maybe she had already decided not to.

As for his parents, he didn't dare even think about them. Adam had been hard enough. He wasn't strong enough to see them, too.

He jumped onto the bus on Wilmslow Road and rode into town. He felt like crying. But what use were tears of sorrow when the most joyful day of all was just around the corner?

CHAPTER 13

COME THE REVOLUTION

JULIE'S SOLUTION TO THE CHRISTIAN PROBLEM WORKED out just right. She was going to lend Lizzie a city flat belonging to a friend of hers who was abroad for a few months. It was perfect — not just for Lizzie, but for Adam as well.

The bus took ages and it was getting dark by the time she arrived in the city center. The shopkeepers were pulling down the shutters; the police were out and about, setting up roadblocks and forming lines outside important buildings. As she came down Portland Street, she saw a group of people wearing rat masks abseiling down the Bruntwood building. Outside, the police leaned on their cars and watched. You couldn't even be sure what side they were on anymore.

Julie had her own flat on Deansgate, and Lizzie met her there to pick up the keys before going on to meet Adam at Piccadilly Gardens. She had spoken to him about his meeting with Jess earlier. He had sounded upset then, but by the time he arrived he was distraught — weeping, raging, ready to kill himself right then just to escape the knowledge of what he had done. Jess had raised his hopes — then snatched them away. Now he was staring right into the void. No more years, no more months, not even a whole week anymore. No going back; no going forward, either. Adam was a teenage Peter Pan. He would never grow up. Just a few days of now, and then oblivion.

"It's the ride, Adam, it's the ride," she kept telling him. He was living his whole life in one week — there were going to be lows as well as highs. Wasn't that what it was about? She hurried him along, keen to get him off the streets before anyone guessed what was going on. Manchester was heaving — commuters hurrying to get away before things got rough, protesters everywhere — camping out in Albert Square and Piccadilly Gardens, marching up Deansgate, groups wandering round with banners or sitting outside the bars and pubs, waiting for the protest to start.

What would the night bring? Lizzie wondered. She'd heard on the news that people were calling for the government to resign. At this rate, there wouldn't be anything left to fall.

They pushed their way through the excited crowds toward the Northern Quarter, where the flat Julie had found for them was. The crowds were thinner there, but as they turned off a main road into a small street, they heard shouting behind them. A window smashed, yells, a scream. Lizzie turned to see a wild crowd rushing toward them.

It was young people, maybe a hundred of them, raging up the road, full of fury. Lizzie pulled Adam into a doorway. There was no mistaking the sense of power and violence hanging over them. An old man was knocked to the ground and trampled underfoot. A woman got caught in the rush; someone grabbed at her and pulled at her clothes, and she was dragged along after them. Their faces were twisted in rage — or was it despair?

What was wrong with them? Lizzie had never seen anything like it.

They drew level to the doorway Lizzie and Adam were hiding in, and stormed past. Lizzie buried her head and hid. *Not me*, she prayed, *not me.* They roared and screamed just a foot or two away — she was certain they'd rape her or even kill her if they caught her — but no one leaned in to grab her, and in just a few seconds they were gone. She waited a moment before she peered out, only to see Adam trailing up the street after them. She darted out and grabbed his arm.

"Not there, Adam . . . this way." She pulled him away, but he resisted and gazed after the crowd.

"Deathers," he murmured.

Was that it? Lizzie stared at the pack as they tore their way up the road ahead of them. These must be the people who had taken Death in the square the night Jimmy Earle died. They'd gathered together somehow, and were roaming the city in a mob, tearing it to pieces.

She shook his arm. "Is that what you want?" she demanded. "To be like that?"

"They're like me. All together," said Adam.

"I thought you wanted to be with me."

Adam looked at her, shook his head, looked back. A siren called farther up the street and a group of police cars sped past. Reluctantly, he turned away. Lizzie dragged him to the building where the flat was and took him upstairs. *I'm a fool*, she thought. *I should have let him go.*

Inside, Adam was inconsolable. He buried his head in her arms and wept like a child. "I just want to live," he sobbed. She held his head and stroked his face. What could she say? There were no words of comfort for what was wrong with him.

"You'll feel better in the morning," she said, and hoped it was true. He curled up next to her on the sofa, drank a bottle of wine that she found in the fridge, and gradually became still. End of Day 1 and they were both exhausted, distraught, miserable. *Poor payment for a life*, Lizzie thought. She woke him up long enough to get him to bed, then lay next to him, while he clutched at her and then, mercifully, fell asleep.

She waited until he was still, then got up and went to sit in the sitting room, feeling deeply shaken. She had never seen true despair before. Adam's eyes had been like black holes leading all the way to death. All the websites she'd checked out had mentioned this, so she was forewarned, but the intensity of it was shocking. There were going to be moments like this — more and more of them, she suspected.

The Deathers on the street had been the real thing, she thought, the ones with nothing to lose and nothing to gain, ready to die. The trouble was, Adam wasn't like that. On the contrary, he was just ready to begin his life. It was the selfishness of the suicide. *Look at me! I'm going to die. Pity me. Be with me. Do what I want.* Suicide — but with all the benefits of watching your friends mourn you.

"It's all about you, Adam," she whispered.

She got up and went to the sitting-room window. It was all going on outside, but she couldn't see much — just police lights flashing blue somewhere and the glow of flames around a nearby corner.

She flung the window open and it came rushing in on her. Shouting, screaming, chanting, singing, cars revving, the wail of sirens. And somewhere, not far away, the pop and rattle of gunfire.

Lizzie felt a thrill. Was it really happening? The world had seemed frozen rigid, stuck in its old ways just a few days ago. Now, everything was melting and the future was being forged here, on the streets of Manchester, right before her eyes.

Only one thing was certain. The government might fall, food and money might become common property, the new order might be cruel or kind, tyrannous or democratic — but none of it was going to affect Adam. His time was already over.

It's going to be so exciting, she thought. She wouldn't leave Adam. She'd keep her promise. But it was hard, so, so hard, to be tied to someone already in the past, when the whole future was up for grabs. What a shame, she thought, that she was going to remember Adam as this selfish little beast, gobbling up everything he could, when just a short while ago he had been so sweet and kind. Which one, she wondered, was the real Adam?

But then, what difference did that make now?

CHAPTER 14

BEING NICE TO CHRISTIAN

MR. B RANG THE BELL TO GARRY'S DOOR AT NINE O'CLOCK sharp, which surprised Garry because he'd said he'd call at eleven. He knew who it was because the caller leaned on the doorbell for a good minute. Who else could it be?

Garry was on the toilet at the time. He flung himself from the seat onto his crutches, levered himself to the top of the stairs, got in the stair lift, and started the thing on its way down.

"Please please please please please," he begged. *Please let him be nice to me. Please let this go as smoothly and as quickly as possible.* And of course, *please make the stair lift work.* Mr. B was the kind of person you didn't want to keep waiting.

"Coming!" he yelled, as cheerfully as he could manage. Halfway down, the stair lift predictably went into reverse and started on its way back upstairs.

"No!" Garry jabbed at the button with a stubby forefinger. Why him? Why his legs? Why his stair lift? At last, after a series of desperate pokes and bangs, the thing ground to a halt and sat there sulking for a full twenty seconds before carrying on its way down again.

Christian did not look amused.

"Sorry, sorry," Garry babbled. "The stair lift has a mind of its own. Up, down, all around. Heh heh heh," he tittered, grinning like an overexcited puppy as he backed away from the door.

Christian stepped inside. He tried not to look discomfited by the fact that the place was damp and dirty. That would be bad manners. Christian prided himself on being good-mannered and expected it in others. It was sad but predictable that Garry had left him standing at the door for so long before answering — an example of bad manners if there ever was.

"Come in, come in!" chirruped Garry unnecessarily. "Sit down. Tea? Biscuits? Piece of cake?"

"No, thank you," said Christian, looking with distaste at the grubby kitchenette tucked away under the stairs. He himself only ever ate the very best quality takeout or ready meals at home, and his house was littered with tinfoil trays full of half-eaten and flyblown meals. Compared to that, Garry's place was almost clean. But there was a difference: Christian's house was covered with rich dirt, while Garry's stank of poverty. And poor dirt, as everyone knows, is so much dirtier and more contagious than the wealthy sort.

The poor, the poor, Christian thought. *They are always with us, but that doesn't mean you have to do business with them.* Vince was right. This man should never have been given access to expensive drugs.

Garry sat there smiling up at him, thinking, *The rich, the rich! Always on the make. Well, just you wait, pal. In a few days our time will come and yours will end.*

"Cup of coffee?" he suggested.

"No. Just the money will do, thank you."

"Ah, the money! I can do better than that. Here . . ." Garry dug about in his pajamas, much to Christian's disgust, and pulled out the polyethylene bag with Death in it. He beamed. "You know what? I'd prefer to give them back. I'm a bit out of my depth, to be honest. It's just not secure enough here. I'm going to get myself into trouble."

"Yeah!" smiled Christian. And they both chortled briefly at the thought of how nearly Garry had got himself into trouble.

"Just one missing," said Garry. "And I have the money for that right here." Digging into his pajamas again, he came out with a handful of notes.

"Thanks for the offer," said Christian. "But we have a contract. I provide the goods. You pay for them."

Garry flinched. "Contract?" he said. "You mean — legally binding?" He snickered weakly at his own joke.

Christian nodded. "Yeah," he said. "In a manner of speaking."

There was a moment's silence. "Please," said Garry. "I'm not ripping you off. I know when I'm out of my depth. I'm giving you the stuff back. Please."

Christian strolled around behind the chair and began to rub his fingers down the back of Garry's neck, feeling his way through the flesh to the bones beneath. With the other hand, out of sight, he took a short-bladed knife out of his coat pocket.

"What are you doing?" begged Garry. The massage felt almost nice. Nothing could have been more terrifying.

"Quad or para?" asked Christian suddenly.

"Eh? Well, para, you know? Hands and elbows, but no knees and toes," said Garry, twisting around to look at him and parroting a phrase his mother used to use when he first had his accident twenty-five years ago.

"Quad," said Christian. He grabbed hold of Garry's head and forced it forward. While Garry squirmed helplessly under his grip, Christian raised the knife, took careful aim, and brought it down with a dull thud into the back of his neck. The blade sank in up to the hilt in the gap between two vertebrae beneath the skull. A thin stream of blood rolled down under Garry's collar, and he let out a muffled squawk. A shudder ran through his body. He twitched a few times and then ceased to move. Christian let go of his head, which lolled at an odd angle onto his chest, and stood back to survey his handiwork.

This particular cut was something he'd been working at for a while. It was a tricky one to get right. He picked up one of Garry's arms and let it flop down like a piece of limp celery. So far, so good. But the guy was being too quiet. Christian bent down and looked into his face.

"How's it feel?" he asked.

Garry blinked at him but didn't say a word. Not good. Christian was going for a C4, severing the spinal column in between vertebrae 4 and 5. Quadriplegic, but the victim could still breathe — if you got it right.

He tipped Garry out of the chair and peered into his face. It was changing color. Shit! He pushed him over onto his face and fumbled at the neck, trying to count the vertebrae below the head. The bastard had a fat neck. Christian hated fat necks. He had miscounted, done a C3 instead of a C4 and disabled his victim's breathing as well. Silently at his feet, Garry was suffocating.

Bugger! Disgustedly, Christian kicked at the limp body. This was the third time he'd got it wrong. It was infuriating.

He shook his head, popped the bag of pills into his pocket, and headed off. He needed more practice. Next time for sure.

Behind him, unable even to struggle for breath, Garry watched as Christian wiped his expensive handmade shoes on the doormat, so as not to dirty the streets outside with the cheap crud from the grubby carpet. The door opened and closed; his murderer gone. Garry turned red, then blue, then white, and died with a murmurous gurgle some ten minutes after Christian had left the building.

CHAPTER 15
THE HEIST

TUESDAY MORNING AND ADAM WAS SITTING IN THE KITCHEN, happily tucking into bacon and eggs. The food was perfect and so was everything else. The day awaited his attention, the sky blowing grubby white and gray clouds across a pale blue sky solely for his enjoyment. Lizzie was in the shower — and he was in love.

Best of all, he was no longer a virgin. Adam grinned at the ceiling. Sex was great. He loved sex. It was, without doubt, the most wonderful thing that had ever happened to him, and he'd done it with the most wonderful person he'd ever met. If he'd been any happier he'd have just melted away with sheer joy.

Lizzie, Lizzie, Lizzie. "I love you!" he shouted out over his shoulder, and he heard her shout back, "I love you!" from the shower. How lucky was he? Maybe they'd go and do it again in a moment. And again, and again . . . Wouldn't it be great just to put on some music and spend the day in the flat? Staying in bed, doing it, chatting, relaxing, doing it again . . . maybe go out for a drink later . . . ?

But he couldn't. There wasn't time. He had to get on with the list.

Overnight, things had sorted themselves out in Adam's brain. That was Death for you — each day was fresh and new — the next twenty-four hours opened up like a whole new life spread before him.

He whipped out the list and scanned it.

Fall in love. Done!

Sex with Lizzie. Done! *Get her pregnant.* Yeah, well. Worry about that later.

Loads of sex with loads of girls. Several of them at once. He felt guilty about it, but he knew he was going to check out that website, regretitforgetit.com, to see how many bites he'd had. Lizzie would understand, one day.

Drink champagne till I can't stand. Done!

Do cocaine. Something to look forward to.

Drive a supercar around Manchester.

Kill someone who deserves to die.

Do something so that humanity will remember me forever.

Die on the Himalayas, watching the sun go down.

He'd work on those later.

Get rich. Leave my parents and Lizzie with enough money so they'll never have to work again.

Too right. He needed money to make the rest of the list happen. That was today sorted out. He was going to get rich.

He'd done three out of ten already and it was only Day 2! Heroic. And more than that. Look at this flat — it was huge! He could have put "live in a fabulous place" on the list and he'd have achieved that as well. Everything was modern, every luxury you could think of. Jacuzzi. A sauna. Yes, you heard right — a sauna. And the view — you could see halfway across Manchester. This was living! The food he'd just eaten had tasted better than anything he'd ever had before. That was Death, his best friend Death, heightening his senses, making everything so much better, so much more real.

Lizzie came in wearing a robe and sat opposite him. Adam jumped up and kissed her. Dreams. He was going to make them all come true.

"You know these protests," Lizzie said.

"Yeah."

"How about going to have a look? Everyone's talking about it. It sounds like something might actually happen this time."

Adam frowned at her. "But it's not on the list, is it?"

"Leaving something behind you is. This is big, Adam. The government could be overthrown. The way you are, maybe you could do something to help it. Legacy, you know?"

Adam thought about it while he took a shower. Yeah, legacy was on the list. Some act of bravery or something, so he wouldn't have lived in vain. But how do you make a life count? Six days left. A thrill of fear shook through him and he found himself leaning on the tiled wall, gasping for breath. Fear; it took him by surprise every time.

And Lizzie, going into the bedroom to get dressed, paused to listen in on the mind of a man with all his youth and love and energy to burn up in six short days, heard Adam murmuring, singsong under his breath, ". . . don't think it don't think it don't think it . . ."

and she knew that the day wasn't going to be spent planning the overthrow of the state. Who would bother to vote, if they knew there were no more tomorrows?

She sat down on the bed and sighed. If it were up to her, they'd have spent the whole day just lying in bed, then gone to the protest in the evening. Romance, excitement, and falling in love. It could have been wonderful. As it was . . . well, the sex had been OK. It was like Sarina had said — it was something that would probably get better the more you did it. But it wasn't ever going to get like that with Adam. So she felt . . . but then, what did it matter what she felt?

Adam banged in on her and grinned.

"Guess what?" he said. "We're going to rob a bank!"

There was a huge HSBC smack in the middle of town — no one would expect them to take that out. Adam would get a Death-powered stranglehold on one of the clerks, force them to let him in, open up the safe, and make off with the cash. Easy.

It took Lizzie a good fifteen minutes to change his mind. There was a reason why no one would expect them to take on the big HSBC — it was like an armed fortress, for instance. Plus the fact that the Zealots were putting all the major banks and companies under attack. There were police everywhere, and armed guards all over the building. The center of town was the last place to try to pull a heist.

Adam came up with another plan — Booze R Us on Wilmslow Road, back in Fallowfield. While the revolution was going on around the corner, the smaller places out of town would be relatively unprotected.

Lizzie wasn't exactly happy about it. She knew that shop. The till and the booze were behind glass and you had to tell the shop assistants what you wanted. They got it for you and you passed your money through a mail slot–sized gap under the glass. You couldn't get anywhere near the cash.

"There's a back entrance," said Adam. "Whenever someone on the staff wants a smoke, they go out that way and leave the door open. All we have to do is take them out, stroll in, and help ourselves." He grinned. See? All you needed was the nerve and commitment to do it.

"So why do they go to all that trouble to keep people away from the booze and the till, and then leave the back door open?" Lizzie wanted to know.

Adam had the answer to that. He had the answer to everything. "Because the system was designed by security consultants, but it's operated by monkeys. Simple. No problem. Loaded!"

They caught a bus on Oxford Road and then walked around the back of the shops to stake the place out. They only had to wait a few minutes before the back door opened up and a tired-looking guy with limp black hair came out. He lit up his cigarette, leaning up against a wall by the door, which, as Adam had said, he left open.

"Let's go," hissed Adam.

Lizzie glared at him. She felt sick with fear. "You owe me," she hissed.

Adam grinned back. "I won't live long enough to be able to pay you back. Just go! You'll get a share of the proceeds, won't you? Let's go-go-GO!"

He stepped forward. Lizzie followed him, and they both ambled casually toward the shop assistant. Not casually enough. Maybe it was the way they were walking — maybe it was the way Lizzie had pulled her woolly hat down over her eyes so she couldn't be recognized that made her look exactly like a robber. Either way, the assistant seemed to know at once that they were up to no good. He was edging toward the door before they were halfway toward him. Adam sped up. The assistant jumped inside and slammed the door shut.

"Run!" yelled Lizzie, scooting backward, but Adam hadn't given up yet. He threw himself at the door — and he was in luck. The assistant was still fumbling with the lock and it flew open under his weight. Lizzie came running in after him and found him in a storeroom, piled high with crates of booze, crouching over the terrified man, who was cringing on the floor.

"Don't hurt him!" she said.

"I'm not," hissed Adam. "Get in there — quick."

She edged her way to the door at the front of the storeroom. On the other side was a short corridor leading through to the shop. She glanced back; Adam nodded and she made her way forward. Behind her, Adam forced the man flat onto his stomach. He felt so strong he could do anything.

"Stay still," he hissed, "and no one gets hurt."

The assistant pressed his face to the floor and nodded. Inside, Adam could hear Lizzie banging about.

"I can't open the till!" she yelled. Then: "Agh! Ads, there's someone else here!"

"Not my name, you idiot!" Adam yelled back. He hauled the assistant to his feet just as Lizzie came charging out. At the same moment, an alarm began ringing. Cursing, Adam pushed both Lizzie and the assistant into the shop. There, cringing by the counter, was an old guy, over sixty, gray hair, balding . . .

"Shit, Lizzie, it's someone's granddad, we're not going to be scared off by this," snarled Adam furiously. He shoved the first assistant into the older man and grabbed them both by the hair. He was so full of adrenaline, he could have wrestled a rhino to the ground.

"Open the till!" he yelled.

"No," squeaked the old man.

Adam banged their heads together gently.

"OK! OK! OK!" the old guy yelled. He reached over and pinged the till open. There it was — the lovely money. Adam reached in, snatched a handful, and kissed it. He scooped the rest of it out, then turned abruptly and dashed out, with Lizzie on his tail.

They ran and ran, the clanging alarm fell away behind them. No one gave chase — they were in the clear. After five minutes they slowed down and ducked into an alley to get their breath back and count the loot. They'd done it! How cool was that? Adam pulled out a big, fat roll from inside his jacket. He counted it up: one thousand pounds. Not bad. He shook the notes in Lizzie's face. "We can blow this lot, then we'll do another one. We know how now," he boasted.

Lizzie nodded, but really, she felt dreadful. Yesterday she was living at home being bored. Today, she had run away from home, had sex for the first time with her boyfriend who had taken Death, was being hunted down by a pervert gangster — she hadn't even bothered mentioning that to Adam — and here she was, committing a major crime with a prison sentence hanging over her if she got caught. She was out of breath, sick with fear, and emotionally exhausted. It was all too much. She started to sniffle.

Adam put his arm around her. "Aw. What's up?"

She looked at him. What's up? Didn't he even *know*? She started to cry uncontrollably — great gusts of tears, crouching there in the alley, while Adam waved the thousand pounds under her nose to try to cheer her up.

"Come on, Lizzie! We pulled it off! Hey — guess what?"

Lizzie shook her head.

"Did you see that guy's face when I banged their heads together?"

Lizzie looked up. Her lip wobbled. Adam nodded at her. *Come on, come on, come on! Please, Lizzie, just feel good. Do it for me!* To his relief, gradually she started to smile wryly and then wheeze with laughter.

"He looked like he was going to piss himself, didn't he?" said Adam. "And how about that kid when I made him get on his knees? I reckon he thought I was going to make him pray!"

Yeah, hilarious! Lizzie began to giggle, although whether it was hysteria or true comedy, she wasn't sure. They laughed and laughed, had to hold each other up but ended up rolling around on the ground anyhow. Finally, snorting and giggling, they made their way to a bus stop to catch a double-decker into town. The fun bit was, the bus took them past the shop they'd just robbed. It was even more hilarious. There were police cars, cops stopping people going in and out. It was great. They'd made fools of everyone.

The bus rolled on its way down Wilmslow Road into town. Past the Curry Mile, past the Whitworth Art Gallery. Adam and Lizzie checked on their phones to see where to eat, what to do, what was on. They were halfway there when Adam realized they'd stopped for too long and peered out the window. There was a cop car next to them. He stood and looked out. There was another police car pulled up in the road right in front of the bus.

He knew at once. "They're onto us," he hissed. He leaped out of his seat and ran for the stairs. Lizzie stood up — then sat down again. Adam was fast, he might be able to escape, but her best bet was to hide here among the other people on the bus. And — Adam had given himself away . . .

Adam almost fell down the stairs. At the bottom, the door was shut. He ripped it open and jumped out — right into the arms of the police.

"I'm guessing you must be the guilty party," one of them said. A couple of them grabbed hold of him, pushed him over, and pressed him down into the road.

"Spotted on the bus laughing your silly heads off," another said, and they all laughed.

It was hopeless. Adam was surrounded, facedown on the pavement, his arms pinned behind his back. He peered sideways and up: handcuffs. Once they were on, he was screwed.

He twisted suddenly and managed to get on his back. *You have to try, right?* He jackknifed — shoulders on the ground, striking up with his feet — and caught one of the policeman square on the chest. The man went flying. Adam flipped down, got his feet under him, and he was hurtling off as fast as he could, vaulting over the hood of a car and away up the road. He ran — ran and ran and ran, the cops hot on his tail. One of them was a bit overweight — he didn't stand a chance — but the other was young, long-legged, and fit. Even with Death in him, Adam was losing ground.

He was going to get caught — he had to do something! He dropped suddenly to the ground and curled up into a ball. The policeman banged his foot smack into his back and went flying. But that foot caught Adam bang in his kidney. He jumped up at once and tried to carry on, but he was crippled with pain. He staggered up the street, his legs buckling under him. The policeman was back up already. He'd skinned his hands and his face on landing and looked dreadful, covered in blood — but his wounds were just skin deep. He caught Adam easily, spun him around, and shoved him down face-first on the road again.

"You little shit," he hissed, and punched him hard in the kidney. "Unavoidable injury sustained during capture and detention."

The other police came running up. They dragged Adam to his feet and marched him off to the police car.

They had Lizzie, too, standing there in her black woolly cap. Except, when he got close, it wasn't Lizzie. It was some other kid, a bit younger than Adam, with the same kind of clothes as Lizzie, looking anxiously at him as he was marched up.

"Tell 'em, mate," the kid said. "It wasn't me, was it? Your mate must have got away."

"Sorry, Al," Adam said. "They got us."

The kid stared at him as it sank in. "You bastard," he squeaked. "Hey, he's lying, honest, he's lying, it wasn't me . . ."

The police led them off to the waiting cars. "It's a setup!" the kid yelled, but the police just pushed him down into the car. Adam went in another one, and they drove off. Before he got in, Adam managed to glance up and saw the white face of Lizzie in the upstairs windows of the bus as it pulled away.

At least she'd got away with it. But as for Adam — that was it. He was going to get tested for Death, locked up, remanded with no bail. They only needed one week. He was going to spend the rest of his short life behind bars.

The cell was a metal box — welded metal walls, metal door, metal floor, a metal bunk, and a metal toilet in one corner. A small square of glass about twelve inches thick let in a thin gray light, drowned out by a bright neon tube that was locked above him in a tough metal cage. It stank of piss and shit, and would have held a dinosaur, let alone one miserable boy. They left him there to stew on his own for half an hour — then, without warning, the door burst open and two big policemen stormed in, shouting and swearing, screaming threats in his face. For a few minutes the cell was full of loud abuse; then, just as suddenly, they went out and left him alone, leaving him shaken and more scared than ever.

That happened twice more; then the questions started. They took him to an interview room and told him how much better it would be for him to confess now. His mate Al, apparently, had already cracked and told them everything. Adam's parents had been called and were waiting outside for him. His mother was crying; so was his dad. It didn't look as though they could afford bail, but he might get a deal if he talked now. Did he really want his parents to be sitting there all night, worrying about him?

Then came more time on his own. More threats. A policeman came in and kicked him around the cell for a bit. Then more quiet, more screaming and shouting, followed by another beating. Adam kept his mouth shut, more by instinct than from any sort of plan. Eventually, hours later, a doctor came for the blood and urine tests. Afterward, back in the cell, sitting on the floor breathing in the stink from the toilet, Adam's last hope died. This moment, this misery, was going to be the rest of his life.

Hours passed. Once again the police came and took him out to a small room where he was charged with robbery and resisting arrest. Then he was marched along a corridor, turned a corner, and emerged in the front of the station where his mum and dad were waiting for him.

He was confused. What about the blood tests? Didn't they know about the Death? The policeman was explaining to his parents what would happen next. The test results would be back in a week or so.

A week! He was free. Suddenly, he was filled with joy. He had never been so glad to see anyone, ever. He grinned at his parents, but they looked back at him dark-eyed, and almost at once, his spirits sank again because — what was he going to say to them? How could he ever explain what he had done to himself, and to them?

All three of them stood there like naughty children while the sergeant gave them a lecture about being good parents and a good son. His mum hugged him while his dad signed some papers, and he was handed over like a lost pet into their care.

The journey home was grim. The bail had been huge — more than they could possibly afford. But they'd found it for him somehow, out of love. His mum drove; his dad sat twisted around in the seat trying to talk to him, but Adam had nothing to say.

"Why?" his dad kept saying. "Do you think this is going to solve all our problems? All you've done is make them worse. All that money for the bail."

"It's not the money," said his mum.

"Not *just* the money, no," said his dad. "But Adam — think! What are we going to do? How are we going to manage?"

Back home, his mum cooked him sausages while his dad sat at the table drinking tea. He went off to bed as soon as he could and texted Lizzie that he was out. There was no reply.

An argument was going on downstairs — obviously about him. Some time later, his dad came up to say good night. He bent over the bed to kiss him, something he hadn't done for years. His scratchy gray beard on Adam's cheek reminded him of when he was little.

"You must remember that we love you very, very much. No matter what, Adam. No matter what. We have each other first, last, and forever. But this has to stop. Robbing a shop! A poor man doing his job — you must have terrified him. You must accept the way life is and help us. You understand?"

Adam nodded.

"I want your word. Your word of honor, Adam, that this will stop."

Adam didn't even pause. "I promise. I give you my word. I'm sorry, I really am."

"Good." His dad nodded. For him, that was that. Adam had given his word. There would be no more questions or doubts. Only Adam knew that his word was worth nothing.

The old man paused at the door to drive his message home. "I love you. I love you and this has to stop," he repeated. He nodded once more, then left.

Adam tried to go to sleep — the sooner this day was over, the better. All he wanted was that wonderful good-morning feeling that came when he woke up with Death fresh in his veins. But he knew his mum was going to come up to see him, too. Sure enough, ten minutes later, there was her step on the stairs. The door creaked open. She whispered his name to check that he was awake. He didn't answer, just lifted his head, and she came quietly in, sat on the bed next to him, and stroked his head.

"I'm sorry," he said.

"I know you are," she said. "I'm sorry, too."

"What for?"

"This mess. It isn't what I wanted for my kids. Your dad handicapped. Me working myself into a shadow. And Jess, of course, especially Jess. But you know what, Adam? The funny thing is, I'm proud of him in a way."

Adam was outraged. "But he let us down!"

"He stood up for what he believed in. And maybe he's right — have you thought of that? Everyone's working harder and harder for less and less. So few people getting richer and richer, and the rest of us getting poorer every year. Kids killing themselves for a good time. Jess wanted to do something about that."

"I can't believe you have any pity for him," said Adam.

"I know he let us down. I'm angry about that, too, but at least he did it for a good cause. People are talking about revolution, you know. It can happen if we want it to. There are half a million people on the streets of Manchester right now, as we speak. Half a million! Something has to give."

Adam said nothing.

"The thing is, Adam . . ." She squeezed his hand and bent down a little closer, to try to push her words deep inside him. "Life is still worth living. There are so many wonderful things. Having a job you don't like — most of us have to do things we don't like, but it's still an adventure. It's all waiting for you. Growing up, having children. Making love. Falling in love." She smiled. "It really is like they say in the songs. Love is the greatest thing. Don't throw it all away just because there are bad things as well. Life can be generous as well as mean. It can be joyful. Always remember that. Promise me, Adam, will you — always to remember that?"

More promises. Adam nodded. But he would keep this promise, he felt. He would remember her words until his dying day.

She bent to kiss him. "Night-night," she whispered.

"Night, Mum."

Adam turned over as she left the room and lay there, keeping himself awake. He waited until the house had gone very, very still before he got up, let himself quietly out the front door, and left.

CHAPTER 16

LIZZIE MAKES A DATE

ON THE BUS, LIZZIE ESCAPED BY SIMPLY STAYING PUT. NO one seemed to realize that she was with Adam, or if they did, they didn't point her out when the police came up and took that lad downstairs. She sat quietly until the bus got into town, and then went straight back to the flat.

That was it, then. Bang. Adam was as good as dead.

On her own at last, she burst into tears. What a couple of days! It was exhausting just sitting next to Adam, watching him foam over with life and knowing he was going to be dead in just one week. And now he was gone forever.

She was relieved; she felt dreadful for feeling relieved. She was sad; she was angry. He'd let her down; she'd let him down . . . she didn't know what she felt.

She drifted about the flat, wondering what to do now. Her parents would be going crazy. She turned on her phone, which she'd kept off to avoid hearing from them earlier, and sure enough, there was a long list of calls and messages. *Where are you? What's going on? We just want to know you're safe.* It was the first time she'd been away from home without telling them. She had planned to be away a week, but it looked like it was time to go home already.

Life was going straight back to zero, she thought. Home. School. Mates. Mum and Dad. And all the time, Adam was in a cell waiting to die.

Not yet. She wasn't ready to go back yet. She turned on the telly and flipped through the Internet to find out more about Death — and there it all was: the gangs rampaging around Manchester, the rumors about the Zealots manufacturing the new cheap Death. The stages people went through. It started off manic, apparently, in the first few days, then calmed down. That was when the despair hit home.

She wept again. It was impossible to think about Adam without crying. He had been a little shit these past two days, but that wasn't him — that was the drug. She dried her eyes and flicked through some more until she found what she was looking for. A page on a Deather site: "The Antidote."

It was a no-hoper — but it was the only hope.

There were a lot of rumors, but no hard facts. A post by a journalist explained how an antidote was impossible because of the way the drug bound itself to the brain. But then there was another by a guy who claimed to have actually taken the antidote after stealing it from a secret government lab. It was real, he promised. It was out there. You only had to look . . .

And another post warning about this cruel hoax.

Who knew? If there was an antidote, she was in the right place. This was Manchester, where it was all happening. The police were pretty sure the illegal Death was being manufactured here. Not only that, but Lizzie had a good idea who might be involved.

It was dangerous, she knew that — Julie was scared by Christian for a reason. But it was Adam's life at stake. She had to at least try. If she didn't, she wouldn't be able to live with herself.

She had his phone number, too — he'd slipped it to her when she was talking to him at the party. She didn't want to lunge straight in, though, so she began by trying a cautious phone call to Julie first.

Her cousin was horrified when she heard that Adam had taken Death, but pleased that he had been caught.

"Thank God he's off the streets," she said. "Deathers are such wankers. It makes me angry. He deserves it. God knows what sort of trouble he'd have got you into. He was lucky to have you for just a few days. These people only get worse as it gets closer."

She went on to tell the story about a couple who had been at her party who'd taken Death.

"It started off, they were so cool. Really Zen and all that. Sitting about watching the sunset and being, like, in tune with the universe? You know. The next day, guess what? She catches him with a pair of prostitutes. He's like, 'Hey it's cool, I'm just, you know, making the most of my last few days.' Next thing, they're at each other's throats.

From love to hate in two minutes. How Zen is that? She forgives him, just about, but now — guess what? Going with those whores has made him realize what he's lost! How insulting is that for a girl? Next day she finds him in the bathroom with his throat cut out, dead as yesterday's hamburger. So now she's got two days left and she's searching, like, for the antidote, you know? Which doesn't even exist. How's that for fun? One more week on the planet? He didn't even make four days."

"So that's right about the antidote?" Lizzie asked. "You know that? There isn't one, right?"

And all she wanted was for Julie to say, *No, there's no antidote. I know that for a fact.* She pretty much held her breath, waiting for the feeling of relief when it came.

But instead, Julie got cross. "Listen to me, Liz," she said. "The people peddling this stuff are very rich, very powerful, very greedy, and very dangerous. They will do anything they have to to get what they want. If there is an antidote, they're the only people who know about it, and they ain't saying."

"So you're saying there might actually be one, then?"

"Don't you even dare think about it. You've just had one fuck of a lucky break. You had Christian Ballantine after you and a total loser for a boyfriend — and by sheer luck, both those things have been sorted out for you. So just leave it, OK? Bloody hell. What are you trying to do? You're seventeen. Stop acting like a silly little girl. Stay away from anyone — especially Christian — who has anything to do with this shit. Get it?"

"I hear what you're saying," said Lizzie noncommittally.

Julie seethed and raged some more, but she had already made a number of fatal mistakes, including calling Lizzie a silly little girl, but mostly by confirming that Christian was involved in Death.

Christian was delighted to hear from her.

"Where've you been? I've been trying to find you," he cooed.

"Oh, round about," Lizzie replied vaguely.

"Shouldn't you be at school?" he asked.

"It's the holidays. Hey — I have a question for you," she said.

Christian was lying in the bath. He settled down in the foamy water with a cup of tea at his side. He had been getting pretty irked with Vince about his inability to find the new girl — and lo! Here she was, delivered right into his hands.

"It's about Death," said Lizzie.

Christian paused, his cup of tea halfway to his lips. "Why are you asking me about that?" he asked peevishly.

"You said drugs. It sounded very glamorous," said Lizzie. "I just thought . . . you know . . ."

"OK," said Christian. This girl was not only desirable. She was also dangerous.

"I was wondering if you knew if there's an antidote. I've been hearing there is one," Lizzie said.

Silence, except for a little splashing.

"Because I have this friend," Lizzie pressed on. "This guy. He's been through a really bad time and he's gone and done it. Taken Death. I was wondering . . . you know . . ."

"I see," said Christian. "Well. We should meet up and talk about it."

"Can you do anything?" she asked.

"If I could help you — and I'm not saying that I can — you'd have to meet me, wouldn't you? I mean, what do you want? For me to put it in the post?"

Despite herself, Lizzie felt a ray of hope.

"Are you saying there is one?" she said. "Just be straight with me."

"Lizzie, this is a phone call. I can't talk about it here."

"I have to know. I can't come to see you unless I know."

"Put it like this," he said. "The things people can do today, huh? You know? The entire human genome. Particle physics. They made a man grow a new leg the other day, I read. Then they say they can't work out something like this. Strange, isn't it?"

"I knew it," said Lizzie calmly. "I knew it. Everyone says there isn't but I knew there just had to be."

"You think."

"Don't you?"

Christian laughed. "Yeah, matter of fact I do. You are going to have to come to meet me, though."

"Can you get it for me?"

"We can't talk about it on the phone."

"How much will it cost? I'll need to bring money with me."

"More than you could possibly afford."

"I can give you ten thousand. I have ten thousand," she said. And she had. Various aunts and uncles had given her the money toward her university fund.

Christian snorted. "Forget it. Nowhere near."

"That's all I have."

"Just come round. You won't need any money."

Lizzie paused. "Will you give it to me if I come?"

Christian laughed out loud. "Oh, I'll give it to you, don't worry about that," he said, and he giggled like a boy.

So it was that. She'd thought so. So — just how far would she go to save Adam's life?

"What exactly do you want, Christian?" she demanded. "Just say it."

"I want *you*, round here, right now. In my bed."

"That's the deal?" she asked. "Sex for the antidote, right?"

"That's the deal."

"How long do I have to think about it?"

Christian's house was right out in the country. Driving there, Lizzie was so nervous she actually stopped the car at one point and started back. But then she turned again and went forward. She was saving a life. What sort of a bitch would she be to let Adam die, just because of sex?

It was the old story. Boys went to the rescue with a gun in their hands, girls with their panties in their pockets. So which was worse? This way, she thought, at least no one was going to get hurt.

When she arrived she sat in the car at the bottom of the drive for another minute or two. Last chance to back out. Then she drove up and parked on the gravel in front of the house.

The house didn't help. It looked wrong. It was a great square thing, an old rectory or something. The curtains were all drawn, but some of them were half off the hooks. The paintwork was peeling, there was glass out in at least two of the upstairs windows, and a hank of ivy had been half pulled off one of the side walls and hung there like a piece of peeling skin. The lawns and shrubbery that bordered the house were wild and overgrown, but the gravel area in front had been carefully raked. Three highly polished and very expensive cars stood there — a Porsche, a Lamborghini, and something else, she had no idea what. There were skid marks in the gravel as if someone had been doing wheelies. If it weren't for the cars outside, she'd have thought she was at the wrong address.

She knocked on the door, which was opened almost at once by Vince, who didn't say a word, just stood aside to let her in. He was huge, she'd forgotten how huge. Standing next to him, she felt very little indeed.

Vince turned and led the way inside, still without a word. It seemed as if she didn't require the pleasantries anymore. It made her feel like dirt. Maybe that was how prostitutes always felt.

They walked along an uncarpeted hallway, past a series of shiny but very dusty doors and expensive-looking wallpaper. The whole house was like that — beautifully decorated with lovely furniture, but filthy dirty. It stank, too, of stale food and old clothes.

Vince opened one of the doors and ushered her into a huge sitting room — no carpet, one enormous couch, and a table littered with old takeout containers. Christian was waiting. He stood up as she came in.

"Hello," she said.

"Hi, you look great," he replied. He walked over and kissed her. She had thought there might be drinks or something, but no, he was straight in with his fat, wet, old-man's tongue. It was such a shock, she pushed him away and backed off.

Christian glared at her. "Are you doing this or not?"

She nodded.

"Kiss me, then." He stuck his face toward her and stood there like a sulky boy, his lips pouted, head forward. Lizzie dithered. Then he tutted irritably and came in again for another kiss, same as last time, full of wet tongue — a nasty porn kiss, she realized. But what had she expected? Romance? She had agreed to be porn for him.

Christian ran a series of little kisses down her neck that gave her the tickles. That was the icebreaker. Then he was easing the shoulder straps of her top down, pushing everything down below her breasts, and grabbing hold of them. It was horrible enough for her to back away from him again without thinking.

"Are you going to be my girlfriend or what?" he demanded. "You're not just playing me along, are you?"

"It felt funny," she said.

"Oh. You girls," he said, suddenly playful. "C'mere, you." He grabbed her again, kissing her and kneading her breasts roughly. But before he could get any further, they were interrupted by a knock on the door.

"Fuck's sake!" roared Christian. "What?"

Vince peeped in. "It's Mr. Mindly at the door, sir," he said.

"Mindly. Of all times." Christian disentangled himself, wiped his mouth on the back of his sleeve, and went to the window to look out, leaving Lizzie standing with her top and bra around her waist. Vince stood at the door, staring at her. As delicately as she could, she pulled her clothes up and bowed her head.

"Bastard!" exclaimed Christian. "Coming to my house. How much does he owe us?"

Vince took out his phone and consulted it. He glanced at Lizzie.

"Never mind her. She's my girlfriend," Christian said.

Vince shrugged. "About fifty thousand," he said.

Lizzie thought, *I shouldn't be hearing this, should I?* But it was too late now.

Christian glanced back at her. "You get upstairs. Go and warm the bed up. It's the third on the left when you get to the top. Front of the house. Go on."

Lizzie hurried up. Vince watched her go up the stairs and into the bedroom before he went to the front door and opened it.

The room was big, freshly decorated, and dirty. There were splashes all up the walls behind the bed, and the smell of rotting food coming from somewhere. She found it soon enough, on a tray by the bed — a half-eaten burger that had passed its throw-away date ages ago.

Lizzie threw it down the en suite loo, flushed, then stood looking at herself in the mirror above the grimy washbasin. The face staring back shocked her. She had never seen herself look so pale. Her eyes were like stones. Her top had been ripped at the neckline where Christian had tugged it down. She looked petrified.

It was time to run, wasn't it?

There hadn't been any talk about the antidote, either. She should have made him hand it over before he got her clothes off. And what if he was lying? Or what if he was telling the truth but then changed his mind once he got what he wanted?

She'd always trusted her instincts, but she had overridden them for Adam, and now she didn't know what was going on or how to cope with it. She was trying to be heroic, but what if she was just being stupid instead?

The smell of the rotten burger still hanging on the air made her gag. Suddenly, she'd had enough. She went quietly to the door, opened it a fraction, and stood there, listening. Voices were being raised. An argument going on. She crept onto the landing and peered over the banister. No one there . . .

Then, just before she began to tiptoe downstairs, out of the blue, there was a single gunshot.

Lizzie jumped, screamed slightly, then froze, utterly unable to move a muscle. A door opened below her and Christian stepped out into the hallway. Behind him, he left a bloody footprint — just one.

His left shoe was dripping gore. He glanced behind himself and got on one leg to ease the guilty shoe off.

"You idiot," he said, speaking into the room he'd just left. "That was too quick, much too quick for the amount he owed us. I could have C4'd him. And on the carpet. Don't tread on it," he yelled suddenly. "Take your shoes off. That's a good carpet. You should have shot him on the tiles, for God's sake. Look. What a mess."

"He was going for his weapon, sir."

"Was he?" Christian turned and went back in.

"His inside pocket, sir."

There was a pause.

"That's his wallet, you fucking idiot. His wallet. Look, he has money in it. *He was going for his wallet so I shot him.* How would that look in court? Vince, you're an idiot. He was going for his wallet."

The two men started to laugh and somehow, this sound brought Lizzie back to life. She had to get out — she was witness to a murder. She jerked back from the banister and ran lightly along the corridor to the back of the house. She was in luck — there was another stairway there. But before she could go down, another door opened below her and Christian came out, carrying his hands before him, covered in blood. She just had time to dash into one of the nearby rooms off the corridor as he came up the stairs. By sheer bad luck she found herself in a bathroom — exactly where Christian was heading. She just had time to climb into the bath, draw the shower curtain, and lie down, before he came in after her.

Christian spent some time at the basin, washing the blood off his hands and trying to get some spots out of his T-shirt. Then he took a pee, shook himself, and left. Lizzie waited a few minutes before leaving the bath and going quietly to the door, which he had left ajar. Below, she could hear the two men arguing.

She had to get out. They'd kill her.

She made her way down the front stairs, but the door was locked, so she had to go to the back of the house, right past the room where they were arguing about the best way of getting blood out of the silk carpet. Her luck held, and she escaped through a kitchen window. All she had to do now was get around the front to her car and drive off.

It was getting dark. She was going to be all right! Keep to the bushes, avoid the windows; she was making it! She reached the front, and was just about to leave the shelter of the shrubs and venture onto the gravel drive for her car, when the front door opened and Christian came out with Vince behind him carrying something heavy wrapped up in black garbage bags. Christian opened the trunk of the Porsche. Vince dumped it in there.

Lizzie was tucked away behind some bushes. It was dusk, she was well hidden, no one could see her. Vince got in the car, started up, pulled away, and as the headlights swung around they shone straight at her. She was picked out beautifully, white as a sheet, hidden badly behind what turned out to be a straggly tree.

"Lizzie!" Christian roared.

She turned and fled for her life, but got no more than a few yards before her feet were kicked out from under her. She crashed to the ground and was picked up before she had time to draw breath.

Christian carried her toward the house in his arms like a hero rescuing a wounded girl. He paused by the car where Vince was still sitting, waiting.

"You go on," he said. "I'll look after her."

"She saw everything," said Vince, and he drove off.

CHAPTER 17

JANET

ADAM ARRIVED BACK AT THE FLAT AT HALF PAST THREE ON Wednesday morning. Lizzie was nowhere to be seen.

He texted and rang her; no answer. Where was she? He wandered from room to room like a lost child, looking for clues, but there was nothing. Then he got angry, and trashed some dishes and cupboards in the kitchen. He needed her! He rang again and raged and wept at her down the phone; then he sent another text begging forgiveness, pleading with her to come back. He turned the TV on to try and distract himself, but it was no use; his spirit was in freefall. Seeing his parents had brought him face-to-face with the feelings he had been trying so desperately to avoid, feelings of failure, isolation, and worthlessness. Lizzie had deserted him, he had destroyed his parents' lives as well as his own; all he wanted now was for it to stop.

He contemplated throwing himself out the window — he even went so far as to open it up and look down at the drop. He longed for the oblivion at the end of it, but lacked the courage to face the fall. He began a search around the house, looking for painkillers that might put an end to it all, but he only found a half-used packet of aspirin in the bathroom — not enough to kill a baby, let alone a strong young man powered up by Death. He went to bed in the end, believing that the only reason he didn't end it all now was because he lacked the courage. He was woken up a couple of hours later by his mum and dad ringing him. He turned the phone off, leaned over the bed, and was sick — literally, sick with fear. Then he turned over and went back to sleep.

He woke up to a headache, and, he realized, a bit of nausea as well. What was that about? Death was supposed to make you feel great, wasn't it?

Don't make me laugh.

Then he thought — *Lizzie.*

He turned his phone on. There were a dozen calls and texts from his mum and dad, some from his friends. But from Lizzie, not a word.

She's dumped me, he thought.

He fell back on the bed. How could she do this to him? He was on Day 3 — it felt like Day 7 already — and she'd left him to it. The thought that he was on his own was so frightening that he lacked the courage to ring around and see if he could find her. He lay in bed

for another hour, feeling too low to do anything, before he got up, show-
ered, had some juice, put the TV on, and sat watching an old comedy
for a while. It was late morning by the time he finally tried to find her.

Her home. Nothing. It just went straight to the answering
machine. He tried Julie — she'd left them a number — but she wasn't
picking up, either. Lizzie must have told her what was going on. His
number was coming up and they were all sitting there watching it,
waiting for him to go away, thinking — *What a loser!*

He had a precious day in front of him and no idea what to do
with it.

The comedy on the TV ended and the news came on. Suddenly
the screen was full of scenes of people massing in the streets of
Manchester. The crowds were immense.

Adam watched in amazement. Of course — the riots. Vaguely, he
started to recall the scenes of unrest he had seen while going in and
out of town. Somehow, it had passed him by. It wasn't about rioting
anymore — in fact, riots were impossible with so many people about.
The Zealots had been joined by other groups: trade unions, student
groups, civil rights groups, you name it. The police had stated pub-
licly that it would not engage in any actions against valid protesters.
A general strike had been called for that Friday, the one-week anniversary of Jimmy Earle's death. Even the state-controlled TV channels
were talking openly about it.

Revolution. Was it really going to happen? The crowds massed
in the streets and roared defiance. And sitting there so close to the
heart of Manchester, Adam realized that the roaring wasn't just from
the TV. It was coming from outside. He went to fling open the

window to let the noise in — and there it was! The roar of a million throats. The TV was showing live action and he was there, right there, listening to it. Up and down the street below him, thousands of people were pushing their way forward, trying to get to the main protests in Piccadilly Gardens and Albert Square. Never before had so many people gathered in one place, all with the same aim.

"Freedom!" roared the crowd.

The future, thought Adam. But it had nothing to do with him.

He closed the window and went back inside. He didn't need to see this.

Of all the crap times in history to take Death! The world was changing. No one knew which way it was turning. None of it was any use to him.

He found the regretit-forgetit site and logged on. The first thing he went to see was his own posting, asking for people to sleep with. And — he had a hit! Yeah! Someone had answered.

"Hi Adam," it said. *"I'm interested — definitely. I'm not posting a photo because I don't want my picture up for everyone to see, so you'll just have to take my word that I'm not hideous! I am a bit of an old lady, though — all of 25. I suppose that seems ancient to you, but if you fancy having a date with an older woman — let me know."*

You bet he would. Adam picked up the TV keyboard and typed in a reply: *"Just let me know when you're free."*

Things were looking up.

He flicked through the rest of the site. So many people were taking Death! He found a page where people were posting up their experiences. He settled down to read a few.

"Hey, to the guys at the BP Garage on Finland Road — thanks for the cash, hope no one gets in trouble. Sorry about the broken arm, big guy with the black hair!"

A robbery. *Way to go,* Adam thought. And, wow, how lucky he'd been to get away yesterday!

"I told my mum and dad today."

A pang shot through him.

Don't think it don't think it don't think it . . . Quickly he flicked on to the next post.

"I finished saying good-bye to the world today. I'm leaving early."

Wow. That one froze him to his seat. Leaving early? There was so little time anyway. He remembered how he had felt last night — but this was different. It didn't sound like despair. He flicked on to the comments underneath.

"You DICK! You threw your life away, man. DEATH is for living, not dying on!"

"What an empty, barren little life you must have had," said another.

"But you guys don't get it," said someone else. *"When you're ready to go, you're ready to go, it doesn't matter how old you are or how long you have left. I think saying good-bye is a beautiful way to go. What did you say good-bye to?"*

And underneath it, the original poster had written, *"I said good-bye to everything that ever mattered to me, and I did it real slow."*

Adam leaned back and thought about it. It made sense to him. Not the killing yourself — not yet, anyway. That stuff about doing it real slow. He'd been rushing around like a lunatic. Maybe it was time to slow down. Lizzie had the right idea after all. *Everything is for the last time. Every little thing matters.* It gives things a different perspective. He'd been going at it all wrong — too fast, too rushed. Today, he thought, he was going to take it slow.

Say good-bye. Yeah. Take time. Take a look at his old school, at his home. He didn't want to see anyone — no friends, no parents. As soon as he did that the peace would be shattered, you could bet your life. Maybe he'd take a few pictures on his phone, post them up for people to see, so at least they'd know he'd been around. Hey, that was an idea. He could leave some messages for them. He could say good-bye like that.

Better than meeting them face-to-face.

The more he thought about it, the better it seemed. It was right.

Before he went, he checked out his message box again — and he had an answer already.

"OK. See you in Piccolino off Albert Square today at 5? I'll be the blonde with the blue coat. I'll know who you are. We can have a drink and if we don't like each other, we can say good-bye. If we do . . . let's see, shall we?"

"We have a date," Adam answered.

Five o'clock. It was almost midday already. Today was going to be a good day. Take it all in, enjoy it. The smells, the sights, the sounds of some of the places he'd been familiar with during his time on earth. Saying good-bye.

He rang Lizzie again. Still no answer. That hurt him, deeply, badly, right down inside. But he didn't have time to let it worry him. He finished his cereal and went out to begin his day.

*   *   *

Adam intended to catch the bus straight to Fallowfield, but as he walked to the bus stop on Oxford Road, he got caught up in the crowds. Hundreds of thousands were converging on Manchester for the protests. There were tents on Piccadilly Gardens, food stalls and soup kitchens were being set up. There were posters and banners demanding that the government must resign, that the banks must be broken, that the corporations that had become more powerful than states be controlled, that capital should be mutually owned. A couple of the big office towers had signs up saying FREE MANCHESTER. It was a declaration, not a request.

People were coming to see the future recast. Something remarkable was going to happen, something that could change your whole life overnight. Adam felt as if he was in a dream, that none of this was really happening to him. It wasn't. He was immune from the future. This was for the living, not the dead.

He wandered among the crowds for a while, but he'd quickly seen enough and walked away along Portland Street. On Oxford Road outside the Palace Hotel, a running battle was taking place. The rebels were trying to take the place over, and the management had hired their own security team to see them off. People struggled in the lobby and on the pavement outside; and in the middle of it, a thin line of people waited for the bus — life still going on amid the chaos.

Adam joined them. He stepped onto the number 42 and rode away out of town. Things were much quieter out there, and by the time he got to the university, you would never have guessed that less than a mile away the world was changing forever.

As he entered his own patch, a sense of the amazement of life filled Adam up — how the world just kept on going on! With you or without you, it was always there. He got off the bus, wandered around, anxious in case he saw his friends or his mum or dad. His mum would be at work, of course, but the old man would be home alone now. He had to turn his phone on to take pictures, but kept the sound down, although it kept vibrating. He checked. It wasn't Lizzie and there was no one else he wanted to talk to.

He stood on the corner of Copson Street and Wilmslow Road, watching the shoppers going to and fro. The old Romanian lady who sold the *News of the Week* was there, calling out to people. Yeah, life went on regardless. It was beautiful but sad, and he tried to take some comfort in the idea that it would still be here, doing its thing, whether he was happy or sad, or high or low, or living or dead. In the end, what difference did it make? After, he went to have a look at his school. Same building, same students, same teachers teaching the same lessons. His death was going to mean so little to the world. Even his parents were going to get over it. Life went on. What did it matter how and when you popped in and out?

Sooner than he expected, he'd had enough. He didn't want to go back to his house but he did, anyway, just so he could have a picture of it and post it up, and his parents would know he'd been there, thinking about them.

On the way back, he stopped on the Curry Mile to eat — a favorite restaurant where he used to go with his dad, and once or twice with his friend Jack. He wondered if he ought to give Jack a call, but it was already four o'clock. He had his date in an hour. He ate up, paid the bill, and caught the bus back to town.

As he got close, in among the big crowds, he started to worry that Piccolino would be closed, but he needn't have worried. People still had to eat. With all these crowds waiting in the city center, it was actually fat pickings for the restaurants.

He pushed the door open and walked in. It was half restaurant, half bar — not the sort of place he'd usually go. People were drinking wine. It was too old for him, and he felt out of place at once.

His date — Janet, she'd called herself — had told him she would be the blonde wearing a blue coat; and right there, sitting at the long table that ran in front of the bar, was a pretty, young blonde woman. She caught his eye, but she wasn't wearing blue. Adam looked around, but saw no one else. He looked back to the woman. She was patting the seat next to her. There was a blue coat lying on it.

Adam froze. She smiled and called across to him.

"Adam," she said. "Sit down? Want a drink? I'm having prosecco."

"Yes, please. How did you know it was me?" he asked.

"How many seventeen-year-olds do you see in here? I wonder if they'll serve you." She nodded to a waiter and asked for another glass. The man frowned at Adam.

"Madam, he looks very young . . ."

"Bring us a bottle of water and a spare glass, then," she said, and winked openly at Adam. The waiter shrugged and went to fetch them.

Janet settled herself back on her stool and gave him a long look. "You'll do," she said, and she laughed. "How about me? Will I do?"

"Of course!" Adam insisted. He would have found it impossible to say no under any circumstances, but he took the chance to look her up and down. She opened her arms to show herself off, and then laughed and blushed slightly. She was quite short with a neat figure, wearing a white blouse open at the neck, a black jumper, and a short-ish green skirt. He was already wondering if he was going to get to find out what was underneath it. The thought made him blush, and he looked up quickly to meet her eyes. Underneath her makeup, one of them looked bruised, he thought.

"Fine," he muttered, and she laughed at him again, but it was a high, tinny laugh, because he'd sounded so gruff and uncomplimentary.

The prosecco arrived with the water. Adam studied her some more as the waiter served them. There was more bruising when you looked closely. Someone had beaten her up recently. There were some laughter lines around her eyes. But they didn't make her look old, he decided.

She waited till the waiter had gone, then poured Adam a glass of wine.

"The world's falling to bits outside, and he's worried about his license. Cheers," she said, holding out her glass.

Adam picked his up, and they tipped their glasses together and drank. There was a brief pause.

"I was worried it would be shut," Adam said, gesturing around at the bar.

"The Zealots use it," she said. "And some of the other rebel groups as well. Oh, it's a hotbed of sedition in here all right. Full of spies as well, I expect."

Adam glanced at the other people sitting around. Most of them were in their twenties and thirties. Well dressed. How could you tell what side they were on? He had no idea. But the thought alarmed him.

There was more awkward silence. Janet smiled tightly. "I don't suppose you have much small talk, do you?" she said.

"Er — do you work in Manchester, then?" he tried, but she lifted up a hand.

"Sorry, my fault. I don't want you to know anything about me," she said. "Do you mind?"

"No. It makes small talk a bit tricky, though."

Janet bowed her head in admission. "You're not doing bad," she told him. She laughed again, more relaxed. "This is funny. It feels exactly like the dates I used to go on when I was a teenager. Oh my God, I used to get so uptight! It brings it all back!"

"Was it that awful?" he asked, because it looked as if it was. He felt vaguely insulted.

She thought about it. "Looking back, I always thought it was awful. But now I think, maybe not so bad. What about you?" she went on. "Do your parents know about . . . what you've done?"

Adam looked coolly at her. He'd thought he'd do anything or say anything to avoid scaring her off, but now that it came down to it, he had his pride.

"I don't want you to know anything about me, either," he said.

"Touché!" she cried. "And that is going to make it rather hard, isn't it? But I like a little chat, it's romantic, isn't it, sitting here with the city burning all around us and everything about to change. Like soldiers of fortune, aren't we? Or spies or something." She smiled. "And with nothing to say to each other."

"I don't want to talk about my family, that's all," he said. "You can ask me about anything else."

"Can I? But isn't your family the whole thing?" she said.

Adam shook his head. He didn't want to go there. They talked about the protests instead, and Adam told her how he had been at the Jimmy Earle concert that had started it all off. She was curious about that. "I'd have given anything to be at that concert," she said. She asked him a little more about himself, about school, about his friends, his girlfriend. Adam was waiting for her to ask the big one — about his decision to take Death. He'd prepared for it. *I couldn't see any future I wanted to be a part of* was his favorite. Something like that. But to his surprise, the question never came.

Finally, she quaffed her wine.

"OK," she said. "Let's go."

Adam gulped and nodded. He emptied his glass and followed her outside. It was a chilly, breezy day, colder than it looked. She walked down toward Albert Square, but it was just too packed, so they headed the other way, through the narrow side streets toward Oxford Road. Janet linked arms with him, dipped her head, and smiled.

They checked into the Palace Hotel on Oxford Road, where there had been a battle on the streets earlier. It all seemed back to normal, the staff in their places, everything quiet. Maybe it had changed hands. If so, there was no way of knowing.

It was appallingly embarrassing going in — the staff had to know what was going on. To his surprise, Janet felt it, too.

"That was the walk of shame, wasn't it?" she said when they got safely into the elevator. "I was thinking all the time, they must be wondering which one of us is the prostitute."

It was a huge room — four-poster bed, two sofas, a desk, a table, and chairs. There was an en suite bathroom, with a bath that was long enough to lie flat in and a separate shower. It was all oversized.

"Do you like it?" she said. She laughed and looked sideways at him.

Adam suddenly thought that he was supposed to make a move and took a step toward her, but she darted off to the cupboards and stared searching through them.

"Here!" she exclaimed. It was a minibar in a little fridge in a cupboard under the desk. She took out a half bottle of champagne, which she gave to Adam to pop while she found some glasses.

"I'm nervous!" she confessed. "Isn't that idiotic?" She poured for them. They clinked glasses and gulped at the wine.

"Have you . . ." she began.

"What?"

"Done this before?"

Adam blushed. "Yeah, of course. A few times," he lied. "You have, I suppose."

"Not with a seventeen-year-old boy with one week to live. I'm a virgin myself in that respect." She laughed again and took another glug of her champagne. "Right. I'm going in the bathroom to undress. You get into bed and I'll come and join you. OK?"

Adam nodded. Janet scurried off into the bathroom. Adam dropped his clothes as fast as he could, hid in the bed . . . and waited.

She wasn't long. She came out wrapped firmly in a white bathrobe, and made him look the other way while she slipped in next to him.

"This is silly!" she said. "I'm supposed to be the sophisticated older woman, but I'm just so shy."

"What are you shy about?" he asked.

"You!" She wriggled close and pressed herself against him. He felt her body all down his — breasts, legs, torso, her little rough bush against his leg.

She kissed him. "You can touch if you like," she said. She lifted his hand to her breast. He rubbed gently and felt her hard nipple in his palm. She put her hand down and touched him under the covers, and came in for a kiss. She tasted of wine. Then she sighed, relaxed, and pulled him on top of her.

Afterward, they dozed briefly. Adam came round before her and lay there with her head on his arm, waiting for her.

So that was it. Second time, second partner. He hadn't had time to think about it much the first time with Lizzie, but now it reminded him a bit of those birthdays he used to have when he'd think — *So I'm ten now*, or *I'm thirteen*, or whatever, and he'd strain to feel a change, but it was never any different. Having had sex wasn't much different from being a virgin. Maybe you had to wait till you were in love. Maybe you had to wait forever to feel anything other than what you were.

He remembered how his dad had told him something his grand-dad had said on his seventy-fifth birthday. "I know I'm old," he'd said. "But I don't feel old. I feel the same as I did when I was eighteen."

You just did stuff. You went on and did other stuff. But it was all the same. Maybe that's what Death was going to teach him. That it didn't make any difference after all.

But . . . it had been very, very nice. He felt guilty about Lizzie, but she'd left him, after all. He was hoping they'd do it again when Janet woke up, but she wasn't interested. She went to the loo, then came back to bed and kissed him on the lips.

"Thank you," she said. "I thought I was going to make you feel older, but instead, you made me feel like I was fifteen again — all shy and sweet and scared. But perhaps a little more confident this time. I loved that, you know."

She propped herself up with the pillows and finished off the wine. Despite her claim that she wanted him to know nothing about her, she started chatting away about all sorts of irrelevant things — bars in London and Manchester, a boy she knew who might have been the love of her life but didn't seem to care, and how heartbroken it made her feel, and how she couldn't get over it.

"I don't think I ever will," she said. "Not till my dying day." She threw back her head and laughed, then gazed sadly at Adam. He knew — he thought he knew — what she was thinking: that he wasn't going to get over anything. His was a story already coming to its end.

When he looked at her again, he saw that she was crying. He wanted to comfort her, but didn't know how. She leaned over for a tissue, blew her nose, and wiped her eyes. "Getting sentimental in my old age," she said. For some reason, perhaps because of the sex, or because of her tears, or because she had shared a secret with him, he wanted to share something with her as well.

"My brother's in the Zealots," he said.

Janet turned to him. "Tell me about him," she said, and it was as if a plug had been pulled. His whole heart came flowing out of him — about Jess, about how much he'd loved and admired him and how angry he was with him now, and how let down he felt. About his parents, and how he'd ruined their lives and was too weak even to tell them he was sorry. And Lizzie, of course; how he'd said he loved her because it didn't matter whether he did or not, but now he thought he really did, but she was gone, and he couldn't really blame her, could he? How could he blame anyone for anything after what he had done?

And most of all, he talked about how he wished he'd never done it. He wished he could go back to a week ago. Life had seemed so terrible to him then, but in fact, it was so precious, so wonderful, so lovely — and he'd thrown it all away because it hadn't been what he'd expected, like a sulky brat throwing his teddy out of his stroller. Now he wanted it back so badly but it was gone forever, and no one could give it back . . .

Janet listened carefully, but didn't offer him any advice or ask him any questions. When he began to cry, she took his hand and stroked it and waited until the flood ended.

"Your brother sounds like a proper soldier," she said. She sighed and looked across at the clock on the bedside table.

"What are you going to do?" he asked her. "Can't you stay?" He didn't want to be on his own.

"The revolution," she said. "Listen!"

From outside came the sounds of chanting — half a million voices calling for change. "I want to be a part of that, just for a few nights."

A few nights? Did that mean . . . "Have you taken it as well?" he asked.

"No. Nothing like that. Don't ask, I won't tell you." She slipped out of bed and began to pull her clothes on. As she dressed he could see more bruises on her body, but he didn't dare ask what had happened. When she'd finished dressing she checked her hair in the mirror and came to sit on the bed next to him.

"Now, Adam," she said. "I want you to listen very carefully to me. I know the Zealots. No, don't interrupt me. I know some of them very well, and I can tell you something not many people can. There *is* an antidote. You understand? And I can get it for you."

She looked down at him, her face almost without expression, as if she was conducting an experiment on him.

"I don't believe you," he said. But he was hoping so hard.

"It's going to take me a couple of days," she said. "But I promise, I absolutely promise I can do this for you. All you have to do is stay out of trouble for that long. Until Friday." She stared down at him. "Well?" she asked. "What do you say? Do you want it? Or would you prefer to hang on to your week?"

Your week. She said it scornfully. Such a tiny measure against a whole lifetime.

"Why are you doing this?" he begged.

"Because I can," she said. She was quite businesslike now, like a doctor, sitting there on the edge of the bed telling him what he had to do.

"But I only have four days left," he said.

Janet smiled sourly. "And if it's not true, and I'm lying, you'll have wasted two whole precious days staying nice and safe. Except, Adam, they're not precious, are they? They're painful and horrible and nasty, because you're going to die when the world is about to change, goodness only knows how, and everyone is looking toward the future and you should have your whole life ahead of you. Well, I'm offering it back to you. Do you want it? Tell me. No questions," she said as he began to speak. "I can't answer them. All you have to do is keep yourself safe and be here when the antidote arrives on Friday night. It's that simple. Yes or no."

"But everyone says there's no antidote," he whispered.

Janet bent down close over him. "Everyone is wrong," she said. She leaned right down and kissed him on the lips. "Everyone except me." She laughed. "Do you agree?"

"Yes," he said. Yes. And now he had admitted it fully. He had made the most terrible mistake possible. Above all things, he wanted to live.

"Good." She stood up and smiled down at him. "Thank you for a lovely evening," she said. She picked up her bag and went to the door, where she paused and lifted a finger of warning. "Stay safe," she told him. "It's dangerous out there. If I were you I'd stay here, right in this room. No risks, Adam — because I'm risking a lot for you. Understand?"

Adam nodded.

As soon as the door closed behind her he jumped out of bed and stood in the middle of the room, exalting, his heart beating in him like a drum. It was a miracle. He was going to live!

He grabbed his phone and rang Lizzie. He had to tell her! Wouldn't it be wonderful if she came round and spent these two days with him? She had to know. Everyone had to know.

"I'm going to live!" he shouted. His voice echoed around the room. He had never felt happier in his life.

CHAPTER 18

CAPTIVITY

AT ROUND ABOUT THE SAME TIME THAT ADAM WAS SHOUTING hallelujah in his hotel room, Lizzie was sitting up in bed with a cup of coffee. Her left eye had swollen up until it was almost closed, and a trickle of blood was coming down her nose. She was very much aware that every time Christian lost his temper and hit her, she became a little more ugly. Becoming ugly was a bad move on her part, because, as he had pointed out to her after the last blow just a few minutes before, he was only going out with her because he liked her looks.

He didn't like her being afraid, either. It made her look stupid, and the way she flinched when he lifted his hand was just plain irritating. Which was a pity because the past day had been the most terrifying of her life. At the moment, she was concentrating as hard as she could on not spilling her coffee. Trembling apparently made her look like a spaz, and who wanted a spaz for a girlfriend?

Christian was standing a few feet away, getting himself dressed up in some new gear — baggy T-shirt, high-tops, and a pair of designer jeans he'd just had delivered. There was a new skateboard as well. He was posing with it under his arm in front of a full-length mirror.

"What do you think?" he asked.

Lizzie licked her lips and tried to control her breathing, terrified that if she spoke she might burst into ugly tears.

"You don't like?" asked Christian. "You don't like?"

"I, I, I, I . . ." she began, and the tears came out — hot, ridiculous, humiliating, ugly.

"What is wrong with you, Lizzie?" demanded Christian. "Look at this stuff — it's quality."

"I need, I need, I need . . ." she began, trying desperately to control her voice.

Christian rolled his eyes. "What *do* you need, Lizzie darling?" he sneered.

"I need to go to the loo," she admitted. She'd been dying to go for ages, but held back because going to the loo involved being humiliated. Being humiliated, in Christian's eyes, was almost as bad as being ugly.

Christian tutted. "Vince!" he bawled. "Girlfriend needs to go to the loo."

There was a pause.

"Vince!" screamed Christian. "Girlfriend! Toilet. Where the fuck are you?"

The door opened and Vince came in. He hiked his immaculate trousers up at the knees and bent to pull the potty out from under the bed.

"You took your time," complained Christian, turning back to the mirror.

"I was making a deal."

Christian closed his eyes tiredly. "You're a servant, Vince. You don't wander around with a phone in your hand when you should be attending to me and my girlfriend and our needs. Duh."

"Sorry, sir," said Vince. He put the potty on the floor and stood up.

"Pee," said Christian to Lizzie.

"Can I have some privacy?" she asked.

Christian shook his head. "I'm your boyfriend. This is a servant. The rich don't worry about that sort of thing. I could get him to hold my dick when I pee, like that guy does for Prince Charles, and it would not be pervy in any way at all. It's how we behave at this level of society. Go on. Pee."

She really was busting. She got out of bed. Her face was swelling up on one side. Ugly, ugly, ugly. Her hand was manacled to the bedpost but, by holding out that arm, she managed to reach the pot and squat on it. She bent her head and pretended she was on her own. At least she was wearing a nightie, even though there wasn't all that much of it.

Both men stood and watched her. When she was done, Christian threw her a box of tissues. While she wiped herself, he came over, flipped her hair to one side, and bent her head down, revealing the back of her neck. On it was a series of lines drawn in black ink — C1, C2, C3, C4, C5. Lizzie knew exactly what it was he had drawn on her, as he had explained that if he did a cut at C3, she wouldn't be doing much saying no then, would she?

Vince bent over to have a look. Christian evidently felt he was disapproving in some way. "It's my girlfriend," he said crossly. "I can do what I want with my own girlfriend, can't I?"

Vince frowned. "I thought we'd agreed that she wasn't your girl-friend, sir."

"She's in my bed. That makes her my girlfriend."

"Only if she wants to be there."

"Fuck's sake. Lizzie! Do you or do you not want to be in my bed?" he demanded.

Both men turned to watch her.

"Yes?" she said cautiously.

"See? Ah, this is boring. I'm going to play on my Xbox," Christian announced. He stalked to the door, shaking his head with exasperation.

Vince stood watching him curiously for a moment, before picking up the potty and going to empty it in the en suite. Lizzie waited until he came back out before she spoke to him in a whisper.

"What do I do?" she begged. "Please. Help me."

Vince said nothing. He put the pot back under the bed and picked up her coffee cup. He headed for the door.

"Please, Vince. I don't know what to do," she begged. She'd seen how Christian treated the big man; there was no way he could like it. He was her only chance.

Vince paused and looked back at her. "Just act like his girlfriend," he told her.

"Is that all? Will he let me go?" she wept.

Vince shook his head. "It always ends the same way. But at least you might not get hit so much getting there. He's making you look a right fucking mess."

He left the room. Behind him, Lizzie closed her eyes and tried to control her shaking. *Act like his girlfriend*, Vince had said. It was the only clue she'd had so far. Because — *Fuck this*, she thought. There had to be some way out of this. First off, though, she had to find some way of not being so hopelessly, pathetically, stupidly scared all the time.

After leaving Lizzie, Vince went down to the kitchen where he opened a cupboard stacked full of boxes of medicines. Christian was worrying him. Up to now it had been nice straightforward kidnap and violence. Now it was girlfriend. That was just plain weird. Something was going on, and he was willing to bet it involved the meds.

He took out a brand-new pack of pills, peeled the cellophane off, and peered inside. All present and correct: right labels, right brand, right everything. He sighed. Maybe it was just the normal ups and downs of being a raving psychotic that was making Christian behave like this.

Vince popped a selection of pills out of their foil wrappers, crushed them in a pestle and mortar, and stirred them thoroughly into a glass of warm milk, checking to see that everything had dissolved properly. Then he went through to the sitting room to give them to Christian, who was glued to his game.

Christian let out a wail of exasperation when he saw him coming, but put out a hand to take the milk. Turning to Vince, he drank it, swilling it around his mouth and gargling noisily before swallowing it down.

"Mmmm, yum yum yum. Yeah. I feel so much calmer already." He laughed, a high-pitched, insane giggle that could have been him being psycho, pretending to be psycho, or pretending to pretend to be psycho in order to hide the fact that he *was* mad, or any combination of the three.

Vince stared impassively at him. He'd definitely have to see Mr. Ballantine about a doctor's appointment, unless the nasty little fuck stopped being so weird pretty quick. They were due to go around to pick up more Death that Friday. He'd ask about it then.

And if you are pulling the wool over my eyes and I find out before then, Vince promised himself silently, *I will abso-fucking-lutely take the opportunity of bouncing you around this room until your balls go ring-ding-a-dong on your forehead. And that, sir, is a promise.*

"You're being a dick today," Christian pointed out. "Tell you what. I had a call from Dad. Apparently someone has reported my girlfriend as missing. Imagine that, Vince! I wonder what could have happened to her? I think you better go around and investigate the matter, don't you? Her parents probably. Pay them a visit. That bitch Julie, too. She gave the wrong address, didn't she?"

"She did." Vince was always happier out of the house. He nodded. "I'll get right on it."

"You do that," said Christian. "See you later, big boy. Lizzie and I will watch a bit of TV. Maybe have a bit of the old hokey cokey, eh?"

"Enjoy yourself, sir," said Vince. *Fat chance of that*, he thought. Christian had been impotent for years. He should have mentioned it to the girl, since it was bound to be her fault when he failed to get it up.

Whistling to himself, he went to get his car keys. A trip into town. Nice. Maybe after he'd paid a call to Julie's parents and found out where she lived, he'd have time to stop off with some mates and have a drink.

Adam awoke the next day feeling cool, light-headed, and very calm. He was in a large and beautiful room, with subdued but radiant light coming in through the windows. He didn't recognize any of it, but it was deeply comfortable. His head felt completely empty. He lay still for a while longer, enjoying the feeling but knowing somewhere inside that this pleasant state wasn't going to last very long at all.

Then he turned over and it all came flooding back. He sat up. He was saved. He was going to live! He just had to wait two days, but he had to have Lizzie here with him — he *had* to. He picked up his phone and rang her number. Again, she didn't answer. And now, finally, at last, he began to worry about her. If she'd really dumped him he couldn't blame her. But it wasn't like her to just vanish. She'd have said. Wouldn't she?

He left a message and started to ring around. Her parents picked up this time, but they had no idea where she was. That was odd. They sounded scared. Adam was getting scared, too. He tried Julie again. Still no answer.

It was almost lunchtime by the time anyone picked up. It was Julie. She didn't sound very pleased to hear from him.

"I'm looking for Lizzie . . ." he began.

"Oh, of course," sneered Julie. "You wanna know where your girlfriend is. Boy, that's good of you. You have SUCH a big heart. Well, let me see? Oh yeah, she got kidnapped by a bunch of gangsters and then her parents complained to the police so their house got torched. Yeah — that was it."

"What?"

"Hey! Lizzie is going to be soooo happy to hear about you trying to get in touch, in between getting beaten up and gang-raped! That is *just* so *nice* of you. It's so much gonna make her day, you wanker."

"What's going on? You're joking me. Stop it. Where is she?"

"And you want to know why, you pile of shit? Because she was trying to help you. She walked straight into their arms asking them if they made Death and if so, could she please have the antidote — which doesn't actually exist, by the way, I'm pleased to tell you — and they said, 'Sure! Yep. Just pop round and we'll chain you up and rape you forever.'"

"The police —" he said.

"The police *know*, you fuckwit, that's why her mum and dad got done over. It's also, incidentally, why *my* mum and dad got done over. They are in hiding. I am in hiding. It was probably the police who did it. You, Adam — just you stay away from this whole thing, right? Unless you want the same sort of shit raining down on your family's heads."

"Who's got her?"

"Oh, yeah, right, I was just going to tell you about that . . . Fuck off and die."

She slammed down the phone.

Adam's brain started babbling away to him at once, giving him every reason under the sun to explain it all away. He rang back but there was no answer. He rang again — no answer. He tried Lizzie's mum and asked her about it and . . . yes, yes, Lizzie was missing and she was very worried about her, and did he know anything about it? For God's sake, they just needed to know that she was safe . . .

"OK, Jean, we agreed not to talk to anyone else about this . . ." said a voice. Her dad. The phone went dead.

Adam got up, put his coat on, went to the door, and stopped. Because . . .

Because if he went to rescue Lizzie, he'd probably die, too — and he had a life to live! Janet had promised him the antidote. A whole life, his life, was going to be delivered to his door tomorrow. He'd only just got it back. He wanted it more than anything else there was. Why should he risk throwing it all away?

It felt like he was going mad. He ran around the room, groaning to himself. How could this have happened? Lizzie wanted him to live, wasn't that why she'd tried to get the antidote in the first place? And now he was supposed to go and get killed all over again for her sake? It was wrong, it was all wrong. It felt as if his head was about to explode.

Suddenly, he stopped running and clapped his hand to his back pocket. The list. It was still there — it had been there all the time. He pulled it out and read through it.

Kill someone who deserves to die. Well, that was going to be the bastard who had kidnapped Lizzie.

Leave my parents and Lizzie with enough money so they'll never have to work again. These people were gangsters; they were bound to have huge amounts of money. He'd take it off them.

Do something so humanity will remember me forever. No one would ever forget how he'd rescued Lizzie and thrown away his only chance for life in doing so. That was noble. Lizzie would never forget. That was what mattered.

There was still time. Three days. The list was back on!

There was so little time, so much to do. He was going to die, that much was certain. But this time, at least, there was something worth dying for. He ran out the door and off as fast as he could. The elevator was busy, so he took the stairs three at a time.

PART 3

REVOLUTION

CHAPTER 19

TO THE RESCUE, HERE I AM

JULIE WAS IN HER MANCHESTER FLAT FLINGING THE FINAL few items into her suitcase when the doorbell rang. Who the hell was that? Her parents had managed to keep the address from Vince despite all his efforts, as her father's broken fingers showed. He and her mother had hastily organized a trip to LA and didn't want Julie to go with them. In fact, they didn't sound as though they wanted to see her again for a very long time indeed.

And Lizzie. Poor Lizzie! God only knew what that freak Christian was doing to her right now. It broke her heart, but there was nothing she could about it. Lizzie was as good as dead. All Julie could do was try and save herself. It was good-bye Manchester and London, hello New York and LA. And in a hurry. If Vince was looking for her, Vince would find her. It might take him a few days, but he'd get there in the end. The sooner she was gone, the better.

Julie ran to the intercom by the door as quietly as she could and listened.

"Are you going to open it, or am I going to knock it down?" asked Vince.

Shit shit shit shit shit. What to do? Think! Escape. Where? The window? Too high. The corridor? Below, she could hear the front door burst open followed by the leisurely sound of someone ascending in the lift.

Panicking, she locked the door and ended up, ludicrously, hiding under the bed like a child. Vince knocked and waited about two seconds before breaking the lock and coming in. From where she lay on the floor, Julie could see his feet in the hallway as he took off his jacket and hung it up in a businesslike way by the door.

"Tell you what," he said. "How about, if you come out on your own, I don't hit you in the face?"

Julie knew it was as good as she was going to get. She closed her eyes and crawled out.

"What's it for?" she begged.

"Reporting Lizzie missing."

"It wasn't me."

"Who knows?" said Vince, and he got on with the beating.

Three minutes later, her ribs were broken all down one side, and her liver and kidneys might or might not have been ruptured. But Vince was as good as his word; her face was untouched. To look at her, no one would even know she'd been hit.

She coughed up a little blood and wiped it away.

"Is it over?"

Before he could answer, there was a tap at the flat door. Vince stepped into the bedroom, out of sight. The broken door opened and Adam put his face inside. Julie lurched to the door and pushed him back out before he got any farther.

"Where is she? Just tell me and I'll go," he begged.

"I have no idea what you're talking about," gasped Julie. Even talking was agony. She went to close the door, but Adam put his shoe in the way.

"Look," he said. "I've got three days to go. I'm going to die. I've got nothing to lose. At least let me try, OK?"

"Piss off, Adam," snarled Julie. But she didn't push him again. The fact was, he had a point. It wasn't a very good point, given what a tosser he was, but still . . . Julie was fond of her little cousin, and if she could throw her a lifeline, no matter how weak, she was tempted to do it. As she'd grabbed the door her wrist had bumped against Vince's jacket, hanging neatly on the hook behind it, and something in one of the pockets had rattled.

Keys.

"Piss off!" she snarled again, and banged the door on his foot, giving him a big, fat wink at the same time. Adam, the idiot, took his foot away. She glared at him and rolled her eyes down. "Put it back!" she mouthed. He did as he was told. Julie banged the door angrily on it, shifted to one side, and while her body hid the movement, lowered her hand quickly into the pocket of Vince's jacket and took out the keys. It was a long shot, but you never knew . . .

"Get your foot out of my door!" she screamed. She put her hand to his chest as if to shove him backward, and dropped the keys neatly down his shirt front. Then she winked at him again, kicked his foot out the way, and slammed the door behind him.

There was a brief silence, and then, to her relief, the sound of Adam's feet pattering away. Whether he'd work out what to do with the keys was another matter. She could only hope. But she'd done her best.

Vince stepped out.

"What did you give him?" he asked.

Julie shook her head. The guy was a monster. How had he seen that? She'd had her back to him the whole time.

"Nothing."

Vince took hold of her by the shoulder and slapped her violently on the side of her face. He waited a moment before letting her fall to the floor, then picked her up by her hair and punched her in the nose. It broke. Blood spattered everywhere.

"What did you give him?" he asked again.

"My face, you promised," she said.

"You won't be needing that anymore," he said. He slapped her again, even harder. She spun around like a top and collapsed. The side of her face began to bleed. Vince sat down on a chair in the hallway.

"You're in shock," he told her. "You need a minute to recover before you can speak." He rolled his cuff up slightly to look at his watch. "Minute's up," he said. "So what did you give him?"

Outside, a car started up. Vince stiffened.

"Your car keys," said Julie, and she turned to watch the look of shock on his face.

The whole conversation had been bewildering. Adam had some idea that Julie was trying to help him. But car keys? What good were they? Down on the street he pressed the OPEN button on the key ring and right next to him, a car bleeped and flashed its lights at him. And not just any car, either — a classic silver Porsche.

"Oh, man. Speed machine," breathed Adam. That was another point on his list — drive around Manchester in a supercar. And here it was! The gods were with him today. He opened the door, got into the driver's seat, put the key in, and started it up. It roared quietly, like a wave of whipped cream breaking on fine gravel. There was a pair of sunglasses on the dash. He picked them up and put them on. They were too big, but he still looked cool. That was the kind of sunglasses they were.

Experimentally, he ran through the gears with the clutch pushed down to the floor. He'd had a few driving lessons and a bit of practice sitting next to his mum in the family car. It was a long way from having a license, but Adam wasn't likely to let a detail like that get in the way of a chance like this.

He'd just got it into first gear when the doors to Julie's block of flats burst open and the huge figure of Vince came rushing toward him.

The guy who'd beaten him up at the party. This was *his car*?

With a scream, Adam slammed his foot on the accelerator. Crunching and snarling, the Porsche lurched off down the street, jumping forward in fits and starts like a crippled pig. The big man screamed at him and launched himself at the car, landing on the hood, his face gnashing at Adam through the windshield.

The Porsche stalled.

"Nooooo!" Adam started it up again and bounced along the road, swaying from side to side. Vince, lying full-length on the hood, swung a fist at the side window on the passenger side. The glass crazed and turned opaque. At the next blow, his huge fist came straight through and started groping at Adam's throat.

Adam leaned away from him and revved the engine; the car shot forward — and stalled again. Vince fell off. Adam got it going once more, forced the gears accidentally into third, and crept forward at a snail's pace over something in the road. Vince? The screaming indicated that, yes, it was. Finally, he got the gear/accelerator ratio right, and shot off like a bullet, the car roaring and swerving violently from side to side. He struck a glancing blow at a parking meter, a Jag, and a garbage truck in quick succession — and then he was away, shooting forward in a cloud of black smoke and the stink of burnt rubber.

Behind him, Vince got to his feet. Adam had driven over his forearm. Even worse, he had crashed his car. Vince loved his car almost as much as his body. He let out a scream of rage. He was going to kill that guy very, very slowly, and he was going to enjoy every minute of it.

*   *   *

Adam had no idea what to do next. He had Vince's car. Great! But what next? He pulled over and went through the glove compartment and rooted on the floor and in the backseat, looking for clues. He found several bars of chocolate, which he ate, but there was nothing in there to tell him what he was supposed to do next. He tried ringing Julie again.

No answer.

He sat there, chewing his nail. What was he supposed to do? She obviously thought this was going to help him. Did she think he already knew where Lizzie was being held? There had to be a clue in here somewhere.

He looked around the car again. CD player, GPS, map in the back. He flipped though the map. Nothing. He turned on the GPS. It was a posh one.

"Where do you want to go?" a voice asked him.

"Er . . . to Christian's," said Adam.

"Going to . . . Christian's," said the voice. It was a woman, with a Salford accent. In fact, it was Vince's mother's voice — a birthday treat for her boy.

"Turn the car round, son," she said.

Adam did.

"OK. Next right. Off you go. And don't go too bloody fast this time!" the voice snapped.

Ignoring her advice, Adam pushed down on the accelerator.

Lizzie's day had started off well enough with breakfast in bed — scrambled eggs and smoked salmon, coffee and croissants, made by Christian with his own fair hands. They had a pleasant chat, watching breakfast TV. The news was all about Death, the riots, and the growing demos in the cities, calling for the government to resign. They toasted the big sales in Death with their coffee cups, scoffed at the Zealots for their revolutionary fervor, and shook their heads at the weakness of the police in not getting tough on the streets and sorting it out.

Lizzie had been practicing her girlfriend act, and felt that she was getting the hang of it. Some of it was pretty traditional — stuff like sitting in bed filing your nails, talking about your next hairdo, or trying on new clothes in front of your boyfriend. In other ways, Christian was rather more modern. A good girlfriend, in his view, should be independent, smart, funny, and sexy. The trouble was that Christian considered himself the very epitome of all those things and, as a result, he expected her to be in agreement with him about whatever he wanted to do.

It was a hard act to get right. The worst part was when he tested her girlfriending skills by closing his eyes and waiting expectantly for her to announce his own desires to him. It was terrifying. At best, she was only putting the next beating off awhile. No matter how attentive she was, Christian was going to make a fool of himself sooner or later — and Lizzie was going to get the blame.

After TV came sex, which rapidly disintegrated into violence as she failed miserably to get him excited. Getting hit was another thing girlfriends did and she had learned to take her beatings in grim silence. The fact was, she was relieved. Getting beaten was horrible, but it was a good deal better than rape, in her view — especially rape that she had to pretend she wanted. At least this time she managed to protect her face reasonably well — she'd found out how important that was on day one, when she had been beaten once for making a stupid remark, and then again for being ugly.

After kicking her around the bed for a few minutes, Christian wandered over to the window to have a think, and decided, suddenly, that today was going to be a lazy day. Tomorrow he had to go pick up some more drugs from his father's factory. Today they'd lie in bed, watch his huge collection of back episodes of *EastEnders*, and just . . . hang out.

Great! enthused Lizzie. *EastEnders*. Amazing. Her favorite show.

Christian beamed at her. "Mine, too! How amazing is that?"

Isn't it, thought Lizzie. Yes — she was definitely getting the hang of this. If only she could survive long enough to find a way to escape . . .

They were several hours into the afternoon when Vince rang. Christian was not happy about it.

"This better be good. He knows not to ring when I'm watching 'Enders," he muttered. Lizzie tutted sympathetically. He put the phone to his ear and listened.

"She gave him your car keys?" Christian was most amused. "You're not very good with girls, are you, Vince? I'll have to give you a few tips. Me and Lizzie are here having a lovely day, aren't we, Lizzie?"

"Yeah — hush, not so loud, I'm trying to listen."

"Hear that?" exclaimed Christian triumphantly. "Someone likes watching 'Enders with me. See?"

He paused the recording and listened some more, then turned red.

"Might be coming round here? How do you work that out? The fucking GPS? You had my address on the GPS? What else do you have on it? The factory? The map reference where you put the bodies? You idiot. Jesus."

He sat there steaming for a bit while Vince rattled on. Lizzie sat next to him, filing her nails and listening in as hard as she could. Someone might be coming round? She had to hold on to anything that might help get her out of here . . .

"Smack her about. Make her suffer. Then get your arse round here. In fact, get round here now. We can worry about Julie later on, when you've sorted this mess out. Jesus."

He ended the call, stared at his phone, then chucked it savagely at the TV. "Right in the middle of 'Enders," he complained. "Calls himself a bodyguard." He got out of bed and got dressed. "Guess what?" he told her. "Your old boyfriend is coming to rescue you. How about that?"

"Adam?" A ray of hope shot through her. "That's dreadful!" she exclaimed. "He must be . . . not accepting that we split up."

"I hate those sorts," snarled Christian. "Some kind of weirdo stalker. We'll have to kill him."

But he was looking at her suspiciously. Had she done something wrong? A thought seemed to occur to him, and he turned to her with tragic eyes.

"Haven't you told him about us yet?" he said. "When, Lizzie? When? You make it so hard sometimes."

"I have told him! He's just . . . won't accept it. You know . . ."

Christian slapped her round the head, but just once. Then he stalked off to make his preparations for Adam's arrival.

Lizzie pretended to weep into the pillow, but actually she was jubilant. Adam! Bless him. In her heart she knew he stood no chance. In fact, he'd probably just make it worse. But he was trying. He was trying and . . . you never knew. She had to hope.

Christian came back into the room with a few items. A golf club. A pair of tights. Some handcuffs, ropes, chains, and a cigarette lighter.

"Sorry, sweetheart," he said. "It's for your own good."

He got her out of bed, chained her tightly to a chair with her forearms and hands behind her back, and gagged her by stuffing the tights into her mouth.

"This is the plan. If he turns up, we stay very, very quiet. Let him get in the house and creep around a bit. Then, when I give the signal, you scream as loudly as you can. He'll come running up, I'll take his feet out with the golf club, and then brain the little bastard. OK? Nod if you agree."

"Mnng," she replied. He looked at her. She nodded.

"But the thing is, Lizzie — don't deny it — I think you still have a little bit of feelings for that boy, don't you? Oh, I know you do," he insisted when she shook her head. "It's not that I don't trust you, but . . . well." He flicked the lighter and waved the flame in her face. "Just in case you need a little help."

He snickered, went to the window, and leaned out, whistling a tune — "Whistle While You Work." You had to hand it to him. No matter how mad he got, he always kept his sense of humor.

Lizzie pulled at her bonds. It was hopeless. Whatever the next half hour brought, she was going to be spending it sitting in the chair, watching. But there was one thing she could do to help; she was not, under any circumstances, going to scream. When Christian got the gag off for her to yell, when the lighter flame flicked, she was going to shout to warn Adam. On that she was determined.

Adam was sensible enough not to drive straight up to the house, but Christian recognized the engine as it approached along the main road. Some minutes later came the soft swish and thud as Adam slid up one of the big sash windows on the ground floor. Next, the creak on the boards as he tiptoed around. Finally the different creak on the stairs as he began on his way up.

Lizzie knew exactly what was going to happen and was prepared for it. Christian put the lighter under the soft flesh of her wrist in advance. As soon as he heard the creak of the stairs, he flicked the flame on with one hand, waited for the burn to get deep, then hoiked the tights out with the other.

"AaaaRRRRRGGHHHH!" she screamed. It was impossible. It hurt too much. Christian shoved the tights back in her mouth and went to hide behind the door with the golf club before she could get out another word.

"Mnng, mnng," she groaned, shaking the chair from side to side. But it was too late. Footsteps thundered up the stairs, the door crashed open, and Adam rushed heroically in. Christian, stooping low to take the swing from up behind his head, swung the club violently down onto his shins. Adam yelled in pain and fell like a rock. Christian stood over him and — whack! Right on top of the head with the club.

And that was that.

He came round to find himself tied hand and foot to a chair, his hands cuffed behind his back. His shins were ablaze with pain, there was blood trickling down into his eyes, and he had a splitting headache. Vince and Christian were standing by the window having an argument about something and Lizzie was sitting opposite on another chair. Her face was covered in bruises.

"I uv ooo," he said. He was gagged. She looked at him and shook her head. He tried again. "Ang . . . urv . . . oo."

"Shut the fuck up, will you?" said Vince. He came across and slapped him round the face with the back of his hand. "You stole my car," he said in tones of disbelief, and whacked him the other way, knocking him out once more.

When he came round again, the two men were still arguing, as far as he could tell, about what to do with Lizzie.

"Mr. Christian, she is NOT your girlfriend," Vince was saying. "A girlfriend does not have to be tied up and burned before she'll lure her ex-boyfriend upstairs so you can brain him. A girlfriend would do those things willingly. She'd be *happy* to do that for you. You wouldn't even need to ask — she'd offer. It would be her pleasure."

Christian was finding this difficult to follow, and he was grinning, grimacing, twisting about, unable to make his mind up. Finally, though, Vince managed to convince him.

"OK! You're right. The bitch has been leading me on," he said. "Fucking cow, can you believe it? I could have been killed," he said, and he bulged in rage at the thought. "Fine. Kill her. Kill them both. Let's not waste any more time. Shoot them both, the little fucks, right now."

But Vince held up a hand. "Sir, that's just more bodies," he pointed out. "I'm always driving to and fro with bodies in the trunk. If I can suggest something else — how about a pill, sir? The boy's already taken it. If we give the girl one now, we can drive them both out to the factory tomorrow, lock them up in a box . . . and that's that. No one's going to go digging about round there, Mr. Ballantine sees to that. In a week they'll both be dead, and we can dump the bodies wherever we want. Everyone will think they're just one more pair of Deathers."

Christian liked it. "Yeah, yeah, good idea. Let 'em die in a box, see how much fun they have then. But not the same box. We don't want them to comfort each other, Vince."

"Certainly not, sir," Vince agreed.

"They can suffer on their own."

"I'll fetch the doings, shall I?" Vince offered.

"Yeah." Christian grinned. "Good. The boyfriend can watch. Then I get to fuck her for the rest of the day — he can watch that, too. Cool, eh?" he said.

"Very cool, sir," said Vince.

They did it with a funnel and water. Christian turned Adam around so he had to watch. He banged his chair and begged through his gag, but there were no offers he could make, no bargains to be struck. Vince tipped Lizzie's head back as far it would go and pushed the funnel down into her throat until she retched. Christian dropped a pill in, then swilled it down with a glass of water. They stood there, holding her mouth shut tight and stroking her throat while she gurgled, turned red, and swallowed.

"All your fault," Christian said.

Adam closed his eyes and wept. He'd failed. Lizzie was as dead as he was.

"Orry," he said. "Orree." She didn't answer. Christian tied her gag back on, and Lizzie bent her head and wouldn't look at him. What could she say? It was, as Christian said, all his fault.

While Christian was gloating over Adam and slapping him around a bit, Vince went to pick up his jacket from the bed, where he had put it out of the way as he worked on Lizzie. As he did so, he spotted the corner of a familiar box half sticking out from under the bed.

He bent to pick it up. It was Christian's meds. But what was it doing here? He kept the meds under lock and key.

Vince smelled a rat. He tore off the cellophane and opened it up.

The box was full of styrofoam. It was a mock-up. A very good mock-up. But what would Christian be doing with a mock-up of his meds . . . ?

A light went on in Vince's head. Christian's increasingly bizarre behavior . . . false boxes of meds . . . The little git had been having fakes made up and swapping them . . .

"You sneaky little shit!"

Christian turned around from what he was doing, took one look, and knew he was caught. Vince shook the box at him.

"How long have I been feeding you fakes? What was in those pills — sugar? It's straight to the funny farm for you, you little dick."

"You're talking complete nonsense," said Christian smoothly, and without another word, turned and dashed for the door. Vince let out a bellow and shot after him, catching him by the collar before he got out. To his delight, Christian swung one at him.

Vince had put some thought into how to do this. He couldn't mark the little toad too much, or Mr. Ballantine would be onto him. He spun him around and delivered a series of knuckle punches to the back of the neck. Revenge, so sweet! One, two, three, four. Christian collapsed to the floor without a sound. Vince picked him up, punched him in the solar plexus — always a good number, because it hurt like hell, made you panic about your breath, and left very few marks. Then, he banged his head against the wall.

Christian flopped to the floor like a doll. Perfect.

Vince took out his phone and dialed Mr. Ballantine. It was time for a much-needed holiday. Where to? New York, Paris, the Bahamas? He smiled happily — but he had made a serious mistake. He noticed that both Lizzie and Adam were staring at a point behind him, and was just realizing what that meant when Christian, who had never lost consciousness, even for a moment, leaped on him.

Vince was a good foot taller than him, and Christian had to more or less run up him like a monkey, getting footholds on his calves, then his bum, until he was able to bury his hands firmly into his hair and pull himself right up onto the big man's shoulders. Wrapping his legs firmly around the big man's neck, he pushed Vince's head forward and down with one hand and, with the other, groped at his belt for that deadly, short-bladed little knife.

Vince knew exactly what that meant. He let out a gargling bellow of rage and fear, and began dancing about the room and shaking himself like a bear, frantically snatching and groping at the deadly imp on his back. But Christian hung on tight and he couldn't shift him. Desperately, he ran backward at the wall, crashing into it as hard as he could and knocking every ounce of breath out of his tormentor; but Christian had all the strength and passion of insanity and he clung on, snarling in his ear as they cavorted around the room: "I'm gonna quad ya, I'm gonna quad ya. C4! C4! Yeehaw!"

Adam and Lizzie, tied firmly to their chairs, were only able to watch in amazement. Adam had no idea what was going on — all he knew was that neither Vince nor Christian was watching him. It was late, it was terribly late, but rescue was still possible. He had to get Lizzie out of the grip of this psychotic monster and back to the hotel in time for the antidote turning up. This was his chance — but what could he do, tied hand and foot to a chair?

Adam began to rock himself backward and forward. He had no idea what this was going to achieve, but he did it anyway, and eventually he rocked so hard that the chair tipped forward. He just managed to catch himself before he went right over and ended up balanced improbably on tiptoes, still sitting in the chair, bent over almost double. He had just a little play on his legs and, with great difficulty, was able to hobble across the floor like an insect toward the door. He got himself out of the room as far as the top of the stairs before he paused to look behind him. Vince was busy trying to bash Christian to pieces against the top of the chest of drawers. Lizzie, sitting still in her chair, was gazing at him with big eyes over the top of her gag.

Adam shrugged. What had he got to lose? Twisting as he fell, he flung himself down the marble stairway and smashed, bounced, and bumped all the way down.

Behind him, Lizzie stared in shock. What on earth was he doing, trying to kill himself all over again? And what did it matter, anyway? She was going to die. She listened as he crashed down like a stack of sticks; then there was nothing.

Vince ran past her, howling. Christian had finally got that nasty little knife out and was waving it in the air, screaming in triumph. Vince swung around, ready to back him into the chest of drawers again, which had a hard edge just at thigh level, when Christian suddenly brought the knife down with a loud thud.

The effect was instant.

The big man stopped in his tracks and stood swaying on his feet, expressions of surprise and horror equally lit on his face. Christian jumped down, like a boy dismounting a horse, just as Vince began to topple. He came down like a tree right at Lizzie's feet, his arms limp at his sides, striking the carpet chin first. He opened his mouth to let out a final bellow of rage and despair, but nothing came. His eyes flicked up to meet hers. Then he closed them and let out the tiniest, weakest, most helpless little sigh of defeat.

Christian bent down to examine the knife in the back of his neck, and then down to the big man's face. He put his hand close to Vince's mouth.

"Breathing," he whispered in ecstasy. "Still breathing."

Then he went crazy.

"C4 — C fucking 4! I done it, you bastard. See you ring Daddy now. C4! C4! C4!" And screaming with triumph, he did a dance of victory around the prostrate body, while Lizzie, in her chair, wept and struggled and did her best not to scream. She was certain she was going to get it next.

It took Christian about five minutes to realize that Adam had gone. For some reason, it flung him into a complete panic.

"Where's he gone? Jesus. Where he is?" he wailed. He ran around the room, looking out the window, under the bed, in the en suite. "Where is he?" he begged Lizzie.

Lizzie shook her head, unable to speak through her gag. Christian stared at her for a moment, then ran out of the room and down the stairs. Below, the front door banged.

Lizzie couldn't stop crying. What next? She looked over at Vince, lying flat on his front, with the knife handle sticking out from the back of his neck. His eyes swiveled around to met hers and they locked eyes briefly, each as helpless as the other. Neither of them could move a muscle.

Then — a miracle. The door opened and Adam came hobbling in. Flinging himself down the stairs had bruised him badly, but it had smashed up the chair enough for him to tread his way out of it and make off. He was still gagged, his hands were cuffed behind his back, and his feet hobbled by the short length of rope that had tied them to the chair — but he was free. He had managed to get back upstairs, hide, and wait till Christian had gone out, and now here he was, hobbling to the rescue.

He ran up to Lizzie and stood in front of her, making weird noises through the gag. Lizzie did the same thing — the pair of them, gurning and grunting at each other. Adam gave up. He lay on his back, lifted his legs up, and kicked her violently in the stomach. Lizzie doubled over with a groan. Had Adam gone crazy, too? He jumped up, turned around, flicked her gag up, and started trying to shove his fingers down her throat.

"Adam," she groaned, "what are you doing?"

"Ergaggnng — dech," he said. And despite everything, she knew what he meant. He was trying to make her throw up to get rid of the drug.

Yes! She nodded agreement and stuck her head out, while Adam groped down her throat with his fingers. She retched and gagged — but couldn't be sick.

She'd had enough. "Adam," she said. "Adam."

"Hmm. Ngg, ngg . . ." he groaned.

She shook her head. "You came back for me."

"Nggg. Ganng. A angoo."

"Yeah, I know you love me. But, Adam, you have to go, right now."

"Nnng? Gno . . . I . . ."

"Yes, you do," she told him. "Christian will come back, anytime now. Get out while you can. I'm stuck."

"Ngg," said Adam. He shook his head. He was rescuing her! He wasn't going to give up. He looked desperately around for some way of getting her out of the handcuffs and rope. No key, no hands, no pliers, nothing. His gag was wrapped around his head, going tightly inside his mouth, so that although his tongue was forced down, his teeth were free. In his desperation, he bent down and started chewing at the rope around Lizzie's hands.

Lizzie sat there and watched the back of his head. Her face hurt, her body hurt. She'd been force-fed Death and she was going to die — and here was Adam trying to chew her free.

She started to laugh.

Adam looked sideways up at her. He wasn't finding this as funny as she was. He went back to his chewing. Lizzie shook her head. "Adam," she said again.

He looked up and honked piteously.

"You have to go."

"Mnnh! Urrg, mmm," he said, nodding again desperately around the room.

"Just — get real for once, will you? Christian will be back in a minute. If he catches you here he'll kill us both. You're no use to me dead. Go! Rescue me later."

Downstairs a door slammed.

"Go!" she hissed. Suddenly she was furious as well as scared. *Just once, Adam — behave.*

"Arie. I uf goo," said Adam, and he turned and bounded across the room like a gigantic rabbit toward the window. He peered out. It was a long way down, and the window was locked.

Feet on the stairs. There was no other choice.

He took a few steps back and made a run at the window at the very moment that the door burst open behind him. He crashed through the glass and went down in a sparkling display of shards, like a gagged angel glittering in the late-afternoon sunshine. Down, down, down . . .

He hit the ground feetfirst in a rosebush and tipped over in a tangle of thorns. He rolled away deeper into the shrubs as a volley of gunshots came from the window above. It should have been an easy shot — but Adam had an advantage. The sun was shining brightly on that side of the building, and Christian was blinded by the light. Adam crawled to his feet — hobbled, hands behind his back — and made a mad dash for the car.

Up at the window, Christian cursed. He turned to look at Lizzie, gun in the air. Havering, he waved it in her face.

"What are you doing, you idiot?" she yelled. "He's getting away!" It was her only chance. In his mind, she was either on his side or against him.

It worked. He cursed and ran to the door and down the stairs. "The fuck! The fuck!" he screamed. The front door banged again and she heard him running across the gravel in pursuit of Adam. Lizzie held her breath to listen, her heart thudding like a machine in her chest. *Please God let Adam get away! Please God get me out of this. Please please please.* Tied hand and foot to the chair, she was unable to do a thing. She remembered what Adam had done, tipping the chair and walking away. She tried it herself — and fell sideways to the ground, her face just a foot or so from Vince's. He lay there unmoving, eyes shut. She assumed he must be dead.

The sounds of gunfire receded. The room, which had been so full of shouting and conflict a moment before, became very quiet. There was only her own ragged, half-sobbing breath. Another shot in the distance. A bird began to sing in the trees outside.

Miraculously, she was still alive, but on Death. That didn't sound all that optimistic, but you know what? It did mean one thing: She had nothing to lose.

If I'm going down, I'm going to take you with me, you bastard, she thought.

She started to sob again and forced herself to stop. She had to be strong. She had to act the girlfriend and stay alive long enough to get her chance to kill Christian.

Opposite her, quite suddenly, Vince opened his eyes. She screamed slightly — it was yet another shock — then caught her breath.

"Vince. You . . . OK?" she asked.

His eyes rolled sarcastically. He tried to speak but his voice was so weak, she could hardly hear it. With difficulty, she jerked her chair closer.

"What?"

"Kill me," he was saying in a tiny little voice. He had hardly any breath — just about enough, she guessed, to keep himself alive.

"Kill you? How?" she demanded. For a moment longer they stayed staring at each other.

"What do I do, Vince? What do I do?" she begged. "Tell me what to do. Maybe I can get him back for you."

Vince snorted derisively. Fat chance.

Lizzie bared her teeth. There had to be something!

". . . phone . . ." said Vince.

"What?"

"My phone." He was looking sideways. His phone lay in the middle of the floor where he'd dropped it when Christian attacked him. It was an iPhone, same as hers. Yes! Jerking the chair with her body, Lizzie made it across the floor, turned herself around, and took it in her hands.

Communication. Somehow, someone, somewhere. Adam — if he was still alive. Her parents. She jerked her way again across the floor to the bed, tucked the phone under it, and got back into her place just as the door banged below. Christian came slowly up the stairs and into the room, the gun hanging in his hand. He stood by her head and looked down.

He was a complete mess. His teeth were bloody and crooked in his mouth. His nose had moved sideways, his eyes almost disappeared in the bruises on his face. Vince had done a real job on him. Only his psychosis was keeping him on his feet. He looked so, so crazy.

"Your boyfriend is dead," he said.

Lizzie had no idea if he was telling the truth or not. All things being equal, he probably was. But she had to say something quick, or she was going to be next.

"Good," she said. "That bastard has had it coming for ages."

She was amazed at her own survival instincts. Christian didn't reply. He just turned to look at Vince and cocked his head to one side.

"It took you bloody long enough," she said, driving on, trying to touch a chord in his madness. "What kind of way is this to treat your girlfriend, leaving me here with this freak?"

Christian looked at her. He licked his lips.

"Girlfriend," said Lizzie.

"Girlfriend," he said.

"Yes, girlfriend. What else am I doing in your bedroom? I can't even do my makeup or file my nails like this. How about undoing me so I can make myself pretty for you?" She began to cry with fear. All she could do was hope that it looked like the sort of thing a girlfriend would do.

"Girlfriend," said Christian again. Suddenly he jerked his arm in the air. "Yeah!" he said. "Right on!"

"Great," said Lizzie. "How about a cup of tea, then? And maybe a sandwich. I'm famished."

On the floor, Vince smiled to himself. *Clever girl*, he thought. Christian nodded. He cocked the gun, checked the ammo, lifted it, and shot Vince through the back of the head.

"We don't have time," he said. "We need to get moving. Things to do, you know." And he bent down to untie her ropes.

CHAPTER 20

NEW ORDERS

JESS WAS LYING IN HIS BOX IN THE CONTAINER TERMINAL, hands behind his head, staring at the ceiling. Anna, after her taste of what was happening on the streets, had refused to go back and had tried to get him to stay with her, but he'd insisted on seeing the job with Death through to the end.

"Such a soldier," she'd said. It was true but she had no idea how it broke him up inside to be like that.

Predictably, Ballantine had responded to him coming back by beating the shit out of him and then locking him up. At least before he'd been allowed to wander about with a guard. Now, he only got out each day for work. The rest of the time he was locked up in his box. Worse, they'd taken away his TV, his radio, and his phone. Outside, the government could have fallen, Parliament could have closed, the world might be upside down wriggling its toes in the stars, and Jess wouldn't know a thing about it.

He had only one link to the outside world — his Zealot phone, the same make and model as his personal one. He held it tightly in his hand now, ready to stuff it quickly out of sight if anyone came in on him. He was dying to make a call, to Command, to Anna, maybe, and find out what on earth was going on outside, but he didn't dare. Ballantine's men had found and taken his only charger, and the battery was almost dead. He was expecting a call — had been for two days now. Surely, surely, Command was going to issue him with new orders? As things stood, he was still supposed to make his way out to the big rally tomorrow, and die for the cause. Public immolation. Self-burning. But they weren't going to waste his life in protest now. Surely — and he prayed for the chance — they'd want him to fight.

Most days he could hear the sounds coming over from the city. Albert Square was less than a couple of miles away and with the wind in the right direction, you could hear the voices of tens of thousands of people in unison, singing and chanting. It was the voice of the people — but how many? One hundred thousand, two hundred thousand? A million? He had no way of knowing.

Jess rolled over onto his front. It was driving him mad! Everything he'd worked for was coming real — and he was stuck in a box. Tomorrow was Friday, a week to the day after Jimmy Earle's death. There was to be a mass demo, a general strike. Maybe more. Who knew how things had changed since he'd been locked up in here? Most important of all, they would be making the big announcement he had been working toward all this time. He had to be there . . . but no way was Ballantine going to let him out. With Anna gone, he was the only one who knew how to make Death. They still needed him.

Jess lifted the phone in the air and weighed it in his hand, a little lump of hope. And at that moment — finally, after two days of waiting — it rang.

"Jess? You there?"

"Anna!"

"You OK?"

"Yeah. You? I can't talk long, the phone's nearly out and they've taken the charger. What's going on out there?"

"Oh, man, Jess, you should have stayed with me. It's fabulous! I don't think the world's ever going to be the same again."

Jess groaned. He was missing it all!

"Can you get away?" she asked.

"No! They've locked me up. Taken my radio and TV. Tell me — what's happening? Tell me quick," he begged, torn between wanting to know and wanting to save his phone for the orders he hoped were coming.

"Everything! The general strike is on. The police, the army, they're all coming over. People are marching on Westminster and no one is lifting a finger to stop them. Just a few army brigades holding out . . ."

It was true, then. "It's happening?" he asked. "It really is happening?"

"It really is. And tomorrow — the big announcement. It's planned for one o'clock. You have to get out, Jess!"

"I'm trying." In his excitement and frustration, Jess got to his feet and paced round the metal box that was his prison. He had to be there! But how?

"Look, I have to go. If they ring with new orders, I need the phone . . ."

"I have your orders," said Anna.

Jess stopped in his tracks. "What are they?"

"Get your arse out of there!" she said, and she laughed. "Just — get out here."

"Really? They want me out?"

"Of course they want you out! What do you think?"

"But I volunteered for the death squad."

"They've taken you off it."

Jess felt his heart leap inside him. Life. Hope! It nearly knocked him down. He hadn't dreamed he wanted to live so much.

"Why?"

"Why do you think? Don't you know what you've done? Without you, none of this would have happened. They're not going to let you go if they can help it. They want you alive."

Jess listened breathlessly. He'd thought he was going to die. He was ready to die. He'd believed he wanted to die — and now he'd been given life.

Suddenly he had a thought . . . "What about Adam? Did you find him?"

"Oh, yeah. He's holed up in a hotel room." Anna snorted in amusement. "That should keep him out of trouble. He thinks I'm coming round tomorrow with the antidote." She laughed out loud.

Jess felt his heart, which had been frozen for so long, begin to move. Life. His family, waiting for him. He could go back to them. It was unbelievable.

"And you?" he asked. "You're off the squad as well?"

"Not me," she said.

Jess stalled. "Why not?"

He could feel her shrug. "I must be a bit more dispensable."

"What do they want you to do?"

"I'm a bomb, Jess." She laughed. "A blonde bombshell, that's me."

Suicide bomber. A lot better than burning. But . . . a long, long way worse than life.

"When?"

"Tomorrow."

"What's your target?"

"Classified." She laughed again wryly. "Sorry, Jess."

His phone began to beep. It was dying.

"I'm going," he said. "Will I see you again? Let me see you again."

"I don't think so, Jess. Just get out of there. They can't send anyone to help you, OK? You're on your own. Get out of there any way you can. And Jess. Guess what. I just want to say —"

And the phone went dead.

"Shit!" Jess looked at the stupid gadget in his hand — dead to the world. What had she been about to say?

Whatever. He was going to war. He was going to fight for the revolution. All he had to do now was get out. And that was easier said than done.

CHAPTER 21

DON'T CRY — KILL

AFTER SHOOTING VINCE, CHRISTIAN WANTED TO GET AWAY as fast as he could. He untied Lizzie from the bed and hurried her to the door, but she managed to stall him by pointing out she was still in her nightie.

"It doesn't matter," he yelled.

"It does!" she yelled back. She nodded down at her body. "For your eyes only."

Grumbling but flattered, Christian allowed her to pick up her clothes and get dressed. In doing so, she was able to recover Vince's phone from under the bed.

Done! She was feeling good — strong, quick, clever. It was only while he was hurrying her downstairs to the car that she realized what was happening; she was feeling the first effects of Death. It was a feeling that was unlikely to last, but if it helped her get away from Christian, it was more than welcome.

Christian drove them into Manchester, where he kept a town flat on Deansgate for business purposes. The fight with Vince seemed to have unhinged him totally. Maybe he no longer had to pretend, maybe the beatings his head had taken against the wall had done some damage, but his mood was swinging dangerously between the sentimental and the violent. At the flat, they spent most of the rest of the evening watching a film on TV, with Lizzie manacled to the sofa. Her coat with the phone in it was in the bedroom, hanging up on the door. She had no chance to get anywhere near it.

As the film progressed, Christian began muttering to himself, at first quietly, then louder and louder.

"Tomorrow we go to the factory," he announced to no one in particular.

"Where's that?" asked Lizzie lightly.

Christian jumped and looked at her suspiciously. He'd obviously forgotten she was even there.

"Don't answer her," he said. "She's fishing. No, she's not! She just wants to know. You trust her?" he asked incredulously. "You trust her? Do I look stupid?" he shouted suddenly.

"I'm your girlfriend, Christian," she told him in a cross voice, doing her best not to show how terrified she was. "Of course you trust me!"

"Do I?" Christian flailed around in a panic. "You? But who else are you?" he demanded.

"Just me," she said. "Girlfriend. Girlfriend. Remember? Lizzie. Girlfriend. When are we going to get some tea, Christian?" she asked, frowning. Getting him to do things for her seemed to help keep him away from dangerous thoughts.

Christian chewed at his knuckle and came to a conclusion. "She's all I have," he explained to himself. He kissed her and went to the kitchen to see what there was to eat. He came back with a single bowl of tomato soup, all he had. He wouldn't go out to get any more because he was convinced that his life was in danger. Lizzie had no idea why. Probably it was pure paranoia, but maybe, just maybe, he was scared of Adam. She hadn't seen a body. It could be that he was still alive.

She could hope, anyway.

They shared the soup, but it was nowhere near enough and in an hour or so, Christian started to get angry about how hungry he was. Lizzie knew better than to offer to go out for him, and made a big fuss about how important it was that they stay put and hide from their enemies. That helped calm him down and convince him they were in it together. She helped him do a search of the cupboards, but all she could find was a single bag of sugar. She spent the evening making gallons of hot, sweet tea for them both, which they drank together, huddled up in bed, like children hiding from the ghosts. The hours and minutes passed slowly by. He beat her up twice: once at midnight, and again two hours later. Toward first light, he fell in love with her all over again and went to sleep in her arms, weeping sentimental tears.

Lizzie watched over him. He had chained her to the bed and to himself. There were no weapons nearby. She wondered if she could strangle him, but thought probably not. It was tempting, but now was not the time. So she waited, watching over him, until at last she fell asleep as well.

After he had crashed through the window in a hail of shattered glass, and pulled himself out of the rose bush, Adam dashed off with tiny steps into the woods, still hobbled and with his hands cuffed behind his back. He had hardly gone more than fifty feet or so when Christian burst out of the front door and began firing wildly through the trees in his direction.

He ran on as fast as he could, tripping and falling over every few steps, until it occurred to him that he didn't actually have to have his hands tied behind his back — he could step over them so they were in front and then untie his legs. Why hadn't he thought of this before? As he paused to do it, he could hear Christian tearing his way through the tangle of woodland, bawling in rage, only forty or fifty feet away. But he was heading the wrong way and obviously wasn't sure where Adam was. He bent, rapidly untied the rope around his legs, and fled. Now Christian spotted him and fired off more rounds, but his luck held. It was another two hundred yards to Vince's Porsche and Adam covered them at full tilt, with Christian, full of fury but out of his mind, tripping and cursing, screaming at him to stop, and letting shots off at every shadow he saw.

Adam got to the car and there was a dreadful moment when he thought he'd lost the keys. He fished desperately around in all his pockets before he found them. He reversed out, burning rubber and grinding the clutch as Christian came out of the trees toward him. He stalled on the road; a truck going past blared its horn and swerved to miss him. But then he got going again — and pulled away, nought to sixty in seconds. A couple of shots thumped into the trunk — he could feel the impact of them right through the car — before he got out of range, driving fast to safety.

But it wasn't over. It couldn't ever be over with Lizzie still in captivity. Christian would be straight back there. Maybe he'd shoot her on the spot, but Adam was hoping that now that she'd swallowed Death as well, he'd follow Vince's plan and let her live out her week. Either way he had to get back. The longer he left it, the worse things could get for her.

He pulled over into a rest stop and waited a few minutes to give the impression he was gone, then turned around and went back. He parked the car well away from the drive and once again made his way up to the house, but he was already too late; the birds had flown. Only Vince remained, dead on the floor with a bullet wound in his head.

Adam had escaped. Lizzie was as good as dead.

That was it, then. He'd lost her and he had no idea how to find her. She'd been fed Death — and what on earth would her last few days be like, with Christian as her jailer? It didn't bear thinking about.

He wandered around the house, trying to find some kind of clue as to where they'd gone, but found nothing. Eventually he went back to the car and sat at the wheel, still trying to work it out.

Christian had been right about one thing: It was all his fault.

Where was he? Day 4; Day 5 tomorrow. Two days to go. He'd lost his life, ruined his parents' lives, and now he'd destroyed Lizzie's as well. Sitting at the wheel, Adam began to cry, quietly at first, then more and more until he was sobbing out loud. It was getting dark, but he remained where he was, with nowhere better to go, nothing better to do, until, blessedly, he fell asleep at the wheel.

The following morning, Friday, Lizzie's luck was still holding: Christian woke up feeling refreshed. He looked almost normal. They kissed, made small talk, watched TV. He even went out to buy stuff for breakfast.

As soon as he was out the door, Lizzie was out of bed. The phone . . . just a few feet away, in her jacket hanging on the door. The bed was a huge oak thing that weighed a ton, and she had to drag it inch by inch behind her to get there. She typed out her text in a panic — the shop was only a few steps away and Christian could be back at any moment. She got as far as **at factory** before the front door went. Back already! She had time to type out Adam's number and send, before desperately dragging herself and the bed back, wincing at the noise of the legs on the boards, certain she was going to get caught. She chucked the phone under the bed and just about managed to get everything back as it was before he came in bearing croissants and jam. She smiled sweetly. Done! It wasn't much of a text, but it was a start. At least something had gone out.

They ate together in bed with coffee. When it was done, Christian wiped his mouth and said thoughtfully, "You know what, Lizzie? I think we need to get away. Just you and me. Big holiday. Thailand, maybe. All points east. Japan. We've always wanted to go to Japan. What do you say?"

"It sounds wonderful! When do we go?" she gushed. Christian beamed at her, and her heart quailed inside her. She had her one week — the most life could offer her now. How horrible it would be if she had to spend the whole time pretending to be in love with Christian. She wanted to see her parents, she wanted to see Adam — she had so much she wanted to do in those few, miserable days. For the first time, she began to wonder if it was worth it, this dreadful struggle to stay alive. She was going to die anyway, probably in a horrible way. Perhaps it would be better to get it over with at once. Anything would be better than this.

But not yet. She wasn't ready for that. In a few days maybe . . .

The holiday idea seemed to be a runner. Christian booked some flights to Tokyo. They could get a hotel when they arrived. It was all set — and then things began to deteriorate. He finished the calls, made them both some tea, which they drank in bed; but then he began to get agitated. The muttering started up. Lizzie tried to distract him by talking about Tokyo, but it was no use.

"You idiot!" he suddenly bellowed. "You've forgotten the business." He swung around suddenly and glared directly at her. Lizzie cringed down — it was a bad move but she couldn't help it.

"Don't call me an idiot!" he screamed. But he had turned away and was talking to someone in his head. "Yeah, but you are, aren't you? You have business. What's Daddy going to say . . . what's he going to think . . . what's he going to do?"

Gibbering in fear, Christian turned his horrified eyes to Lizzie, as if begging her for an answer. At any moment it could turn to rage. She tried to smile.

"Er . . . we ought to get the business side of things sorted out before we leave, though, don't you think?"

Christian looked at her suspiciously. "What do you know about my business?" he demanded.

"Nothing. But you always have some. Isn't there something you need to do? Weren't we supposed to be . . . going to the factory today?" she asked, digging into her memory as she spoke.

His eyes swiveled anxiously. "Factory . . . yeah. That's it. Right. The factory. Good girl. Good girl, Lizzie!"

He ran to kiss her, and then dashed off to sort things out. Lizzie had time to sob twice before he was back, ordering her to get dressed. They were going right now. This time, to her disgust, he stood over her, watching her like a hawk, and she had no time to pick up the phone.

Fifteen minutes later, after tying her to the passenger seat of his car with several yards of rope, he was driving her east. The phone was still lying under the bed. She just had to hope that Adam was still alive and that, if he was, he would manage on his own. It wasn't a thought that filled her with confidence, but there was one thing, to her surprise, she felt confident about. If he was alive, he would try.

She had no doubt about that. Adam was an idiot in many ways, but this much was true: He was her idiot, and he would never give her up in a million years. She didn't think there was anyone else in the world she could say that about. And she wasn't sure she knew anyone else who had that, either.

What a thing, she thought. *And what a way to discover it.* It was just a shame that they had only days left to live. And with that thought, suddenly, she was fighting back tears.

There wasn't much time to mourn, though. Christian, who was obviously very nervous about the trip, started to explain to her that he wanted her along for moral support.

"What sort of moral support?" she asked.

He rambled on, half to her, half to himself, but from what she could gather, he needed her to reassure his dad that he was, in fact, taking his meds; and that Vince was, in fact, not with them because he had another important job to do rather than having been murdered; and that he, Christian, was, in fact, as sane as the next man.

"No problem," said Lizzie brightly. She settled herself into the seat and looked out the window. Adam was going to die, if he wasn't already dead, and she was going to die, too; she knew that. But with a little bit of luck, just a tiny wee bit of luck, she might manage to take some of the bastards who'd been making this horrible drug with her. Christian was there, at the top of the list, and his dad was right below him.

Why not? she thought. *This one is for you, Ads. Leave the world a better place, like it said on the list. Go for it!*

Christian looked sideways at her, his eyes rolling like marbles. Lizzie smiled back. *Don't cry*, she thought. *Don't cry — kill.* Even if she took just one of them with her, it would be worth it.

She was expecting a long ride, but very quickly they were driving through a strange wasteland of shipping containers. Lizzie was amazed. She had no idea that such a place existed so close to Manchester city center. There were hundreds of containers, maybe thousands, some stacked on top of each other, all laid out in endless rows.

The car pulled up in the middle of nowhere and Christian got out. He stood there a moment, flexing his shoulders and looking around him. She thought, *Is this it? Has he taken me here to kill me?* But then he bent into the car and kissed her on the cheek.

"Won't be long, love," he said.

"Aren't you taking me to meet your dad?" she asked.

"No." Christian was most amused. "No way."

"But you said —"

"Don't be ridiculous, Lizzie," he said. He shook his head irritably, and walked off. Lizzie watched him disappear behind a container. Suddenly she was on her own. She tugged at her bonds, but he'd tied her good and tight. Her hands were free, but there was no way she could reach around to the knots that had been tied behind the seat. She was stuck — and if she didn't take her chance now, she might never get another go.

There was only one thing she could do. She leaned across to the driver's seat and pressed on the horn. *Please God let there really be someone there.* The horn blared out into the silence of the container terminal. And it worked. All around her, doors opened in the containers. The whole place was full of people hiding in them. They ran toward her. One of them was Christian.

CHAPTER 22
THE DEATH FACTORY

ADAM WOKE UP IN EXACTLY THE SAME POSITION HE'D fallen asleep in — sitting in the car with his head resting on the steering wheel. He felt dreadful — headache, nausea, aches, the lot. What had happened to that beautiful glad morning of Death? Why was he so shot? It made no sense.

He clicked the key in the ignition and checked the time. It was already eleven A.M. So late! He'd slept for hours.

And . . . Lizzie. He'd lost Lizzie.

He couldn't see any way out of it. It was Day 5 — Friday — the day Janet had said he should meet her and collect the antidote. Was that what he had to do — save his own skin? He might as well, if he couldn't do anything for Lizzie.

He felt so bad about it — but it would pass, wouldn't it? He had it all back. His parents, his life, work — all waiting for him. He could go and wait for the antidote, and just get on with it. He'd have to live with what had happened to Lizzie, but he'd forget. He'd learn not to let it ruin his life. That's what happens. We live, we move on. We persevere.

Adam took out his phone and turned it on. As he expected, there were maybe fifty messages from his parents. Looked like they were going to be in luck after all. Loads from his friends, too, who had obviously been brought in on the act by his mum and dad. *Where are you, we miss you, we just need to know you're OK.* He scanned through them.

Then, an unknown number. He opened it up. The message had two words: **at factory**.

Adam stared at it. Where had he heard that word before? Vince, was it?

He turned on the GPS and said the word "factory." And up it came. Adam sat there, staring at it. The text *had* to be from Lizzie. And now he had a choice. He could go back home to life — to all the things, good and bad, he'd thought he'd lost forever. Or he could try to help Lizzie — and probably die in the process.

Adam sat there at the wheel, not thinking, not feeling, just waiting. As if somehow, if he sat there long enough, maybe he'd think of a way he could stay alive and bear to face it.

Jess was in the lab running tests when the commotion started up outside. A car pulling up, a door slamming. It was shocking. No one, but no one, made any noise during the hours of daylight in the container terminal. Even Florence Ballantine avoided moving about by day, and he owned the place. Everyone in the lab, guards and techies alike, paused, got to their feet, listening, trying to work it out. Then, the horn, blaring like a siren — and off went the guards like dogs after a rabbit, the guns coming out, faces intent.

They left the door open. Casually, Jess strolled toward it.

"Hey, where are you going?" one of the techs yelled.

"Don't worry, just looking. Having a smoke," said Jess. He leaned against the door and took one out. The techies didn't like it, but it wasn't their business to stand guard over him. Besides, they were curious themselves. Some of them were already drifting over to the door after him to have a look themselves. Jess yawned, but inside he was burning with excitement. It was midday. He had one short hour to keep his date with Anna. Outside, in Manchester city center, the crowds would be gathering right now. Even here, miles away, the noise was immense. Every day it had been growing louder — the roar of a million voices asking questions the government was unable to answer. It felt as if the whole country was there, just out of sight, waiting to claim the future. Jess had been given a chance to join them, to be with them — to die for them, if he had to.

All he had to do was get there.

He glanced behind him. Some of the techies were still watching him. Not yet . . . not yet. Steady. If he ran too early, they'd be onto him at once.

He leaned out the doorway to take a look at what the fuss was. There was a car with a girl sitting in it who looked familiar. She was yelling, "He's not taken his meds! He's not taken his meds!" at the top of her voice.

He knew her. Where had he seen her before?

Then he remembered. Lizzie, wasn't it? Adam's girlfriend. What on earth was she doing here? And if she was here, could Adam be far behind? But Anna had said he was in a hotel room. Jess groaned. *No! Not here, not here of all places. Adam! You idiot!*

There was a crowd gathering around the car. Christian Ballantine was there, bawling like an animal, batting at Lizzie with his hands through the window while the big guys tried to pull him off. He looked crazy, as if his brain was melting. The girl cringed back in the car, shielding her face with her hands. She'd already taken a few batterings by the looks of it. Florence Ballantine himself was out there, too, striding over with a face like a fist, wanting to know what all the noise was about.

The techies had stepped out past him to have a look — it wasn't the sort of thing you saw every day round here. No one was paying him any attention. Holding his breath, Jess silently slipped around behind the lab. As soon as he was out of sight, he began to run, weaving in and out of the other containers. After a few hundred yards he paused to listen. There was shouting. He'd been missed — but they had no idea which way he'd gone.

He began to run again. He was away. He was almost free. And . . . he was going to live! To Jess, it was a wonderful thing to give your life for something you believed in. He had been living with the idea of his death for so long, it felt almost wrong, as if he'd been cheated, to have it taken away. But today was the day — the one-week anniversary of Jimmy Earle's death, the big announcement in Albert Square. Perhaps, too, it was the day the government would resign. It had to happen. If he could be there when it did, he would not have lived in vain.

But what about Adam? Jess loved him — but he loved the cause even more. It was a shame. He'd have helped if he could, but today was booked. Today was the revolution. This was what he had sacrificed everything for — his friends, his family, his own life if need be. He couldn't let anything get in the way — not even his own brother.

He ran fast toward the perimeter fence.

For a few seconds, Lizzie thought they were really going to let Christian tear her to pieces. But the big guys pulled him off and then a shorter, older man, obviously in charge, turned up and started roaring at everyone. But it was Christian he was most angry with. He grabbed him by the lapels and bawled at him, "Is that right, you little shit? You've not been taking your meds, is that right? Is that right?"

"Lizzie!" cried Christian in a tormented voice. "How could you? How could you?" And bursting into tears, he began to cry like a child.

Ballantine let him go. That kind of answered his question. For a moment, everyone stood around watching in embarrassment; but Ballantine had reckoned without his son's cunning. Christian suddenly lashed out, pushing the older man back, and ran off at full speed.

"Catch him, you dicks!" yelled Ballantine. Some of the men shot after him in pursuit. His eye fell on Lizzie, cringing in the car, waiting to see what was going to happen next.

"What's going on?" he demanded.

Lizzie bent her head onto the steering wheel. *Out of the frying pan,* she thought. But she wasn't dead yet. She looked up and smiled at him as calmly as she could.

"If one of your men will untie me," she said, "I'll explain."

Ballantine gestured to one of them to cut her loose. He stood watching, arms crossed, scowling. "So where's Vince?"

"Last time I saw him he had a knife in the back of his neck," said Lizzie.

Ballantine paused and looked closely at her. "Are you having a laugh? Don't try and be funny with me," he told her. But he didn't look so angry anymore. "Bring her to my box," he told his men.

"Yes, sir," one of them said, still fumbling at her bonds. A couple of the other guys dithered a moment, getting up the courage to tell their boss that the chemist had done a runner. Sorry, sir, but . . .

You could hear the shouts of anger all the way to the railway line, half a mile away.

Ballantine's container, to Lizzie's amazement, was fitted out inside like a posh office suite. There was a staircase leading up to the container above, and for all she knew, another one going up even higher. It was like a house.

The older man sat down behind the desk and told one of his minions to fetch tea and biscuits. It made her start to giggle, and once she started, she couldn't stop. They all stood around and watched her being hysterical for about five minutes, until she finally got control of herself again. Then the older man asked her again what the fuck was going on.

Ballantine listened very carefully to her, nodding, urging her to take more biscuits and more tea — very polite, very calm. When she paused in the middle and needed a pee, he got one of his men to show her upstairs to the toilet, and she took the chance to wash her face and sort her hair out. They were treating her nicely. She wanted to look good. Mr. Ballantine looked like the sort of person who didn't respond well to weakness.

He shook his head when she was done. "What can I say?" he said. "I apologize for my son's behavior. I'm sorry that he's treated you so badly, and I'm devastated that he made you take Death. I wish I could make all of these things go away, but . . ." He spread his hands, in a gesture of helplessness. "What can I say?" he repeated. He looked around at his men. "Box her up," he said.

"Box her up?" repeated one of the men. "Are you sure, Mr. Ballantine?"

"Of course I'm sure. She knows Christian. She saw him murder Vince. She knows about this place. What do you want me to do, put her on the next plane to the Costa Brava? I apologize," he told her again. "Like I say, I wish I could make all this go away, but I can't."

One of the men took her arm. She stood up shakily. "Box me up?"
she asked.

Mr. Ballantine smiled reassuringly. "It's not as bad as it sounds.
Not like being buried alive or anything. Just putting you away in a
container for a while. Just to keep you safe."

Lizzie shook off the hand of the man at her elbow. "Safe?" she
said. "For how long?"

"'Bout a week." Ballantine shrugged. "Like I say . . ."

"But — what about the antidote?" she begged. "Can't you do
anything?" She ran out of words. If they wanted to make sure she
never told anyone what she knew, they were hardly going to help her
live longer, were they?

"If it's any consolation, which I don't suppose it is," said Ballantine,
getting up as if to see her out, "there's no such thing as an antidote.
Death binds itself to the brain in the first few hours. After that, you're
dead meat. Everyone agrees about that. I wish I could offer a better
way of spending your last few days, but that won't be possible, either.
Unless you want a quick way out? A bullet?" he offered.

"Mr. Ballantine," complained one of the men. "She's so young."

"Only fifteen," said Lizzie. She thought maybe taking a couple of
years off her age would help.

Ballantine shook his head irritably. "What is it with you guys?
You're happy to shoot your own grandmothers, but as soon as you
come across a girl a few months underage, you start making puppy
eyes at me. Tell you what," he told her. "Spend a little time in the box,
have a think. If anyone can work out a better way of dealing with the

problem, I'll be happy to look at it. Meanwhile — box her up," he told the heavies. "Don't forget — that bullet's still on offer," he added as she was led out. He was still trying to be nice.

It was just a short walk to the place that was going to be her final home and prison. Inside, it was pitch-black. No lights, nothing. She turned around and looked at the man accusingly.

"Sorry," he said. He shrugged, embarrassed, and pushed her gently inside. He paused a moment. "You've had some pretty bad luck," he suggested.

"You reckon."

"You want me to drop by later?" the man asked. "Mr. Ballantine is a gentleman, he won't let anyone molest you, but he might look favorably on a date."

"A date?" she said, amazed. "You're asking me for a *date*?"

The guy shrugged. "Your last week and all that."

Lizzie shook her head. "The answer's no. I've got better things to do . . . like sitting in the dark crying. You know?"

The guy stiffened. "Have it your own way," he said, and shut the door on her.

Left on her own, she did as she said — sat in the dark and wept. She had been holding it together for so long, it had to come out somehow. She had nothing and no one to help her. The phone had been left behind in Christian's flat, Adam was probably dead, and even if he wasn't, would those two words she'd texted really be enough to lead him to her? But — she wasn't giving up. She had Death inside her, souping her up. She finished her tears and started to feel her way around the box. There was some rubbish scattered around — some bits of old furniture that someone had dumped for the prisoners to sit on, perhaps. A mattress, a table, an old armchair, a dusty leather sofa.

She stood very still for a moment, getting control of herself, then went back to the door and felt her way around it. It was locked tight, so she began to feel her way around the walls of the container, looking for some kind of a crack or opening, no matter how small, that she could use to her benefit. She was full of Death. She was strong. She'd survived so far. There had to be something in here that could help her escape. Somehow or other, she was going to do it. And when she had, she was going to fulfill her bucket list. There was only one item on it — killing as many of these bastards as she could. And boy, she was really looking forward to that.

CHAPTER 23

HIDE-AND-SEEK

ADAM WAS ON THE M56, HAMMERING IT TOWARD MANCHESTER. The Porsche was a mess — bullet holes in the back, a couple of windows smashed in. If the police got to see it, he was going to get done. His driving was improving, but it still wasn't all that great. Other drivers were making as much space as they could between him and them as he went swaying past them at 120 miles per hour in the fast lane. The GPS kept nagging him to slow down, but it didn't stop telling him where to go.

He drove more calmly once he hit Manchester — no point asking for trouble. But when he arrived at his destination, his heart sank. It was an industrial wasteland — miles of it! The GPS directed him to a set of gates in front of acres of parked-up shipping containers and told him to drive straight on. But the gates were locked.

He got out and climbed the fence to have a look.

To one side was what looked like an abandoned waste disposal site. He could see heavy machinery — trucks, bulldozers, tractors — rusting where it had been left. Beyond them, a huge warehouse crumbled in the damp weather. In front of him was the container storage area. It just went on for miles.

Lizzie was somewhere in there . . . maybe. He had no chance searching on foot; it would take him forever. He needed satellite navigation, which seemed to be working on a map reference. Only one thing for it . . .

Adam reversed the car to get a decent run at the gate. He hit it at sixty miles an hour, ducking as he struck — just as well, as it took the roof off as he went through. He smashed the remains of the glass from the buckled window so he could see properly, and shot off in among the boxes. He heard engines behind him and peered back. Two motorbikes had pulled out and were on his tail already. Damn it! He went faster, wobbling furiously from side to side.

Adam's car was fast, but the bikes were more maneuverable and he was losing ground. He had to get rid of them. He twisted ninety degrees, skidding violently, clipped a container, put his foot down flat, and powered up along the long avenues in between the boxes. "Turn left. Slow down. Turn round. Turn right," ordered the GPS. Then — "You have reached your destination. You have passed your destination." Adam looked desperately around. What had he passed? There was nothing there — just yet more containers sitting blandly under the clouds. He twisted the car around another ninety-degree corner and headed back up, but a bike appeared ahead of him. He cursed, swerved around yet another corner, then another, then another, braked to a halt, and jumped out. At least he could hide on foot. He just had time to get out of sight before the bikers turned up. Peering from behind a container, he watched them dismount and come to examine the Porsche.

While the men conferred, Adam tried the door to the box nearest him: locked. So was the next one, and the next. Chances were they were all locked. Behind him, out of sight, the bikes started off again. But where were they going? Adam paused, not sure which way to run. It was a nightmare place for a chase, with a million corners but nowhere to hide. He could run, he could look, he could dodge — but he could never get out of the endless avenues in between the boxes.

He began to jog away, back to where the GPS had told him his destination lay.

If Adam could have flown a mile into the sky and taken a view of the terminal from above, he would have seen that it was far from empty. There were a number of people moving about in between the boxes, each hidden from the other, like rats in a maze.

Jess was there, zigzagging his way across to the northern perimeter fence where the waste disposal site was. Like his brother, Jess paused to hide away when the bikes came close, and started on again as soon as they drove off. In the distance he could just make out the bells of the town hall chiming the quarter hour: quarter past twelve. He had forty-five minutes before the announcement.

He hurried on his way. He, Adam, and Christian at that point were all no more than twenty yards apart, but none of them had any idea where the others were. Jess heard someone scuff their feet on the tarmac, and paused. Who was that? Friend or foe? He paused again and hid, listening carefully, trying to make out which way the feet were headed and who they belonged to.

Ballantine's men were out as well — some walking, some on motorbikes and quads hunting Jess, Christian, and Adam. Their orders for the kid who had broken down the gate in Vince's car were shoot on sight. Jess they wanted alive; he was useful. And Christian, of course, had to be taken alive as well.

Christian himself was still there. When Lizzie had busted him, he had run to the edge of the docks to hide and weep. He'd thought they were in love, and she had betrayed him like a dog. His heart was broken. It would never heal. She was the same as all the rest.

Now, muttering to himself in a low monotone, he was creeping his way back into the heart of the container terminal toward the secure unit where his dad had no doubt locked Lizzie up. In his hand he cradled his knife — the short, stubby-bladed thing that had seen Vince away.

"See how she says no then," he muttered to himself. "See how she does as she's told, with this sweet baby stuck in her neck. See you soon, Lizzie."

A motorbike roared nearby. Christian froze, but it shot past the gap in between a pair of containers ahead of him and vanished without the rider seeing him. Christian grinned. He had killed Vince; he had run away from his dad. Nothing could stop him now. "Soon, soon," he crooned, and crept forward.

Adam rapidly began to despair of finding anything among all those containers. It was hopeless. He was sure he'd gone past the place where the car had told him his destination was — but he had no way of telling, since everything looked so much the same.

He heard it before he saw anything: a low, muttering voice. But from where? He froze, unable to work out where the speaker was. But then a figure crept out in front of him from in between the boxes, its back to him. It was a man; Adam recognized him from the strange clothes he wore.

Adam's first instinct was — run. Get some distance between him and Christian, who was the scariest person he had ever met. But where Christian was, Lizzie must be nearby. He peered out again. Christian had already gone. Adam had no idea which way.

He ran lightly forward. There. To his right. A scuffing noise. Bending low, he inched forward again. At any point he was visible along half a mile of box edges. Which way had Christian gone?

He paused to listen. Whoever it was, they were close — very close. Just behind that corner there . . .

He peered around the edge of the box — then jerked his head back. Christian was less than ten feet away. He'd changed. It wasn't just that his eyes had gone dark, or that his mouth was slack. His whole face seemed to have altered shape, as his madness deformed him from within. He was squatting on the ground, head bent low, talking to himself. Listening closely, Adam could just about make it out.

"Let me down. Betrayed me. No, no, no. She was scared, you idiot, that's all. Too scared. Not scared enough. Betrayed!" he groaned in a hollow voice. "Ask her. Kill her. Ask her! Why should I, what excuse is there? She was scared, she was scared. And so am I."

Christian panted and sobbed briefly. From his hiding place just around the corner, Adam could hear his feet on the gritty tarmac and was just about to risk a brief peep, when Christian actually appeared, crossing directly in front of him. Adam froze, but Christian, focused on his murderous intention, did not look to either side, and moved straight on. Adam held his breath, waited until Christian was a box or so ahead, and then, as quietly as he could, stole out after him.

After another five minutes, Christian stopped outside one of the containers. To Adam it looked no different than any of the others, but Christian bent down and pressed his ear against the side of it. After a moment he bared his teeth, punched his fist against the metal wall beside him, and stood up. Adam darted back out of sight. Then, there was the creak of metal, and he peered out again.

Christian was rattling at a padlock attached to the container doors. He fished a gun out of his pocket, and, glancing anxiously about, struck at the padlock with the gun handle. It did nothing. After a couple of tries, he gave up, held the gun the other way, took aim, and shot the lock off. He opened the door, and squinted into the darkness.

"Lizzie!" he called softly. "Lizzie! You there, sweetheart?" He leaned around the doorway, lifted the gun up, and took aim.

Adam screamed, "No!"

Christian jumped in surprise and swung the gun around toward him. Instinctively, Adam jerked backward, but that was no good — he had to act. With a yell, he flung himself forward, zigzagging as fast as he could toward his enemy. Christian had the gun on him, following him with the barrel, taking aim, ready to fire. But before he could, the door burst wide open and Lizzie ran out, wielding a lump of wood. She flung herself straight at Christian and, with a wild swing, caught him on the side of the head. Yes! Christian staggered a few steps, but he wasn't down. Lizzie paused, blinded in the sudden light, unable to see. Christian took his chance, and swung the gun into her face.

"Lizzie!" screamed Adam. The gun connected, Lizzie went down, and Christian had her in his grip in a moment — her kneeling down, him behind her, her hair in his hand, head pushed forward. In the other hand, held high up in the air, was the short, stubby-bladed knife. He turned to grin at Adam.

"Don't," he sneered. "Daddy, don't. She's been a naughty girl."

Adam rushed forward, but as he did a figure stepped out from behind the container. Christian must have seen Adam's eyes move, and he began to turn — too late. The man clouted him on the side of the head and Christian hit the floor like a block of stone.

It all happened in a moment. Adam ran forward to Lizzie. She knelt as Christian had left her, still dazed, holding the side of her head where the gun had caught her. Adam put his arms around her, and looked up at the man standing watching them. It was Jess.

CHAPTER 24

RUN FOR YOUR LIFE

ADAM STARED AT HIS BROTHER IN DISBELIEF, STRUGGLING to make sense of his presence; but he had someone even more important to him there. Lizzie had had a bad blow to the head but the drug she'd taken was working strongly in her, and she was already getting to her feet. Adam helped her.

"Got your message," he said proudly. Lizzie groaned and shook her head, still dazed from the blow. Adam looked over to Jess. "You turned up in the nick of time," he said.

Jess scowled at him and glanced at his watch. Like Adam, he'd heard Christian making his way back into the terminal, muttering about killing the girl, and had dithered about whether to follow him or not. He'd had no idea that he was about to save his stupid brother. Now, he felt weak with relief that he had. But he'd severely damaged his chances of getting to Albert Square in time for the announcement.

Even as Adam spoke, there was the growl of motors somewhere near. They'd been heard. In the echoing alleyways of the container terminal, Christian's gunfire was proving hard to locate, but it wouldn't be long before they were discovered.

"We have to go." Jess peered down one of the long avenues to see if he could work out where their pursuers were, but Lizzie had recovered enough to get her wits back and she was more interested in Christian, who lay flat out before her on the ground. This was the man who had held her captive and in a state of terror for two days. This was the man who had forced her to swallow Death.

"Bastard!" she yelled suddenly, and stamped on his leg. "Bastard! Bastard!"

Adam grabbed her. "Shhh!"

"What for? He's bloody murdered me," she hissed.

Adam turned to Jess. "He made her take Death, too. We need to get the antidote," he said.

Jess shook his head.

"Don't you care?" demanded Adam. "I know there's an antidote. You must know something about it. Jess, we're going to die. You have to help us."

There was shouting — already so near.

"Look, you've got it so wrong," Jess said. "You're going to live. I promise. But we have to run — right now!"

"But —"

"Now!"

Jess ran. They ran after him.

Around them, the bikes revved and skidded on the damp asphalt. Adam and Lizzie had no idea where they were going, but Jess did. He stopped running and opened a door in one of the containers — *"In here."* They ran in and he slammed it shut behind them. At once, they were enclosed in darkness. Outside, a bike sped by, but it didn't stop. They held their breaths and listened as the sound of the other bikes grew fainter. They were safe — for now. Until they wanted to move on.

"We'll be OK here," said Jess. "Most of the boxes are locked, but the Zealots got this one opened up for us in case we needed somewhere to hide. Ballantine and his men don't know anything about it."

He sighed and slid down the wall to sit on the floor. He was going to miss it — after all that! Beside him, Adam reached out to touch Lizzie's arm.

"You OK?"

"What do you think?" she snapped.

"I'm sorry . . ." he began.

But she had other things on her mind than sorry. "So what's been going on? What about the antidote?" she demanded.

"A girl I met. She said she knew the Zealots. She —"

Jess cut in. "She doesn't just know the Zealots — she's one of us. And she wasn't telling you the truth: There is no antidote." He pulled himself back up to talk to them. "But you're not going to die. The drug you took is fake. I know. I worked out how to make it."

Fake Death? Adam stared at Jess's shape in the darkness. "But that's crazy. Why?"

"For life," said Jess.

But Lizzie wasn't having it. "Oh, fuck off talking in riddles," she hissed. "Just tell us what's going on. So we're OK? Is that right? We're going to live?"

"Yeah. You're going to live. If we get out of this alive, that is."

"But it doesn't make any sense!" said Adam. "I felt so great. I was stronger, quicker. Just like they said. How come?"

"Fake isn't quite the right word," Jess said. "Adapted. This version does a lot of the things that the original does, but I found a way of stopping it binding to the brain. You get a comedown — a long comedown. You're both going to get pretty sick. But it won't kill you." Jess smiled wryly. "I could have been rich. It's going to be a pretty popular drug when people realize what's going on."

Lizzie couldn't believe her ears. She had been through all this — for what? "Are you telling me it was all some sort of stupid trick?"

"No! More than that. Have you any idea how many people have taken Ballantine's cheap Death since Jimmy Earle died? Tens of thousands. Over three thousand took it that first night. Imagine all those people out there right now, believing they're going to die. Believing they have no future. In the past week, nearly all of them will have found out the same thing — the thing you've found out, Adam: that life is actually the only thing worth having. They don't want to die at all. They want to live and it's the one thing they can't have." Jess laughed. "And we're going to give it back to them. In spades."

They could hear the excitement in Jess's voice. But Lizzie was outraged.

"So it was a lie," she said. "The whole thing, one big lie."

"A good lie!" insisted Jess. "You've seen what's happening out there on the streets. Things are changing — and this drug sparked it all off. It's shown people how much life means to them. It's shown them it's worth fighting for. People are taking a stand. Isn't that worth a lie, no matter how big? At one o'clock there'll be a Zealot announcement about it in Albert Square: 'You're going to live.' Can you imagine how people are going to feel? The hope? The world's been changing around them. Suddenly, they'll be a part of it again. Just like you two." In the darkness, he tried to embrace them. "It's life," he said. "You've got it back. The future is yours to take . . ."

Lizzie pushed him away. "You took our lives away and now you're going to give them back? Great. Playing God. You are so arrogant. God help whatever revolution people like you are planning."

"We didn't *plan* it. We never dreamed it would turn into this. We just lit the fuse. And it's not just us anymore. There are all sorts of people getting into this now. Different rebel groups, the unions, political parties. Everyone's involved." Jess moved to the door to peer out of the cracks. "I want to be a part of it. You can join me, if you like . . ."

Adam was listening to Jess's confession in a trance. So the whole thing, his whole week, had been nothing but an illusion. The despair, the pain, the rage, the love, the fear — all for nothing. The raw emotions

he'd been through — the emotions so many people had been through —
had all been just to help the Zealots make a political point.

But what a point . . .

"What about the antidote?" he said. "That girl . . ."

"Her real name is Anna," said Jess. "She worked here with me, but
she got out. I asked her to see if she could find you."

He looked at his watch. Half past twelve. He needed to be in
Albert Square in half an hour. He was wasting time!

"But . . . why did she tell me to stay in the hotel?"

"People on Death take risks. A lot of people don't make it through
the week. We were hoping that if you thought there was an antidote,
you might keep yourself safe."

"You didn't think of just telling him then?" said Lizzie.

"No," snapped Jess. "We couldn't jeopardize the whole plan by
letting that information out too soon. It could have ruined everything."

"All that pain. All those people. You sick bunch of bastards,"
Lizzie hissed. "And what about the people who did die? Good job you
won't have to explain yourself to them, isn't it?"

"There are always casualties in a war. I was prepared to die, too.
I still am."

"So you taught them a lesson. Bravo!"

She clapped, the noise echoing hollowly in the little chamber.

"We made a revolution," said Jess.

"You don't believe that," said Lizzie. "If that's what it is, it was
coming anyway."

As Jess and Lizzie argued over his head, Adam sank down to the
floor, overwhelmed by the whole thing. It was fake. It had been fake

all along — but it meant he was going to live. Lizzie was going to live. A moment ago he had nothing. Now, he had it all.

Trees, he thought. *And . . . chocolate. And fresh air and cars. Apples and pears. Music. Jokes. Falling in love* — like his mum had said. *The whole damn adventure.*

"Being in love," he said out loud.

"What?" said Lizzie.

"We're going to live. We get it all back. Everything! Ice cream cakes and summer days and new clothes, and . . . Sunday dinners, and fish and chips. The lot!"

In the dark, Lizzie made a face. Adam carried on. "Growing up and growing old and having kids and getting a mortgage, and getting your heart broken and scraping your knees, and bacon sandwiches, and being bored and . . ."

"Being a dick," she said. "And dragging people down with you and . . . nearly getting them fucking killed!" she yelled.

"Yeah, my brother's a dick," said Jess. "And maybe I am, too. But you know what, Lizzie? He thought he had the antidote, but he came to find you anyway. He really does love you."

In the darkness, Lizzie could just about make out Adam's shape. It was true; he really did love her. But after everything that had happened, she wasn't even sure how much she wanted it anymore.

"Sometimes, Adam . . . you know what?" she said. "What if love isn't enough?"

Adam just looked at her, dumbfounded, as if he'd never even considered it.

"There will be love," said Jess. "And looking after Mum and Dad. And working hard. And getting up on freezing cold mornings, and worrying."

"Yeah. All that," said Adam. He was sore, he felt sick — the comedown from Death was taking hold. But he was going to live. Nothing else mattered. He stood up and shouted out loud for sheer joy.

Jess smiled. Adam was going to be OK. He was pleased about that. But now he was in a hurry to get on.

"I have to go," he said. "You want to join me? Come on! Don't you want to be in Albert Square when they make that announcement? Or are you going to play it safe and wait until it gets dark?"

Adam looked at Lizzie. She shook her head angrily.

"Come on, Lizzie," he said. "You were talking about the demos. You wanted to take part."

"Forget the past," said Jess. "It's over. This is the future, and it's happening right on our doorstep."

Lizzie hesitated. She was furious with Jess, angry with Adam — but it was true. She wanted to be a part of the future as well.

"We haven't heard the bikes for ages. I reckon they've got Christian and packed it in," Jess said.

Lizzie groaned. "OK," she said. "But not for you, Adam. It's because I'm not going to miss out just to make a point to you two assholes. Understand?"

Adam leaped up to grab her, and she let him. Love, eh? Maybe. Maybe not.

"What are we waiting for?" she said. "Let's go."

CHAPTER 25

WASTE DISPOSAL

THEY HEADED OFF, PAUSING, PEERING AROUND EACH CON-tainer, running on. There was no trace or sound of the bikes or cars. Maybe, their luck was in. Within minutes they had arrived at a line of containers at right angles to the usual rows. They walked around them and there they were, face-to-face with the perimeter fence. On the other side was the waste disposal site, with old machinery rusting on collapsed tires and the huge, open-fronted warehouse Adam had seen when he first arrived.

One look sideways and they stepped back. This was dangerous. A long line of boxes ran parallel to the fence right to the far ends of the terminal. The fence was high, about ten feet — climbable enough, but as soon as they stepped out they would be in full view for half a mile in either direction.

The question: Who else was watching the fence?

The answer: Christian was.

After he had been brained by Jess, he'd woken up with a vile headache and an even viler temper. His beautiful looks had been ruined. Worse, so had his beautiful brain. He knew this by the fact that he was in a permanent rage, and because he was able to remember barely anything of what had been happening recently. Only one thing remained in his mind: betrayal.

Lizzie. That bitch! She'd told him that she loved him, then given him up to his dad, and now, to cap it all, she'd run off with another boy. They were all in it together. They all had to die.

He had no doubt that he would get to kill his enemies. He had right and justice and a gun and loads of ammunition on his side. He guessed that they'd try to get out by the old waste disposal site — it was the quickest way out, and not bounded by either canals, or private sites like most of the other perimeters. He made his way there and settled himself down to wait, tucked away among the line of boxes by the fence. It wasn't long — there! Just a flash, a brief glimpse as they popped out to look at the fence. They dived back in fast enough, but it was them all right, only a couple of hundred yards away.

Now he was going to end it. They were going to run for the fence, and when they did, he'd be waiting for them with his gun and his knife.

Creeping down, low to the earth, Christian began to weave his way through the boxes closer to where they were hiding, to give himself a better shot.

"We'll get them, precious," he said to himself, and giggling at his own joke, wriggled his way forward.

"Over there," whispered Jess.

"What?"

"A hole. See? The wire's torn."

They peeped out. There was a hole in the fence about fifty feet farther up from them — just big enough for a single person to squeeze through.

Still dangerous. But quicker than climbing.

"When I say go, we go together," said Jess. "On the other side, run for the warehouse — that's our best chance to hide if we need to."

"OK," Adam said. Lizzie nodded.

"Go!" yelled Jess.

They dashed out. Almost at once a gunshot rang out. Christian wasn't as close as he'd hoped — ten containers away. He should have kept quiet but the sight of Lizzie was too much for him. In a blind rage he rushed out toward them. "Bitch! Betrayer!" he howled. He fired off more shots, but nothing hit — they were out of range. But not for long.

There was an awful moment while they struggled, one at a time, through the hole in the fence with Christian powering toward them. Then they were through and running in between the decrepit bull-dozers, diggers, and trucks, slipping on the wet ground underfoot.

"I'm coming!" screamed Christian. He had already reached the hole in the wire and was squeezing his way through, less than fifty yards behind them.

"The warehouse," gasped Jess.

They rounded a heap of bleeding paint tins, in under the roof of the warehouse, and straight into an enormous rusting heap of metal. The building had been used to store old white goods — fridges and freezers, mainly — sent there to be recycled long ago. The recession had come and rendered them valueless, so there they remained, a mountain of abandoned metal carcasses, towering above them up to the roof. Jess had hoped they could slip away through another exit, but the only other way out had been blocked by a landslide of rusting appliances years ago. There was only one way in or out — and Christian was coming through it right now.

"The roof — we can get out up there," Jess panted. They had no choice but to climb. Christian, yelling behind them, paused to try a shot, but he was still too far off. He cursed and ran forward. He was in the shed with them before they had made it more than a few yards up the mountain of scrap.

Adam clawed his way up, but the cost of the adapted Death leaving his system was catching up with him. He felt nauseous and weak. The metal carcasses were often precariously balanced on top of each other and to make matters worse, not all of them had been emptied before they had been thrown away. As they climbed, fridge and freezer doors swung open like stinking mouths, dribbling black slime, all that remained of food that had been rotting inside for years. The stink was overpowering. It got on their hands, on their feet, on their faces. But they couldn't stop. Another bullet whistled past. Christian was at the bottom of the mountain now. He stuck his gun into his waistband and began to climb after them.

"Bitch, I'm going to kill you, bitch! I'm gonna C4 you all . . ." His voice choked as he breathed in some vileness, but his madness had given him an inhuman strength and recklessness, and he didn't stop. Even now, clawing his way over the fridges and freezers, he was gaining on them.

It was a horrible effort. Their feet plunged suddenly into cavities, or slipped on a slimy surface. Underfoot, the rusting units tipped dangerously. It had to happen — an accident. As he pushed forward, Jess slipped; his foot jammed in a gap, caught tight in between two heavy units. He tugged — it refused to move. In a panic he tugged again and pulled it out — but badly wrenched. As soon as he tried to put some weight on it, it gave way under him.

Below him, Christian saw and grinned. "C4," he hissed excitedly, and then bawled up at them, an incomprehensible cawing of rage and madness that no one could make out. Jess lunged forward, desperate to escape, but he slipped and fell back down several feet. Christian screamed in triumph; Adam and Lizzie turned back to help.

"Go. Go!" Jess demanded. But Adam shook his head. He and Lizzie tried to pull Jess up after them, but as they did the area they were standing on rocked and shifted downward. They were balanced on the side of a huge industrial chilling unit, some kind of ancient meat refrigerator, one of a cluster of several towering over them like small cliffs. The whole lot was highly unstable, tipping under their weight, shifting down.

"Get off this thing — maybe we can push it down," said Adam. The three of them slid off the corner of the big unit, got down behind it, and pushed. The mass of metal moved a few inches — then ground to a halt.

"Together," hissed Jess. They heaved again. Nothing moved. The unit had jammed.

"I'm gonna have you, you little fucks!" bawled Christian. He was no more than thirty feet away, clawing, shoving, and heaving his way toward them. They were hidden behind the unit, but he'd be on them in moments.

"Again!" said Adam. "One . . . two . . . three . . . push!"

Together they heaved. The huge unit shifted, moved down, slid sideways slightly — and at last began to go. One more push and it was on its way, picking up speed, sliding down, twisting as it went, dislodging and crushing everything in its way, straight toward Christian. For a second it looked as if it was going to jam — but then the units under it crumpled and it shot forward. Christian leaped desperately to one side, but the unit was just too big to avoid and it passed straight over him. For a second or two afterward they could see him, looking curiously flattened and smeared into the metal beneath him. One of his arms twitched, then the whole thing went — an avalanche of fridges. A great mass of them toppled down on top of him, with a grinding, crunching noise, like a metal river passing over a tin mountain. Distantly, caught up in the noise, they heard a scream, cut suddenly off.

The avalanche slowed, petered out, and stopped. Lizzie stared down at the place where he had disappeared. It was over, wasn't it? Finally. Christian was dead.

She turned to look at Adam. "Yeah?" she said.

"Yeah," said Adam.

She grinned. "He was on my bucket list, too," she said. She whooped. "Hey! High five!" They slapped hands.

"Sorry to break things up, guys — but it's not over till we're safely out of here," said Jess. "Ballantine and his men must have heard that racket. We just killed his only son." He nodded to the top of the mountain. "It's safer to go up, I reckon. There's ladders on the roof." He glanced at his watch. Quarter to one. He still had time . . .

They began to climb the final leg.

The heap of fridges and freezers was unstable now, and it was hard to see what they were doing in the deep shadows right up by the roof. But they made it OK. After that it was just a short walk across to the ladders at the back of the building. They were halfway there when a group of men appeared on the roof.

There was no chance of escape. They were fifty feet off the ground — it was certain death to jump. There were six or seven men waiting for them, all armed. One of them was Florence Ballantine himself.

Jess sank down, sat on the roof, and hung his head. They had been so close — so close!

"Yeah, innit?" said Ballantine. "Thought you'd got away with it. Fake Death." He shook his head. "Oh, yeah — I know. A couple of our, eh, experiments should have died a few hours ago. Wasn't difficult to work out after that." He shook his head and wagged his finger at Jess. "Clever boy. And look! I'm not even angry. Why would I be? This drug is going to be a whole lot more popular than the real stuff. You get a great week — and then you live! What's wrong with that? And it gets better! Despite your bad manners trying to run out on me, I still want to work with you. Son, you and me are going into business, only this time, you are going to show me how to make it myself, regardless of what your Zealot bosses say. Then — maybe I'll let you go. Maybe I'll let your brother go. Who knows?"

He smiled broadly.

"And as for you two," he went on to Adam and Lizzie, "only one question. Christian's around here somewhere — we know he came in after you. So. Please. Where's my son? Don't tell me you've done anything bad to him because if you have, that's going to make me very angry indeed."

Lizzie licked her lips. "He was chasing us," she said.

"Yeah."

"He was on the fridges last we saw of him," began Adam. But Ballantine wasn't interested.

"What I'm thinking is," he said, "who to do over? I need the boy to put pressure on Jessie here. I guess that means — Lizzie, isn't it? Sorry, love. You're looking very expendable to me." He spread his arms. "So who's going to talk first? Before I start snipping the young lady's fingers off one by one. Or perhaps the boys here would like a go at her first. Hmm?"

No one spoke.

"I will find out," said Ballantine. "And you know that. So I'm going to ask you one more time: Where's . . . my . . . son? Come on. No one got anything to say?"

"I have."

Ballantine spun around. The voice, a female one, was coming from behind him. The slight figure of a young woman was standing at the edge of the roof by one of the ladders.

It was Anna.

"You! Stupid enough to run and then come back. So now I got the full set. You guys got her covered?"

"She's covered, boss."

Anna smiled. "Mr. Ballantine," she said. "I know how to make this stuff, too. I'll show you — if you pay me."

"And what makes you think I need to pay anyone?"

"It's easier this way. But I don't expect you to take my word. I have the formula and the chemical route to it right here — minus a line or two, of course. That'll be put back in once I get my money. Here . . ." Slowly, she lowered a hand toward her coat pocket and began to advance toward him.

"Stay where you are!" shouted one of the heavies.

Ballantine held up a hand. "OK, let's have a look. Take it out," he told her. "But move very, very slowly. Understand?"

"I understand."

Carefully, she put her hand in her pocket and took out a notebook. "It's all here. All you'll have to do is follow the numbers."

The gangster nodded. With her arms up, Anna advanced slowly toward him and handed him the book. Ballantine flicked through it.

"I'm going to bleed a chemist to check this out," he said.

"Then why don't we go and get one?"

He paused, then nodded. "It's not going to do any harm checking it out. First things first, though. You two," he said, turning again to Adam and Lizzie, "this might — might — just let your brother off the hook. But — I still need to know where my son is."

Over beyond the waste disposal site and the container terminal, there came a roar from the city. The speeches had begun in Albert Square. Even though the distance turned it into a dull murmur, you could tell it was a noise formed in a million throats.

Anna smiled. "Listen!" she said. The gangster paused and cocked his head, and as he did she suddenly launched herself at him, seizing him around the neck.

"Run!" she yelled. Ballantine swatted out at her, catching her in the face, but she had a grip on his neck and was holding tight. Adam, Jess, and Lizzie turned and fled. One of the men turned to give chase, but Ballantine was screaming at them to get the girl off him, and they all turned to help. She disappeared in a mass of bodies. It gave Adam and the others enough time to cross the short distance to the ladder, and begin to climb down one at a time.

"She's wired!" someone screamed. Adam, last down, paused to see what was going on. The heavies had fallen back; Anna had been pulled away from Ballantine and was on the floor. The gangster and his men were beginning to run, but it was too late. Anna got to her feet in an almost leisurely movement and opened her coat wide, to show off the odd-looking packets tied to her body. Adam saw her stand there for a moment longer, the little control box in her hand, her coat spread, head up, proud like the soldier she was. Then, she exploded.

There was a flash of blinding light ripping open the sky and a dull boom. Adam ducked down below the wall and clung on to the ladder for dear life as the blast ripped across the roof toward him. Shards of blazing roofing plastic rushed over his head and high into the air, caught in a wind of burning dust and fire. But it wasn't a huge explosion; it didn't need to be. On the other side of the wall, the roof crumpled; Ballantine and his men fell down, down into the space beneath. Their bodies flamed and twisted as they descended, until the dust thickened over them and they disappeared forever.

Anna had been given her target. The last thing the Zealots wanted was a gang like this working against them so close to the city. One of the first things they planned was to cut down on organized crime. The cleanup had begun.

The blast died down. Adam put up his head to see what was left. Most of the roof was gone. High above him, pieces of it were still falling, some still ablaze. A cloud of dust and ash was boiling in front of him but it was already settling, and through it he could see the city beyond.

"Adam! Are you OK? What happened?" Adam looked down to Lizzie's shocked face. Hidden below the wall, she hadn't seen a thing. He shook his head, unable to speak.

Jess hadn't seen, either, but he could guess.

"Anna?" he asked.

"She had explosives. She . . . just . . ."

Jess rested his head briefly on the rungs of the ladder, then looked back up. "Move over," he said.

Adam edged carefully onto the wall while Jess and Lizzie made their way up.

"Suicide bomb," Adam said, in answer to Lizzie's horrified look.

"She blew herself up? My God, that's terrible!"

"She saved our lives," Adam said. *But why?* he thought. She'd smiled as she did it. He could see her face now, gazing at him serenely in the moment before she detonated. He remembered her in the hotel room a few days ago. She had loved life, he had no doubt about it — and yet it seemed as if she wanted this. How was it possible that you could choose to die, while you still loved life?

"You don't understand," said Jess. "It's what she wanted." He looked down in the smoking cauldron of dust below them, where the wreckage was still settling. The mountain of old appliances was moving again under the weight of the debris that had fallen on top of it and a new cloud of dust rose slowly below them. "She was a soldier. She didn't do it just for us; she died as a Zealot, for something she believed in. Ballantine was her target. What she's done is noble. I'm not sure she even saw it as a sacrifice."

"Noble?" demanded Lizzie. "She can't know what she's done. She's lost everything . . ."

Jess was looking down with a tender expression into the open warehouse where his friend had died. He seemed almost pleased for her.

"Do you envy her?" Adam asked him.

Jess turned to look at him. The question obviously took him by surprise. What Anna had done was something he had believed for a long time was going to be his fate. There had been a time when he wanted it more than anything else in the world.

"No," he said at last. "I wish I did. But I don't." He looked back down. "God bless, Anna," he said. "You got 'em right on the nose."

Across the other side of the container terminal, the town hall clock struck one.

Adam looked at Jess, stricken. "You're not there," he said.

"You know what?" said Jess. He pointed across the terminal. "Grandstand view, isn't it?" Adam followed his gaze. The smoke from the explosion was blowing away in the wind and Manchester lay spread out before them. There was the Hilton Tower, poking up above the city. There were the apartment buildings, the shops, the cathedral, the town hall. It was a beautiful sight. Everything went very quiet.

"The announcement," said Jess. "They'll be making it right now."

"I'm sorry you missed it," said Adam. Now that they were all safe, he felt dreadful. They had survived — but beautiful, kind Anna was dead, and he had been through a week more intense than anything he could ever have imagined. What had it all been for?

"I haven't missed anything," said Jess. "I'm alive. I'm up here with my brother, and I can see the whole thing. Look at it! No one else is going to have a view like this." He waved his hand again. "It's the future. And you know what? For the first time, Adam, it's ours."

But Adam was inconsolable. Lizzie took him in her arms. "What is it, Ads?" she said.

"I made such a mess," he wept. "I ruined everything. I nearly killed you and Jess. I owe both of you my life." He looked up at them. "What shall I do?" he demanded. "Tell me what to do with my life, and I'll do it."

Jess shook his head. "Just live it."

"Yeah," said Lizzie. "Enjoy!" She paused. "Listen! There it is."

Across the container terminal, a great roar went up, louder than ever, as several thousand people realized they were going to live and that the future was theirs for the making. High up on the warehouse wall, Adam, Lizzie, and Jess got to their feet and made their way down to join them.

ACKNOWLEDGMENTS

The first I heard of this book was in a phone call from Barry Cunningham, boss of the Chicken House, with an unlikely story involving A-level philosophy students, their tutors, and an idea about a recreational drug that killed you in a week.

"And I thought — now, who do I know who doesn't mind working differently?" Barry said.

Intriguing . . .

The Hit is an unusual book in that it has so many parents. It wasn't my idea in the first place. Some of the settings — in particular the container terminal — and most of the characters all started somewhere else. In some cases only the names are left and I hope I've made it my own, but it's a matter of fact that this book would never have been written if it hadn't been for other people besides myself. I feel like a sort of foster parent to it. Without a number of folk and their generosity in handing the baby over, I would never have had the pleasure of this story, these characters, or the fascinating experience of bringing someone else's baby into the world.

So more than the usual special thanks, then, first of all to Brandon Robshaw and Joe Chislett, for coming up with the brilliant idea of using a thriller to touch on the big issues, as well as for so many of the settings and characters, and especially for the basic idea of a drug that kills you in a week and the wonderful response — how would you spend that week? Thanks are also due to their students for helping those ideas along.

Having a good idea is great, of course, but the other side of the coin is recognizing it. Most of us in the course of our lives no doubt have countless ideas that would make good books, films, and TV shows, but without the gift to work out which are good and which are bad ideas, you're no better off than if you never did. You need to be able to sort the seed from the fluff. So big thanks to Barry Cunningham for picking this idea out of many others, and then picking me out of many authors. Putting the right idea in the (hopefully) right hands is a rare skill, and I'm delighted to be on the receiving end.

Thanks as well to my editor Rachel Leyshon, for showing such great patience and making so many useful suggestions — a pleasure to work with.

And to Banksy for the Zealot logo inspiration, and everyone who worked on the book, cover, blurb, PR, the lot — thanks!

Melvin Burgess

January 2013